IT BEGAN
IN GREENWICH VILLAGE

where the New York sexual underground and the Mafia rubbed more than shoulders, and the weirdest crew of bank robbers ever assembled was put together by a man named Littlejoe

IT SWUNG INTO ACTION
IN A BANK IN QUEENS

where a dream heist suddenly exploded into an out-of-control nightmare of violence and terror

IT CLIMAXED AT J.F.K.
INTERNATIONAL AIRPORT

where a fueled-up Boeing 707 waited to take off, and the police knew they had just minutes for one last desperate gamble before the most successful getaway in history

DOG DAY AFTERNOON

Don't reveal the ending!

"Grippingly authentic, far more exciting than the ordinary thriller."

—*Library Journal*

DOG DAY AFTERNOON

by PATRICK MANN

A DELL BOOK

DOG DAY AFTERNOON
is based in part on
material created by
Frank R. Pierson.

Published by
DELL PUBLISHING CO., INC.
1 Dag Hammarskjold Plaza
New York, New York 10017
Copyright © 1974 by Dell Publishing Co., Inc.
Dell ® TM 681510, Dell Publishing Co., Inc.
Reprinted by arrangement with
Delacorte Press, New York, N.Y.
Printed in the United States of America
First Dell printing—July 1975

★ PROLOGUE

IT HAPPENED ON THE HOTTEST DAY of the year during the last soap opera of the day.

Flo usually didn't watch the soap opera, not in summer, because summers her husband worked nights and slept mornings. By the time the day had heated up to its fullest, mid-afternoon, he was awake, bitching, yelling for his six-pack of Piel's and whatever game was on TV.

This day had begun even hotter than usual, a real dog day afternoon in August, when New York City was a pizza left too long in the oven, burnt around the edges, damned near poisonous, impossible to swallow.

Irritably, Flo's husband switched channels back and forth. The heat was so fierce inside their tiny house in Queens that even a cold beer and a baseball game failed to keep him quiet.

"Shit," he told Channel 2. "Shit," he informed Channel 4. "More shit," he announced as he kept switching. The only reason he paused at Channel 7 was that a rather attractive young woman had just allowed an older man to pull her into his arms and kiss her.

"No, Doug, no," she was moaning. "I'll never be able to look Amy in the eyes ever again, don't you understand?"

"Look 'er inna twat," Flo's husband suggested, switching to Channel 9. He paused because the word BULLETIN filled the screen.

Flo had stopped behind his chair, because she wanted to see whether Amy's husband, Doug, would now let the girl alone. She found herself wondering what could be so special in the middle of a broiling afternoon to warrant the word BULLETIN.

"Will you shaddap?" her husband asked, although she had said nothing.

Now a man seated at a desk filled the screen. The camera pulled back for a moment, then started to close in on him as he began to read from a sheet of paper, barely looking up now and then.

"This special bulletin just in from Police Headquarters. A neighborhood branch of the Chase Manhattan Bank is in the process of being robbed by two armed gunmen in Queens. With the robbery in progress, this now from Channel Nine's camera crew on the scene."

Her husband's knuckles whitened as he prepared to turn the dial. "Augie," Flo said. "Wait a second."

"'F' what? Some cockamamie heist?"

"Wait a second. You got something better to watch?"

The picture changed: a section of a street baked in the sun. Uniformed police milled around. A storefront bank with one rather small picture window stood in the center of the screen. Two men seemed to be arguing in front of the door of the bank.

"Here at the scene of the armed robbery now in progress," the announcer was saying, "and a dramatic confrontation between one of the armed robbers and Detective Sergeant Moretti of the Two Hundred Seventy-fourth Precinct. Moretti here wearing the hat with the confrontation in progress and Channel Nine's camera crew on the scene for this confrontation."

"The robber," Flo said. She could hardly get the words out.

"What?"

Her throat started to close over in fright. "Th-the robber!"

The zoom lens was closing down inexorably on the two men in front of the bank, the detective in the hat gesturing, the other man, younger, in chino pants and a white shirt with rolled-up sleeves, looking cool and calm. "Augie," Flo said. Her voice came out in a moan. "That man. That armed bandit."

"Fuck 'im," Augie muttered. He switched to Channel 11, but the tube showed the same scene from a different angle.

". . . here with Channel Eleven's camera crew at the scene of the crime to bring you the latest developments in this bizarre and unprecedented—"

"Shit," Augie grumbled. He snapped the dial back through 9 to 7.

"Amy is my best friend," the woman was telling Doug. Beneath the image, a line of white type was moving slowly past from right to left. ". . . ARMED ROBBERY OF CHASE BANK BRANCH NOW IN PROG . . ."

"Shit again." Augie twisted the dial to 5, and once more the man in the light shirt was arguing with the detective in the hat.

"*Mamma mia,*" Flo moaned. "*Maria e Gesu Cristo.*"

"What?" Augie demanded. "What's all the guinea cursing about now?"

"Don't you see him, Augie?"

"I see they ain't nothing on the tube but some shithead holding up some bank."

"It's Joey," Flo moaned. "It's our boy, Joey."

"*What?*"

Augie sat up in his armchair, his scrawny neck stretched as he stared fiercely at the screen. "Shit and shit again! It's him."

"Joey's holding up . . . a bank," Flo said, her voice swimming in tears like an anchovy in olive oil, shimmering, drowning sleekly. "My son, my little Joey, he's robbing a b—"

"Your fucking son maybe," her husband cut in. "Not mine."

"Yours too."

"Not any more." Her husband got to his feet suddenly. "I ain't got no son. I never did have no son. Not that shit-ass little bastard, not ever and especially not no more." He stamped out of the room.

Flo moaned wordlessly for a moment, then sat down in her husband's chair. She adjusted the fine tuning to get a better image and turned up the sound to make sure she heard every word.

Her son was all over the tube. All of New York City was watching him. The whole tri-state area was seeing him rob a bank. She wanted to be sure she didn't miss any of it.

J OE WAS OF TWO MINDS.

He sat in the waiting room with the rest of the people who had come to be interviewed. Some had been far-sighted enough to bring newspapers to read. Being out of work, they brought smudged copies of the *News* or the *Times*, that morning's newspaper salvaged from subway trash baskets. Nobody was reading the afternoon *Post*, Joe noticed. Nobody had the extra fifteen cents to blow on it. *Post* want ads weren't worth fifteen cents.

Joe surveyed the four people in the room, all men, all about his age, late twenties. He wondered how many of them had been in Nam. Half, maybe? They were the right age for it. A third?

He felt of two minds because he needed this job badly but the idea of getting it made him want to puke.

Okay, he told himself, cool it. The ad had been running all week and the job wasn't filled yet. The bank was a big one with hundreds of offices around town. The job was not one of your crappy beginner's jobs like teller-trainee. The ad said very plainly: "Must have yr's exp. or equiv."

Okay, he had the experience. He knew the ropes. He could talk bank talk. He had the job in the palm of his hand, even without the interview. These guys sitting around reading their stolen *News*es were shit out of luck.

But, Jesus, the idea of actually working in a bank

again. That day-in-day-out, punch-the-clock, wall-to-wall, buttoned-down boredom. When he remembered how it felt, something heavy and indigestible inside Joe moved up against the bottom of his lungs, like a beast turning over in its sleep and you better not wake it up. It made his lungs smaller. They couldn't seem to pump enough air. His stomach felt as if it were being wrung out like a dishrag. All the sour juice dripped on his liver.

Don't wake it up, baby. Cool it. Keep the beast asleep. "Come on cool 'cause you ain't no fool." Who used to say that? Some spade cat, some black sergeant back at the copter base in Nam, a mechanic in the Air Force.

Joe's eyes lidded halfway as he continued to look over his competition for the job. Run of the mill. None of them had a prayer. Not them. He had the job. The only question was wheth—

"Mr. Nowicki."

Nice-looking legs, small tits. Joe's glance moved up the young woman's body. He liked them slender, tender and tall. This one was shorter than he liked. He took his time getting to his feet, because that was his style.

Then he stood there without saying anything. That was cool, wasn't it? Any jerkball could holler "Here!" or whatever. The four doggies in the room would hop to and hit a brace if you yelled their name. But the girl didn't seem to understand that he was who he was. Her big eyes locked into his glance.

"Are you, uh, Mr. uh?"

Joe nodded. Just once, cool, but it failed to stop the girl from mispronouncing his name again. Not that anybody ever got it right except another Polack, and this one was no Polack, he thought, not with those big wet eyes and that full, hot mouth. How would those lips feel when he rammed the old Avenger between them?

"This way, please."

Joe had not expected the interviewer to be a woman, much less one this young. But after the girl had escorted him into the room, she sat herself down behind the big desk. "I'm Miss Panetta," she said.

How the hell could she be guinea meat with those baby tits, Joe wondered. No hips, either. He sat down across from the interviewer. "I'm here for the systems job you people advertised for."

For a moment he toyed with the idea of letting her know his mother was a wop. Not only that, but he was tied by blood on her side to one of the really big Maf families. Should he mention it? He decided to hold off awhile.

Miss Panetta nodded, and her dark hair seemed to bounce for a moment after her head was still. Tina's hair had done that once, years ago, before Joe had married her. Tina had been one cute cunt in those days. Short, like this one, but massive breasts and thighs. That had been back in the days, he remembered, when you could still see the cow's shape. Nowadays there was nothing to see but acres of soft, drippy meat. Her tits hung down like—

"Could you give me an idea of your experience?"

Where had she learned that trick with the pencil, pushing it against her lower lip until it almost popped into her soft, luscious, wet mouth, but not quite?

"Sure." He leaned back in the padded armchair they provided for interviewees, the kind of chair made with chrome-steel legs and soft black leather everywhere else. Style was the thing. He knew how to come on with this one, oh yes. Easy. Cool. He dropped one elbow behind the back of the chair and held on to the edge of the back with his hand. Calm. Careless. He crossed his legs. He smiled.

"Sure," he repeated. He ran the tip of his tongue across his lower lip, to get it as wet as hers. "I used to work for Chase. I did about eighteen months with Chase, as a matter of fact, before I shipped out to Nam. I was teller-trainee for a few months but they realized I had a certain style so after the first week I was put in charge of the other recruits, I was kind of a supervisor-trainee, you could say, and I showed them the ropes in a way because, let me tell you, some of them were nervous, and I'm putting it mild. Some of them were shi—some of them were shaking in their shoes, and I was a steady hand who was their age. I set an example of how you go about that kind of thing. I mean, you get your average teller-trainee, they're pretty raw. I say they're fresh out of high school and worried because they think they have to be a whiz with numbers, which I know isn't so, and I knew it even before they told us, I figured it up front, you might say. I knew machines would do the figuring, because machines nowadays do the whole thing, like, faster and without mistakes. Am I right? And I got that over to the recrui—the new people picked it up from me and in no time at all I had them calmed down. 'Come on cool 'cause you ain't no fool,' I used to tell them. You know, a lot of them were colored, and I had to talk to them in their own language if I wanted to get through on their level. So I said—"

"What branch of Chase were you in?" Miss Panetta interrupted.

Joe's hand, holding easily to the back of his chair, lost its grip and fell. He repaired his stylish posture and moistened his lip again. "Fifty-seventh and Broadway."

He was disheartened to see her scribble a note with her pencil. Would she check the reference? Who was she kidding? Nobody checked references any more. "And your immediate supervisor was . . . ?"

He blinked. She was going to check. "Mr., uh, Fo—" He stopped. No sense handing it to her on a silver platter. Fogarty was the bastard who had fired him. "Mr. Fogel," he lied.

"F-o-g-e-l?" she spelled.

"Uh, double l."

She nodded. "And the dates you were there?"

He started to sigh, then stopped himself. They didn't leave you much room, did they? All these interviews were the same. Once they started closing you out, they began slamming doors faster than you could find new ones to open. "That was three years ago," he said. "Before I volunteered for Vietnam," he added, stressing the verb.

Her pencil ticked off a few more words. "Volunteered?"

"I know," he said easily, recrossing his legs the other way. "I sound stupid, don't I? I mean, what guy in his right mind volunteers for a mess like Nam, right? But I didn't know that at the time." He hunched forward in his chair, to try to rivet her attention. "I was a kid. I believed what I read in the newspapers. I was a loyal Republican, too. I believed my President. I thought the President of the United States had to be Number One in everything. What does a kid know? They told me things and I did what I was supposed to do, I volunteered. Call it patriotic. I'm half Italian and there's nobody more patriotic than the guin—I mean, you know. Three long years. Purple Heart twice. Air Corps Medal for—"

"You were wounded twice?" she cut in.

"Four times, but only two Purple Hearts. I—"

"Did you bring your papers with you, by any chance?" Her big wet eyes looked up at him. "Discharge papers?"

"I, uh . . ." He patted his chest pocket, then stopped the charade. Okay, she had him. The last door was slamming shut. "I can bring them in tomorrow," he said then. "I can—"

"That won't be necessary, Mr., uh. We can check it out if we have to." Slam.

"Right." He nodded authoritatively. The clock on the table behind her showed close to five o'clock. Joe found himself wondering how many of the dummies waiting outside would be sent home without an interview and told to come back tomorrow. Bastard banks. All alike. Do what they want. License to steal.

No sense letting her know she'd won. "Can you tell me something about the job?" he asked. Best defense is an offense, right?

"It's in systems," she said, getting up. "We are looking for a few people who understand work flow and we hope to train them to go to the smaller branches and handle routing and re-check and that sort of thing."

He refused to stand. "Pushing around pieces of paper, huh?"

She smiled faintly. "That's just about what everyone does in a bank, isn't it?" She started past him for the door and swung it open. "Thank you very much, Mr., uh . . ." Her voice died away.

Joe sat there, enjoying her embarrassment. He liked throwing her off base. He was supposed to get up like a good little soldier? Fuck her. She could wait till he was goddamned good and ready to get up. They were all alike, these guinea broads. Tina was the same way, always had been. So was his mother, only not as bad. It's always whatever they want, not what you want. Never once.

And now that Tina had the two kids, it was even worse. The only people who needed things were her and the kids. Nothing Joe wanted carried any weight. She used the kids like clubs, slamming his head with them, calling him selfish and a rotten father and a lousy provider and all the garbage that collected in her meathead mind, spilling all over him, and the kids watching their old man eat shit until he couldn't take it any more and just took off for a bar somewhere. Not one of those creep hardhat bars in Queens, where he lived. A bar with class. Like the one down in the Village where Lana hung out. Now, Lana was something else.

He pictured Lana's figure against that of Miss

Panetta. Lana was tall, sleek, like a racehorse or one of those greyhounds. This one here was sleek but small, like a chihuahua or a whippet.

Smiling lazily at her, Joe got to his feet. He moved slowly, insinuatingly, the way he liked to come on with Lana in one of those classy Village bars. There the men moved slow and sure and sleek. Nobody rushed around yakking and hollering like Tina, the pusbag he was married to. Everybody cooled it.

"Thanks a lot, Miss Panetta," he said, making a point of repeating her name when she had already forgotten his.

"If there's anything forthcoming," she said, "I have the form you filled out and we'll call you. However—"

"However," he interrupted smoothly, "I have as much chance of getting this job as I have of sprouting another cock, right? But if I do, Miss Panetta, I'll call you and we can make it two ways at the same time, right? You'll love it, Miss Panetta."

He shoved past her so closely that she shrank back, eyes wide. Okay, that was that. Nobody could say he hadn't held up his end right to the finish. He went on one of these cockamamie interviews almost every day. Jobs were scarce, even jobs that made you puke.

They were all the same, anyway. Qualified or not, you didn't get the job. Veteran or not, no job. But nobody could say he didn't go through the motions. Tina couldn't fault him on that. He tried. He hauled his ass down here and smiled and the dumb cunt couldn't even remember his name for five minutes. Okay. Cool it.

He strode angrily through the waiting room. The looks on the dumdums' faces made him want to puke even more than the job did. They were all kidding themselves. None of them had a chance. There was no job. The whole thing was a cruel little s-m gimmick to let Miss Wetmouth get off her rocks making people crawl. He'd love to humiliate her the way she'd just humiliated him.

The picture of himself with two cocks rose in his mind with such hot speed that he tripped pushing out into the corridor. His face burned with excitement. Then he laughed as he walked along the corridor to the elevators. This was one of those very modern buildings where you needed roller skates to get around. Miles and miles of miles and miles.

He shifted from foot to foot as he waited for the elevator. Damned banks, everything slow, sleepy, dead. They didn't deserve him, not as an employee. The only way they deserved him was raping them with his two avenging cocks. Up the banks. Up all of them.

And that wasn't such a bad idea, either, he thought as the elevator doors opened slowly. They had all the time in the world, those doors. As the elevator crept down to the main floor, Joe considered the idea of raping a bank or two. Easy. Nothing to do but cool it and rake in the cash.

Solve a lot of problems. Get Tina off his back, pay for everything the kids needed. Lay a few bucks on his mother. Get Lana off his back, too, with that operation she wanted. When you're loaded, nobody bugs you. They all suck around.

The smile on his face as he walked out of the elevator was a tiny one, almost not there. But it was a smile nevertheless.

THE AUGUST HEAT was a living presence moving soggily beside him as Joe made his way out of the cool bank building to the subway stairs two blocks away. It was after five. The streets were filling with moist, despairing people in thin dresses and shirt sleeves. The heat walked beside them all, making their skin flushed and damp.

Joe squeezed into a D train and tried to shut everything out of his mind: the interview, the heat, the moisture, the smells, the rumps and elbows shoving against him. Like every other subway rider, he avoided looking into anyone's eyes. The only way this torture could be borne was if you maintained a certain false distance. If you didn't look at them, nor they at you, and eye contact was thus cut down to a bare minimum, then it was possible to play games in your mind, pretend they didn't exist.

He got out at the front end of the West Fourth Street station in Greenwich Village, and as he trudged up the stairs the traffic along Sixth Avenue beat at his ears. Its fumes were choking. Its heat was worse than the subway heat.

Joe wasn't going to his own home tonight, but to his mother's. He'd miss Larry and Lori, but that was the breaks. First, though, after the humiliation of yet another job gone wrong, he needed a bit of class. He needed to hole up in a quiet, dark, cool place where classy people gathered. He needed to reward himself.

He walked west toward Sheridan Square and

beyond, moving slowly along the shady side of the street. A clock showed the time to be five thirty. The bar where Lana hung out would be empty at this hour. Classy people didn't fall right into a bar after work. They cooled it. Delayed the moment. He loosened his tie and took off his seersucker jacket. Hot.

He hated wearing this square drag in the Village. He hated ties and jackets. But there was no other way to dress when you went for a job in a goddamned bank. At least his trousers were tight enough up top, and flared at the cuffs. At least he had that going for him.

Village people moved past listlessly. The same giant hand pressed down on all of them. By the time Joe entered the bar, his shirt was soaked. The cool darkness was God's blessing, laid upon his forehead with the smoothness of the priest on Ash Wednesday, a light, powdery touch.

Joe sighed as he sat down on a bar stool. He nodded to the bartender, whom he knew only slightly. "Draw one," he said.

"Michelob?"

"Whatever's cold."

Joe's eyes hadn't yet adjusted to the gloom. "Lana come in yet?"

The bartender shook his head. "Kind of early."

Joe nodded in agreement and took the mug of beer. He sipped it in long, slow swallows. He liked delaying such pleasures, but by the time he ended his first taste half the stein was empty.

"Hits the spot, Littlejoe," a voice said from the far end of the bar. Joe peered into the darkness and made out the face of a man he'd seen in here before, called Don, mid-thirties, plumpish, always dressed very square, the way Joe was dressed today for a bank interview. Come to think of it, Don worked for a bank, didn't he? Didn't Lana tell him once this guy . . . ?

"You're overdrawn, baby," he told the man. "Insufficient funds."

"What?"

"Forget it. I'm pissed off at banks."

Don got up and carried his gin-and-tonic around the bar to sit beside Joe. "What did the bastards do now?"

"Forget it. Which one d'you work for?"

The other man watched Joe empty his beer. "Chase. Give him another," he told the bartender.

"How did we get to be such good friends?" Joe asked.

"Any friend of Lana's is a friend of mine." The chubby man giggled. "Anybody hates the banks is a bosom buddy. If the public only knew."

"Huh?"

The man watched the bartender deliver a new mug of beer and a fresh gin-and-tonic. "If the public only knew how the banks take them. If the dumb mouth-breathing bastards in the street only understood about loans. Christ, if the hoods only realized how easy it is to knock off a bank."

Joe nodded. "That I know about."

"Robbing banks?"

"On that subject"—Joe stopped to take a mighty swallow of the fresh, cold beer—"I happen to be an expert."

Don nodded politely, falling in with the fantasy. "How many you knock over, Littlejoe?"

"Recently or altogether?"

The chubby man shrugged lightly. "Either."

"Recently," Joe said slowly, as if trying to remember with great accuracy, "I been thinking about heisting a certain bank that just turned me down for a systems job. Your bank, I think."

"Got a plan?"

Joe nodded solemnly. "Everything. Even accomplices."

It was the other man's turn to nod. "That's important," he said sagely. "You can't heist a bank without you got accomplices. It's like, uh, when they make like some new detergent. They got ingredients. Nobody can make a new detergent without they got ingredients. It's the same with accomplices. Am I right?"

Joe stared into his beer. "I'm not kidding, baby," he said then. His glance darted toward the bartender, who was at the far end of the bar, taking an order from a youngish, slim man in tight jeans and a batik shirt open to the navel. "I'm serious. It could happen any time."

The chubby man's glance followed along the bar for a moment. "Oh?"

"Yeah. Oh."

Don shook his head pityingly. "Amateurs are all the same," he said then. "You watch a heist job on the TV and you think, what the hell, I can do it as easy as they did it. But you can't." He sipped his fresh gin-and-tonic. "You don't have the right ingredients, Littlejoe. An amateur don't even know what he's missing. For instance, what kind of info have you got?"

"Info?"

"Info," Don repeated loudly. "You think you just walk into some crummy branch bank and they'll have more than a few grand lying around? You gotta have info. You gotta know when they're loaded, like when they have cash for the local payroll checks or whatever. That's one ingredient, info. And the other is follow-through. That you don't have either."

He fell silent, sitting there with an accusatory look on his pudgy face, as if Joe had somehow let him down very badly. "How come you know so much about what I haven't got?" Joe demanded.

Don flapped his hand at him in a don't-kid-me gesture. "Because you're an amateur is why. An amateur can start a heist, but it takes a pro to follow through. There's a hell of a lot more goes on between the time you yell 'Hey, this is a stickup' and the time you split the joint holding heavy bread. Don't even talk to me about amateurs. They're all alike."

Neither man spoke for a while. Whether this was because the bartender had come back into their area or not, Joe didn't know. Normally Joe reacted badly to fat creeps with superior airs. But for some reason he didn't now to Don. Instead he pulled some change from his pocket and fed two quarters into the jukebox. He punched up records at random and returned to the bar. Dietrich's toneless rasp filled the place, chanting some German refrain against a tinny orchestra.

"Ich bin von kopf bis fus . . ."

Joe sat quietly for a moment, judging whether the jukebox noise made his conversation with Don more secure from eavesdropping. Then: "Maybe you're the guy with info."

The chubby man blinked. "Me? What for?"

"For a cut."

". . . das ist meine welt . . ."

They sat quietly for a while. "Not for a cut," Don said then. "For plain ordinary bitchiness." He started to giggle again and grew almost instantly breathless. "Eleven years an assistant chief teller," he gasped after a moment. "Fifteen years all told. They open branch after branch after branch, and not once do I make head teller, not even in some suburban nowhere branch. Not even there."

The two men listened to Dietrich's moan for a long time, sipping their drinks and saying nothing. Finally Joe motioned to the bartender for refills, pulling a five-dollar bill from his wallet. It was the last of his money.

"Lana won't love you tonight," the chubby man murmured.

"Shit she won't."

"She likes a lotta green, baby, and that ain't it."

"She likes a stiff one, too."

Don's glance moved sideways slightly, as if observing Joe without wanting to be caught. "Regular stud, huh?" He giggled softly. "Regular top man on the old totem pole, Littlejoe?"

"You better believe it." They watched the fresh drinks arrive.

"You married?" Don asked then.

"Yeah."

He giggled again. "Me too."

The giggle was beginning to get on Joe's nerves. He didn't mind freaks. After all, this was supposed to be one of those Village gay bars, wasn't it? But creep freaks he didn't need. "Tell me about some branch in Queens," he said then. "Tell me about a nice neighborhood branch, small, where they put together a payroll the afternoon before payday. You got one, or are you full of shit?"

"Got kids?" Don persisted.

"Yeah, I got kids. I asked you something."

The chubby man nodded. He lifted his gin-and-tonic in Joe's direction. "Here's cheers," he said. "I got a branch for you, baby, but you better never bring my name into it. That's why I don't want no cut, no way. If I don't get a cut, I can deny it and the cops have nothing to go on."

"*. . . und sonnst garnicht.*"

"Then why tell me anything?" Joe asked. "If you're not in it for loot, what's it all about?"

The chubby man pursed his lips into a cupid's bow. The Dietrich record ended and a Garland song began. "I got my reasons."

". . . where, over the rainbow, way up . . ."

"No good," Joe told him. "I get the loot. You get nothing. It don't figure. When something don't figure, I don't like it."

". . . a place that I dreamed of, once . . ."

Don's mouth pressed together so tightly that his lips went white. After a moment he glanced at Joe. "Revenge, baby."

"Ah, come on."

"You better believe it. Re-fucking-venge."

"On the bank?"

"A little of my own back, after fifteen years, that's all."

Joe laughed. "You'd pass up a cut, in cash, for that?"

The chubby man's head began to nod. After a moment it seemed as if he couldn't stop the motion. "Right," he said. "Right. Right."

"Working for them did that to you?"

"Right."

"Jesus." Joe sipped his fresh beer. "I heard of lousy jobs. I had most of them myself, one time or another, for the shittiest bosses in the world."

"Not for fifteen years," Don reminded him. "That's what makes the difference between you and me, baby. Fifteen years gives you a hate that nothing can make you forget."

"Except fingering a heist? That'll make you happy?"

Neither man spoke for a long time. The bar was beginning to fill up now with young men in tight, open clothes. The odor of sweat and perfume began to fill the room.

". . . if bluebirds fly, then why can't I?"

★ **3**

I**T WAS NOT A SPECIAL NIGHT**. Joe knew that in some families there was a special night when the married kids came over to eat dinner with their mother. Went back to their mothers' homes to eat their mothers' food. He had never wondered at all that no one ever returned to, say, his father's home to eat his father's food. Joe knew, without having bothered his head over it, that if you called it home and you came for food, it all was your mother's.

Flo was not that bad a cook. You had to hand her that. Not that Tina ever admitted for a moment that her mother-in-law's cooking could even be eaten. Thinking about this as he rode the IND subway out to Queens, Joe smiled crookedly at Tina's ideas about cooking. A five-buck barrel of fried chicken from Colonel Sanders was her idea of a family feast, with French fries and buttered buns, plus a jumbo pizza, a six-pack of Rheingold, potato chips, and Hostess Twinkies or Devil Dogs for dessert.

At age twenty-four, with a shape on her like a Mack truck made of lard, Tina was still eating like a pimple-pussed teen-ager. She still had a cute, kewpie-doll mug on her, though. Not that hard to look at if you draped a flag over the rest of her. And she was the mother of his kids. The Queen of the Take-Out Dinner.

Joe had folded his jacket and laid it on his lap. He'd been lucky to find a seat. At this hour, well after seven in the evening, the hot, tired mobs of people were still going home, still clogging the subway with sweating flesh. He watched a man his age, but gross with fat the way Tina was, hanging from a strap like a sack of pus that dripped on the floor.

It was a wonder, with an Italian mother and an Italian wife, that he hadn't bloated up himself, Joe thought as he swayed damply with the onward rush of the F train. As it rounded a curve, a shriek of steel numbed his ears for a moment.

But, as Joe told himself, he'd always watched his weight. A guy his size, light, fast on his feet, slim-hipped and flat-bellied, had to watch out for even a pound of extra weight. Not that he had a weight problem. At five-five, Joe barely weighed a hundred and twenty, all of it muscle, sinew, and sheer nerve, fast reflexes—a goddamned tiger you'd better not mess around with.

He got off in Corona and slogged tiredly up the stairs to the still-baking streets, his clog heels clattering. What a change from Greenwich Village, he told himself, looking around at the bars with their television sets flaring turquoise and cerise through the tightly shut doors, small islands of air-conditioned chill.

He almost walked into one of them for a quick shot before facing up to Flo, or, rather, to "her" home and dinner. But as his fingers grasped the handle of the door, he looked through the glass and saw two more of those sad-sack Corona asses draped over bar stools, fat cheeks drooping down on each side of the hard cushion, as if the stools had been rammed up into the rear ends of these two Corona battleaxes, mothers of fled sons, of sons clawing at ass-fat that smothered them, clawing their way up and out of Corona and into the fresh air.

Joe's stomach turned over warningly, the caged beast under his lungs shifting uneasily in sleep. It was true, he told himself as he turned away in disgust from the bar and began walking slowly along the hot, dark street toward his mother's home. It was true that he was drowning in cunt meat, Tina's and his mother's, waves of it flopping all over his face, flabby, raw meat that stank softly of secret juices. But what guy wasn't? They tried to drown you inside them, shove you back up where you came from and encase you in a prison of meat where you screamed for air, twisting, blue-faced, dead.

Joe had paused. The heat shimmered up from the pavement in waves. A man in shirt sleeves, a contemporary of Joe's father, paused, nodded, wiped his face with a red bandanna, and moved slowly on to a rendezvous with a bowl of hot, steaming *pasta e fagioli,* a gigantic dish of soft-cooked spaghetti awash in hotted-up sauce from a jar, veal and peppers emitting clouds of heat—

Joe stopped himself. You had to cool it. You couldn't let them know what the sight of them and their flesh and their food did to you, to the sleeping animal that wakened so easily under your heart.

He turned the corner and surveyed a long row of single-family bungalow-type houses, stretching into the dusk as far as he could see. The sky was still bright in the west, but the street lights were on already, in case any cruising gangs of blacks decided to invade this tight Italian enclave.

Once, his grandmother had told him, these houses had been heaven, these shacks tightly crowded next to each other with only a narrow passageway between them, chunks of pepperoni sliced and left standing in a line. Heaven. Their little screened porches had caught the summer breezes. The moment a family could work its way out of the Mulberry Street slums, it made a down payment on a house of its own in Corona. Ignorant Sicilian farmers! As if this corner of hell, with its cramped, squeezed-out-turd houses, was a better place than Mulberry Bend.

Joe felt as he always did walking down this street past houses no amount of ingenuity or work could any longer disguise. They tried. They spent money on cheap tarpaper shingling, on curiously shoddy siding that was painted to resemble mortared stones. They glassed in the screened porches to make living rooms, while the original living rooms were chopped up into bedrooms. They planted flowers, saw them die, planted trees, watched the sulfuric air of Corona kill each one.

He shivered, even in the thick heat of August. Corona had this effect on him, not because it was where he had grown up—what the hell, everybody grew up in some side-chamber of hell, didn't they, some back shithouse like this?—but because this Corona street was so much like the street on which he and Tina and the kids lived. Instead of one-story houses, it had six-story apartment buildings in dark red brick. Thick with soot. But the feeling was the same.

It was incredible, in a way, that no matter how you clawed your way out of it, you ended up in the same place. It wasn't called Corona. It was a few miles farther away from Manhattan and it was called Forest Hills. Yes, where the rich-bitch assholes played tennis. Although Joe always told people it was Forest Hills, the real name was Rego Park, which a lot of the neighborhood people called Corona East, smiling bitterly. One thing you could say for Rego Park, it had Jews. When the wops and the kikes got together, they had enough political clout to keep the niggers out. For a while.

Joe had already walked past his mother's home and was two houses down the street when he heard Tina's honeyed voice, filtered through pads of fat, the voice you might expect to hear if a plate of gnocchi could talk.

"Littlejoe, honey!"

He whirled, eyes blazing. Where the hell had she picked up his nickname? It wasn't the one he'd grown up with. It was his Village name, the one the class people downtown called him. "Y'bring the kids?" he grunted, walking back to his mother's home and up the cracked concrete walk to the front door.

"Huh, honey?"

He examined her face through the screen door between them. She was his height, even in the slop-slop slippers she was wearing now. She announced herself a mile away, in the house, on the street, in supermarkets, all that meat slipping and slapping and sliding and slopping from one fat foot to the other in heelless slippers.

Her face was round, like one of those idiot smiley-faces people used to wear as buttons or sewn-on patches. Her mouth was big, with big lips, and her cheeks were smaller mounds of their own, equally circular. Tina's nose was tiny but perfectly formed, like Elizabeth Taylor's, classy, with a slight arch, thin nostrils. Her brown eyes looked like two ripe Greek olives swimming in fat that was only start-ing to melt, still white as suet, but liquefying around the edges. She had no forehead, or, rather, her un-plucked eyebrows, arching over the pools of suet, left only a half-inch gap of pale skin before her teased-down bangs, curly as pubic hair, took over.

Tina let him shove the screen door hard against her immense breasts as he came in. She turned up her face as if Joe were a head taller than he really was, and pouted her big soft lips into a kiss. He bit them and, as often happened, felt as if he were biting ass instead. They tasted of garlic and cigarettes, and for some wild reason he could feel an erection coming on.

She was chewing something that still tasted faintly of clove. "Wa' my Dentine, honey?" She propelled the chewing gum toward him with the pulpy tip of her tongue. He took the gum and chewed it for a moment, then spit it out.

"Big deal," he said. "You chewed the flavor out."

"I got another stick." She was fumbling in the shapeless apron tied around her belly. She found the gum, stripped the wrapping, and popped it in his mouth.

He removed the stick and put it between her lips. "Warm it up for me," he said. Then, watching her chew: "Y'bring the kids?"

She shook her head from side to side, chewing strenuously. "Stella's house f' the evening. Honey . . ." Her voice dropped to a low, snarling whine. "How soon kin we blow this place? They got that *French Connection* movie in Sunnyside."

He put his finger between her lips and extracted the wad of gum, then chewed it. "When's the last show?"

"Ten."

"Good. We split this joint right after dinner." He gave her a tight smile. She knew the movie was a weakness of his. He'd already seen it fourteen times in the last year, and he was ready to see it fourteen times more. That wasn't true of every movie. Some he only saw five, maybe ten times. But this one was different, special. "You sure the kids're okay at Stella's?"

"Sure." Like most of the people Joe knew, Tina pronounced this word "shew-uh." Joe made it a point not to talk as goddamned Queens-Brooklyn as all that. He turned and and went inside the house.

His father, reading the *Daily News* in his narrow rocking chair by the side window, looked up as Joe passed, but said nothing. Joe thought of nodding to him, coolly, but decided not to. The miserable bastard deserved nothing, not even that. It was enough that Joe sat down once a week or so at the same table with the rotten piece of shit. Between the enveloping smother of his old lady and the sadistic beatings of his old man, a guy was smart to volunteer for Nam ahead of the draft. Nothing Viet Cong

Charlie could do to him would ever be half as bad as what his own flesh and blood had tried over the years.

He stuck his head in the kitchen and inhaled the smell of garlic, oregano, and stewing tomatoes. "Hi, Flo."

His mother looked up from the old gas range. Actually, Joe told himself, she wasn't fat. Her face was sort of long and thin, actually, and so was her torso, like Lana's body. But Flo had fat hips and thighs, of course—what ginzo broad didn't? On the first look she didn't produce the impression Tina did, a mound of Jello that moved, or the sleek look Lana had. More just a solid feeling.

"Hi, baby. You wanna taste something great?"

"Four pounds of shit in a two-pound paper bag?" he snapped.

Her face, with its big, narrow nose, darkened. "Is that a mouth to bring your mother?"

"Can't help ribbing you, Flo."

Her head shook up and down fast, as if this was only what she'd expected. "That the kind of talk your faggot friends use with their mothers?"

He glowered at her. "I don't like that word."

"Your queer friends. Christ, you're getting just like them. Sensitive."

"Don't use that word, okay?" He glanced around the steaming kitchen as if trapped. How the hell could she stand the heat in here on a night like this? It was a garlic-flavored Turkish bath.

Flo held up both hands, palms turned toward her son as if begging forgiveness. "Your gay friends," she amended. "How are they, your gay buddies?"

Joe felt his face set in a permanent frown. He had to watch the way she did this to him. If he wasn't careful, by the time he was thirty he'd have those deep lines between his eyebrows, the way his father did, permanent frown lines that told the world how bitter and eaten-up inside you were.

"I wouldn't know," he said slowly. "What're you cooking?"

"A little Progresso minestrone, a little cheese canneloni from Fusco's deli, with my own sauce on it. Some cutlets parmigian', and those French-fried onion rings you like from the Chicken Delight place."

He could feel his gut rise up like a trapped tiger, lurching to claw its way to freedom. On a night like this, when the class people down in the Village were drinking cold white wine and eating a little Caesar salad, this tub of shit was mixing up a furnace of food.

He turned away from her because he knew what he was thinking showed on his face. She had always been able to read his face. His father had never even bothered to look at Joe's face, and to Tina his face was only a kind of mirror in which she could see her own fat moon reflected. But Flo was different. She looked. She saw. She dug. Therefore, she was dangerous.

"Where you goin'?" she called as he left the room.

"Outside for some air."

"Dinner's in fifteen minutes."

"Right."

He walked past the immobile form of his father, hidden behind the *News*. "Where you goin'?" he heard the old man rasp.

"Air. Air."

He shoved past Tina, still rooted to the front porch near the screen door. "Air," he told her as he threw open the door and clattered down the wooden steps two at a time, his four-inch clog heels making a volley of sound like a gunfight. "Fresh fucking air," he yelled back at her over his shoulder. He fled down the cracked concrete to the sidewalk, turned right, and strode blindly toward the subway station on Queens Boulevard.

No dinner. No family scene. They could all rot in their own pus. Corona had never been the place for him. Nor Rego Park. At the boulevard he glanced both ways, anxiously, as if he were as trapped here in the hot open air as he had been in that steamy kitchen. A cabdriver, seeing him paused irresolutely just off the curb, slewed toward him. Joe jumped in.

"Sunnyside," he gasped at the driver. "The theater where they're showing that *French Connection* flick."

It wasn't even eight o'clock. He could see the movie and be out of the theater long before Tina's lard-head brain put two and two together and she went looking for him. He fingered the change in his pockets. A dollar for the cab. A couple of bucks for the movie. That left him flat. Maybe enough change to get the subway back to Rego Park. But why go back?

★ 4

HE LEFT THE MOVIE HOUSE after that part of the movie he liked best, where Popeye blasted the rat on the steps of the El station and shot the big cop as they searched the abandoned warehouse, but before the part he hated to watch, where the French crook escaped for good.

He strolled for a while in the somewhat cooler night of Sunnyside, the elevated tracks over his own head as they had been over Popeye's during the big car chase. Christ, that was really it, wasn't it? The chase, the tires squealing, the rammed fenders and dented doors, the people diving out of the way.

He stood for a while in the shadow of a red brick building, a branch of the Chase bank, and watched a train rattle through Sunnyside on the tracks overhead. Joe jingled the coins in his pocket, then, on a sudden impulse, pulled them out and counted them in the red neon glare of a bar across the street.

A dime, a quarter, a nickel.

Not enough for anything. Standing next to a bank, but he didn't have enough to fucking live and breathe and get through this hot night. He saw his father-in-law's light blue Mustang pull up in front of the theater. After struggling with her immense flabby bulk, Tina managed to pull herself out from behind the wheel and slosh up to the box-office window. Trust her, cheap little gash, to con the theater out of a freebie instead of paying admission. Maybe, while she was inside . . .

Joe watched the woman's head behind the glass of the box office nod up and down once. She called an usher, who took Tina inside. Joe walked slowly across the street and along the sidewalk until he was directly opposite the box office and the bank. His father-in-law's car hid him from the ticket seller's gaze—not that she knew him, but maybe Tina had given her a description.

He knew Tina. He knew she was too lazy to take the keys out of the car. He loped across the street and got in behind the wheel. Not only were the keys in the ignition, but the engine was still running. He waited until the ticket seller was lighting a cigarette, threw the transmission into "D," and roared off down Queens Boulevard toward Manhattan. He revved the car up to fifty miles an hour.

The gauge showed an almost full gas tank—no help from Tina, just that her old man was good about such things. Joe gunned through as the green changed to red and raced up a slight incline onto the lower level of the 59th Street Bridge. Funny, her rescuing him. Funny her not even knowing she was giving him a way out. She'd come to recapture him, and instead she'd handed him his escape.

In Manhattan he turned left on Second Avenue and moved easily downtown with the progressive lighting, darting in and out between trucks moving in the same direction. He wondered if she'd report the car to the cops, or if she'd guess he'd taken it. Better phone her old man. Yeah, smart.

He braked at a lighted corner telephone booth, listened to the dial tone, dropped a dime—thirty fucking cents left for the night—and phoned Tina's father.

"Yeah, it's Joe. Listen, I got your Mustang, Gino. Okay?"

"Wha'? You ga' wha'?"

"It's me, Joe, Tina's husband. I got your Mustang. Okay?"

"Whadya mean you goddit?"

"Just tell Tina I got it."

"Don' she know you goddit?"

"Christ!" Joe slammed the telephone back on its hook, jumped into the car, and continued downtown on Second until he reached Fourteenth Street. You couldn't waste your life trying to make these old goombars understand. Gino didn't know anything about his daughter except that she was happily married, had two gorgeous kids, left them with Gino and his wife almost as often as she left them with her sister, Stella, and had a good job in Chase Bank. Not that Tina had worked at Chase for the past three years. Just that Gino still thought she did.

He turned south on Seventh Avenue and slowed the Mustang slightly as he cruised through Greenwich Village. It had been through Chase that he'd met Tina.

They'd both worked for the goddamned bank, him in a branch in Manhattan, her in a Brooklyn office. They'd met on a bank picnic up in Westchester, a whole day's outing with barbecue lunch, barrels of beer, baseball, even boating and swimming at a little lake. He'd enticed her out on a boat in the middle of the water. It had been almost time to leave, the sky getting dark, half an hour before the buses showed up and everybody went back to town.

He'd been her first, pulling her down into the bottom of the boat, yanking up her dress, ripping her little bikini panties because he pulled them too hard. Her muff had been as neat and stiff as brunette Brillo. She had had no idea what to do, how to help him. It didn't matter. He didn't need any help. In a way it was a real kick making a virgin, because there were no smart cracks about his size. Christ, what did these whores know, anyway? As if size meant anything. It was whether you knew what to do with it or not. Miss Panetta was going to get two of them, the bitch.

In the end, even after they were married, he felt something special for Tina, even after she bloated up like a slab of rotten pork. Whatever he did to her, she loved it. No matter how fast he came, she adored it. Nothing he could do to her was anything but beautiful. She said as much, over and over again, maybe not in words but in the way she let him abuse her.

No other broad would stand for the way he treated her. It was almost like not being married, the way he almost never showed up except to play with the kids a little. And this thing tonight, walking out on her and leaving her with his mother, then stealing her father's car. She ate it up. She loved it. To her it was marriage.

He grinned as he steered right onto Bleecker and started looking for a parking place. The good thing about breaking a broad in from the start, especially a religious guinea like Tina, was that she didn't know what any other man was like. You were it. You were everything. She took it and liked it.

He parked the Mustang on Bedford, not far from Christopher, and carefully locked it up. The first thing Tina would do when she found the car stolen was call her old man, and he'd tell her the news. So there wouldn't be any cops staking out the car when he came back to it again. Now the trick for tonight was to find himself a sponsor. He didn't dare show his face at the bar where Lana hung out until he had a few bucks to spend.

He walked quickly along Christopher, nodding to this passerby and that. He was well known in the Village. Littlejoe was a name people had heard of. Even these leather freaks knew him, because he could outleather any of them. They'd all heard of him. It wasn't like Rego Park or Corona. This was Ground Zero for excitement. And where classy, exciting people put it together, Littlejoe was a well-known person.

Maybe Mick would stake him to a night. Mick wasn't a bad guy. He was even some sort of distant cousin, although Flo claimed never to have heard of him. Being Italian, naturally Mick was Flo's cousin, but she refused to recognize him because people said Mick was Maf.

Labels. Until they had a label slapped on them, nobody was a person to people like Flo or Tina. Everybody had to have a label, and if they could label a guy "faggot," oh, man, that tickled their insides. Sure, Mick ran a few leather bars at the river end of Christopher, dark, hot places where you could find yourself somebody who liked getting whipped. Sure the cops had to be paid off steady, right up to the lieutenants, in order to keep the places open and running. Did that mean Mick was Maf? It was a business expense, just like the monthly rent.

Littlejoe checked the front bar at the first leather joint. Since the time was just ten o'clock, the place was still not filled to capacity. He signaled the bartender.

"Yah?"

Joe was glad he'd left his jacket in Gino's car. Even now, in sweaty shirt and loose tie, he looked too square to get within five city blocks of a place like this. "Mickey around?"

"Who's asking?"

"His cousin, Littlejoe."

The bartender squinted through the cigarette haze at him. "Oh, yah," he said in a throaty purr, as if his voice had been left too long in a solution of tobacco and whiskey. "I di'n't see you. You're kinda small." He laughed to himself in a velvety series of chuckles. "No offense, pal. Uh, Mickey is, let's see. He's over at the other joint right about now. If you don't catch him there, try back here after he makes a night deposit at the bank."

Joe nodded, favoring the bartender with a severe frown. Nobody made jokes about his size. But, shit, he couldn't stop for a fight now. He needed to find Mick and hit him up for a ten or two. He left the bar quickly, pacing along Christopher, past Hudson, pressing west toward the distant elevated road where the West Side Highway ran.

The second bar was far raunchier than the first, which was still east enough to be considered a sight-seeing stop on the tours of more daring visitors from uptown. The second joint was a real bucket of blood, originally a sailors' joint where they traded off stolen merchandise to be retailed in fake Army-Navy stores around town: Japanese cameras, transistor tape recorders, small, expensive items, often still in their original packaging.

Joe cased the front of the place without finding his cousin. He moved toward the back room, where, later in the evening, orgies were staged for the insiders. New boys in town were broken in. Old boys, newly on the loose after a bust-up, would advertise their liberated state there.

"Hey, Littlejoe, man."

Joe turned to see a friend of his, Sam, sitting at one of the tables with two older men. Sam was barely twenty, but he'd already done time, not only in training school but in state prison. It was there that he'd gotten so peculiar about making it with big men. He'd been so badly broken in at prison—nine guys gang-buggering him till he needed four stitches before the bleeding could be stopped—that he had a deathly fear of big men. The two at his table were. Joe was not.

"Hey, Joey, man, what's shaking?"

Littlejoe shrugged. "You see my cousin, Mick?"

"Nah." Sam's face was small, neat-featured, pretty and dark, like one of those wop angels they used to paint on church ceilings, but very, very serious.

Something next to his right eye twitched at Joe. A signal? What? "You ready to go, baby?" Sam asked.

Joe nodded. He got the message: Sam needed to be rescued. "Let's go, sweets," he said. "I got the engine running."

Sam got to his feet. One of the two bigger men, in his forties, placed his palm on Sam's skinny chest and shoved hard. Sam toppled over backward, taking the chair with him.

"Siddown," the man yelled. "You're with us, you cheap hustler."

"I'm his date," Littlejoe said. He watched Sam getting back on his feet again. Would he have to tackle this big goon?

"Shit you are."

Joe nodded solemnly. He reached over to pick up the fallen chair as if righting it on its legs again. Instead, he swung it up from under with such force that when it broke against the man's front teeth blood spurted from his mouth and nose. The other man turned pale, and got up and ran out.

"Thanks, Littlejoe." Sam's eyes were darting nervously around the darkened back room. His normally serious face looked especially grave. This wasn't really his scene, and he knew it. One by one was his scene, gently, not with force. "He may be laying for you outside, the other guy."

Joe shrugged. "Let's go find Mick."

They walked back to the bartender, asked him where the owner was, and received the news that he'd left for the bank already. That meant Mick had at least one, maybe two gorillas with him. No sense bracing him for a touch until he was alone again. Give him half an hour.

"I need bread," Littlejoe said conversationally. They were strolling along Christopher, moving back east at a leisurely fashion. The sidewalks were filled with male couples like them, except that Sam and

Joe weren't touching each other. "Gonna ball Lana tonight, man, and that broad don't ball without I lay a few solid blasts on her."

Sam shook his head sadly. "I hate to see you in a relationship with that," he said. "You're a pal, man. That Lana is an animal. You know that."

"Ever meet my wife?" Littlejoe asked. It seemed to end the discussion. They stood at the corner of Washington Street and watched a heavy refrigerated meat truck trundle by. The driver in the cab waved at them. Joe had never seen him before, but Sam waved back.

"How much bread you need, man?" Sam asked then.

"Double saw?"

"Too heavy." Sam had been reaching for his hip pocket. Now he stopped and watched morosely as the trucks rolled by. "I got two fives to my name," he said glumly. His usual mood of depression seemed to deepen.

"More'n you usually hold. Where'd you score?"

"That Hertz truck lot near Twelfth Avenue," Sam said. "I blew a guy twice. You never saw anything like it in your life. Little redneck cracker from Georgia or Alabama, your size, horny as a bull. I go down once for a finnif. I'm ready to move along and what the hell, he's up again, just as big but twice as swole. You know, it had a head on it like a tennis ball, man. Some guys get that way the second time. So, what the hell, another finnif. I'll split with you, Littlejoe. You saved my ass real good back there. I don't forget favors."

Joe shook his head. "You gotta stop working the trucks," he said. "Those bastards will rip you in two some day just to see what your guts look like. They're all crazy, those drivers."

"I don't make it with big guys. Just the short ones."

They crossed Washington and headed east. Littlejoe wondered what his mother would make of someone like Sam, a nice Italian boy, face like an unsmiling angel, giving head to Jimmy Hoffa's finest patriots along every West Side truck route in the Village. Not that Sam liked it especially. But it was steady money.

"There he is," Joe said, pointing, as Mick and two huskies pulled up in a cab and started inside the more respectable of the two leather bars.

"*Eh, cugino, come si dice?*" he yelled.

The heavy-set Mick stopped, turned, and saw Littlejoe. "*Eh, Giuseppe,*" he called. "Who's that, Sam?"

As they reached him, Joe pumped his cousin's hand. "You're just the friend I'm looking for, Mick, baby."

His cousin was older by ten years, taller, and heavier without being fat. He came from the dark side of the family, olive skin blackened by the summer sun, blue-black hair glinting under the street lamp, white teeth bared in a welcoming smile. "How much?" he retorted.

"What?" Joe asked, blinking.

"*Cuanto?*"

"I need twenty, Mick, pay you back the first of the month."

"When your welfare check comes in?"

"Naturally."

"Which check?" Mick said, laughing. He pounded Littlejoe's shoulder so hard he rocked his frail frame. Then, turning to one of his bodyguards, he said: "This boy has moxie, Frank. He's got three addresses and each month he collects three welfare checks. Plus unemployment, right, baby?"

"I do okay." Littlejoe was embarrassed. No one knew his finances, not these gorillas, not Sam, who was only a casual friend, not a close one. He hated the idea of his big-mouthed Maf cousin making fun of him in public. But Mick had already drawn out his wallet, and was peeling off two twenties.

"Here, *piccolo Giuseppe,*" he said. "I hope that Lana

woman of yours enjoys every cent of it."

Joe almost, but not quite, cringed. It was no one's business about him and Lana. If he liked someone, why did all of Christopher have to know about it? But they did already, he reminded himself. He'd never kept Lana a secret. He was proud of her. Not like that cow he was married to. One of these days he was going to divorce Tina and really marry Lana. He considered himself married to her already, in the sense that one stoned night they had held a mock wedding with equally stoned friends.

"Thanks, Mick. You're a pal." Joe pocketed the two bills.

"It's only good business, baby," his cousin said. "Lana is inside my joint right now. You're gonna blow the whole thing back into my cash register anyway." He gave Littlejoe a wink and went inside, his body-guards moving easily in front and in back of him.

With Mick gone, the street was suddenly much quieter. Joe turned to Sam. "Coming in?"

The small, dark boy shook his cherubic head. "I don't like to see you with that animal," he said, his face deadpan empty.

"Come on. I'll buy you a blast."

Sam's head continued shaking. "No thanks, Little-joe. Be good." He started to leave. Joe reached for his arm and held him. "Lemme go, man."

"No, listen, Sam, I got something to talk to you about."

Sam turned back. "What?" His voice was sullen.

"Business. I heard you were very cool with a cannon."

Sam frowned. "So what?"

"You holding a piece now?"

"I'm on parole, man. They jug my ass if they find me packing iron."

"I got an idea how we can make big money."

Sam's face went sour. "I know those ideas. One of them got me two to five." He shook off Joe's hand.

"If I'd been carrying heat it would've been seven to fifteen for armed robbery."

"I said I had an idea. It don't include getting caught."

Sam's eyes widened for a moment; then their lids lowered. "None of them do." He moved off along Christopher. Littlejoe watched him disappear into the crowd. Jail had taken all the joy out of Sam, permanently. He found himself wondering how hard it could be if he too landed in jail. Could it be worse than Nam? Nobody tried to frag you in jail. There was a lot of asshole banditry, but, Christ, they had that in Nam, too.

He entered the bar and moved into the back room. This was a classier place than Mick's other back room. The orgies here were refined. The impromptu shows had a little class, a few laughs. And women were allowed back here, as long as they came with a man. He spotted Lana at once.

She had gotten up on a table and was singing a song whose words didn't make sense, maybe because she was drunk and couldn't remember them. Two men were seated at her feet, clapping time for her. Every once in a while she would flex her long foot in its spike-heel slipper and shove the toe under one of the men's noses. "Kiss, kiss," she lisped.

Then she resumed her song, something about a man who played a piano in old Hong Kong, but the music never made any more sense than the words. Littlejoe started toward her. She had decided to strip now. She was a tall girl, almost six feet in height, which Joe loved, and she was slender, poured into a gold lamé dress that sparkled in the dim light and barely covered her shoulders and breasts. She pulled one shoulder strap free and her left breast popped out, firm, lush, big, with a nipple as hard as a bolt screwed into her rather small areola.

People at other tables were clapping now and yelling encouragement. A woman against the wall had tucked two fingers in her mouth and was producing a shrill wolf whistle in time to Lana's sinuous movements.

Littlejoe stopped a table away.

He didn't mind her theatricality. After all, that was what she was all about. A lot of people badmouthed her for the way she dressed, that spun-sugar wig she flaunted, with its long back flip and bangs, those huge upcurling fake eyelashes flecked with glitter, the dark eyeshadow, the dark lipstick, rouged out to make her mouth bigger than it was, the hectic spots of color on her cheeks. But that was Lana. Take her or leave her.

She had worked her other breast loose and was stroking it admiringly. People began to hoot and yelp like dogs. She was wriggling up out of her golden sheath now, pulling it down over her hips while she writhed and mouthed nonsense words to the rhythm of the clapping.

Her navel came into view and, an instant later, the top of her muff, flaxen and flat, like an expensive linen towel. She turned and stuck out her ass at the crowd, slowly unveiling it with a back-and-forth bump in time to the clapping. "Kiss, kiss." Then she turned back and her penis, engorged, arose from between her legs like some primeval sea monster searching for its mate.

The crowd went wild. Littlejoe glanced proudly around him. He had no idea how many of the people here tonight had known Lana was a man. A few. Himself, of course, included.

Even at midnight, the apartment on East Tenth Street was hotter than the street outside. Or so it seemed to Joe.

The damned trouble, he told himself as he lay beside Lana on the old king-sized mattress shoved into a corner of the living-room floor, was that they had no cross-ventilation. Few of these tenements had been built to let air flow through from front to back. Or, if they had, over the years greedy landlords had so chopped and walled them off into cheap little apartments that the air had long ago stopped moving, stopped clearing out the stink, stopped cooling people on hot August nights like this one.

It was, nevertheless, not a bad little pad for what he wanted. He needed it as an address for the welfare people and as a place to bring Lana after he'd gotten her high. He'd been pretty selective as to whom he brought here. This wasn't just any of his welfare pads. He'd even brought his mother here. This was where he crashed in the Village, even though it was a little too far east for the real action.

"Unreal," Lana muttered, rolling over on her back and snuffling.

"What, baby?"

Littlejoe liked it when Lana was stoned out of her skull and nine-tenths asleep. He'd brought her home in something like a fireman's carry, her long, slender body half draped over his shoulder. He might be a head shorter than she, but he knew how to handle

weights, always had. She lay naked now in the darkness, only a faint glow coming through the grimy
front windows from the street lamps three floors
below on Tenth Street, her lovely breasts firm and
young. He stroked her face for a moment. She
needed a shave again.

Joe grinned to himself in the darkness as he
stroked Lana's long, slender flanks. Sam had called
her an animal, and he was right, of course. She was
like a racehorse, a thoroughbred animal, fast and a
little wild. He understood why people like Sam hated
people like Lana. There had been a whole change
among the gays in the last few years as they came out
of the closets, a change to being natural like the
blacks. The slogans were almost the same: "black is
beautiful" and "gay is beautiful." One promoted Afro
hair and looked down on skin-lightening and hair-
dekinking as a form of slave mentality. The other,
among gay males, led to dressing like men, perhaps a
bit freer and more creative than most, and looking
down on drag queens.

Well, that was Lana. The bitchiest drag queen of
them all. And Littlejoe had her.

Maybe drag queens were on their way out as part
of gay life. Maybe not. In any event, it was too late
for Lana, with her silicone-injected breasts. She had
lived the life so long now that she was comfortable
only as a woman.

"Real dumb," she murmured and rolled away from
Joe's stroking.

"You okay, baby?"

She had taken on quite a load even before Joe
had found her in the back room of Mick's Number
One bar. And it hadn't been till maybe four stingers
later that she'd been willing to pull herself together
and go home with him—or, rather, let herself be
carried away.

"Last of the big-time unreal spenders," she said

very distinctly now, spitting out the words with an excess sibilance that told Joe she was angry.

"Yes, baby."

"Couldn't even spring for a whole, entire cab," she went on viciously. "'S'matter, didn't your welfare check come in, Daddy Warbucks?"

"Next week, baby."

"Carrying me through the Village like a common baggage." She had started to sniffle. "Unreal little jerk-off."

"Now, baby."

"If you loved me," she said, suddenly whirling to face him, "you'd think enough of my reputation not to expose me to every insane prying eye in the Village."

He saw that her mascara was running in black rivulets from under her eyes. Because she was lying on her side, the black was running sideways from the corner of her lower eye into the hair around her ear. He watched, fascinated, as the mascara from the upper eye began to run over the bridge of her rather large, aquiline nose.

"If you really loved me," she was saying, "there'd have been a cab. How much, I ask you, does a cab cost? Can it possibly be more that one of those insanely overpriced stingers that Mafia cousin of yours sells? Um?"

"No, baby."

"What is he charging these days, three whole dollars a whole entire blast?"

"That's about right."

"Everybody knows the drinks cost, like, unreal, because nobody goes there to drink. They go there to look up my asshole. The old tunnel shot. I really showed it to them tonight, too." She shifted from a sob to a giggle and wiped her eye, smearing the wet mascara into a blotch like a black eye.

"If you honestly loved me," she went on then, in a

calmer voice, shifting out of her high register into a throatier one, "you would somehow get it all together for a change and help me with my problem, wouldn't you?"

"What's that, baby?"

"What's that?" Her voice slid up an octave in irritation. "You of all people have the insane nerve to ask what my problem is?"

"Oh, that."

Littlejoe lay in silence for a while. She was back on that again. He'd checked it out with friends. Even if you could get them to do it for you in the States, say at Johns Hopkins down in Baltimore, it still cost about three grand. That included the whole thing, castration and the making of a cunt. If you had to take your problem to Casablanca or Stockholm because the doctors in Baltimore said no dice, it cost less for the surgery and hospital but you had the air fare thrown in. So it always came to about three grand. And what for? Some whim of Lana's? Who needed the whole thing?

"You'll love me when I'm a real woman all over," Lana said then, her voice dropping to a point where it was lower than Littlejoe's, and very arousing to him.

"No I won't."

"You'll adore me, baby."

"You're fine just the way you are."

"Uh-uh. No way. Like this it's unreal, love."

"Not to me," Littlejoe insisted doggedly. "I like you this way. I don't like you with parts missing."

"But a new part put in."

"That's bullshit," Joe corrected her. "I talked to guys who know. They say it's a lousy substitute. I know what the real thing is, remember. Even on Tina. What they'll cut for you is no way like the real thing, no muscles, no juices to make it nice and slick, no nerve endings. You won't feel. It'll be like I'm fucking somebody else."

"And you," she snapped waspishly, "won't have this all-day sucker, will you?" She sneered at him, her nostrils widening fearsomely. "It's everything for you, isn't it, bitch? You want that fat slut out in Queens at your beck and call. Roll over, have kids, drop dead, on command like an insane doggie. And you want me to take any way it strikes you, upside down, up the rear, in the mouth. It's, like, unreal, a circus act. They warned me about you," she added darkly.

Neither of them spoke for a long moment. "What's that?"

"You heard me," Lana retorted. "They warned me you were no good. A real waster. They warned me you'd fuck anything that'd stand still for it. Oh, baby, were they right or were they right."

"Who warned you?"

"Ev-ry-body," Lana drawled scornfully. "Ab-so-lutely every mother on the street told me what an insane cunt you were, not even a proper gay, AC-DC, swings any way he can get it with anything that he can tie down and ram it into. What you are, you're a nymphomaniac."

Joe laughed softly. "Is that what I am, huh?"

"You got, like, an unreal itch," Lana told him. "Sometimes I can't believe what you do. Other times, of course, it's so easy to figure."

"No kidding."

"So easy," she taunted him. "You're an open book with that baby tool of yours. Talk about Tiny Alice. I had a thirteen-year-old once that had three times as much as you, and he didn't stop growing for another five years."

"Cradle-snatching, huh?"

"People say to me, 'Lana,' they say, 'it's, like, unreal how that Littlejoe carries on,' they say, and I say, 'You wouldn't believe what I know about him,' and they say, 'Like what?' and I say nothing. I protect your insane reputation. Don't ask me why."

"Because you love me, that's why."

"Love? With that kind of love, who needs suicide? You'll murder me with love." She had started to cry again. "You won't even pay for the one thing I need to become a real person."

"Maybe I will."

The tears stopped. "Yes? When?"

"One of these days."

"The same promises." Lana shook her head, and the long flaxen wig slid uneasily over one eyebrow. "I don't know why I believe them, why I keep sticking with you, why I protect your good name, even now. Let the whole world know what kind of unreal creep you are, why should I care? I got everything about you figured out, and there isn't even one good reason to keep it to myself."

"What's my secret?"

"Never mind. We both know what it is."

"No, tell me," he coaxed.

"I've said it before. It's not exactly the hottest news in town." She rolled on her back and stared at the ceiling. Passing cars in the street below set up strange shiftings of light and shadow with their moving headlamps. "It's that insane minicock of yours. Anybody who calls you Littlejoe has probably heard how small it is. He's probably even seen it, the way you flaunt that tiny thing."

"I never heard anybody complain about it," Joe said.

"It's because you're so touchy. Nobody wants to run afoul of you. You're small, but everybody knows you're, like, insane strong."

"You better believe it."

"Then if you're really strong," she said, "be a man. Get me what I need. Don't think of it as a favor to me. Think of it as an investment. I'll keep repaying you for the rest of my life."

"You will?"

Lana lay without speaking for a moment. Littlejoe decided she'd gone too far, promised too much.

Part of Lana's charm was her selfishness. It turned him on. "You really want the operation that bad?"

"I want it," she responded in a low, dramatic voice, "more than life itself. If I don't get it soon, I'm doing away with myself."

"Don't put me on, baby."

"I'll kill myself. And you'll be responsible."

"That," he said, "I've heard before."

"You won't hear it again. The next you'll hear is from the coroner."

Littlejoe watched the patterns of light on the ceiling. Somewhere in the distance somebody was strumming a guitar, probably sitting on the front stoop of one of the brownstone tenements. Whoever was playing the guitar wasn't very good, but he kept at it, slamming into one chord after another as if he knew what he was doing. The jangling began to irritate Joe.

"What if I told you," he said then, drawing out his words in the same tantalizing way Lana had, "that very soon I'll have enough money to buy you a thousand operations."

"What would I say? Bullshit is what I would say."

"I'm not kidding."

"I've heard that before," Lana mocked him.

"You won't hear it again," he said, mimicking her ultimatum. "The next you'll hear is what you read in the newspapers or see on TV."

"That boring bank job again. Like, unreal."

"You won't find the bread boring."

"You're still into that whole fantasy schtick?" Lana said.

"It's no fantasy."

"If I wait for you to pay my operation from a bank job," Lana told him, "I'll have a long gray beard and my tits will be swinging around my goddamned navel."

Littlejoe sat up on the mattress. He was covered with a coarse dew of perspiration, but whether it was from the heat or from thinking about robbing a bank, he had no idea. "I told you. I said I wasn't kidding. And when I say something, it's so."

"Dream on."

"You'll see."

"Shit I'll see. And I'm already looking at it." She turned to stare provocatively at him, her eyes imbedded in soggy swamps of mascara.

Joe got to his feet, anxious to be on the move, to get himself out of range of such talk and move his plans along. There was a pad where Sam and a few other kids crashed at night. This thing was moving along faster than he himself knew.

"Where you running away to?"

"Business."

She watched him dress and move to the door. "You're just leaving me dumped here? I don't have a crying dime to my name, you insane bitch."

"Here." He reached in his pocket and threw a bill at her, not sure what denomination it was. He opened the door. A wave of piss smell wafted in from the hall, laced with the oily stench of roach killer. "I'll be moving around the Village a few hours. Clean up your face and I'll see you at one of the bars around maybe two or three." He slammed the door behind him and clattered down the stairs on his clog heels.

Outside the street was cooler, but not by much. Across the way a young man, wearing only overalls, was tapping his bare foot as he attacked the guitar strings with amateur zeal.

Littlejoe frowned. He remembered what the closet queen Don had said earlier about amateurs. This bank thing couldn't be anything but a professional job. Nothing connected with Littlejoe could be amateurish. He was too much of a name in his own right to do anything but a total pro job.

He set out to find Sam.

THE PAD WAS SOMEWHERE on Barrow or Morton Street, on the far west side of Greenwich Village. Littlejoe had been there once before—or, rather, he had been strolling past the place when someone mentioned that it was where Sam crashed with a few of his friends.

Most of them, like Sam, were barely out of their teens, if that. They had a sort of den mother, a middle-aged writer type who had left his wife and given up the straight life for what he was doing now: taking care of the group, clearing out rats and roaches, making sure there was always a hot mug of soup for the boys, or hash if they smoked, or Band-Aids if they bled. Hard drugs were out, but almost anything else was in, Joe had been told.

Naturally, in order to live, in order to bring home a gallon of cheap California red or a carton of butts now and then, they had to work the trucks, like Sam, or else steal.

From things Sam had said, Joe gathered that all of them had homes they might once have gone back to, but not any more. They'd rather scuffle and steal than take from their parents, many of whom had long ago given up trying to get them back, or even trying to find out where they were. After the age of eighteen it became a lot easier, Sam had told him, to kiss off your home. Now all of them had their own home, loose-knit but happy enough. And the older man who looked after them didn't require any special kind of servicing. He wasn't into that scene, Sam had reported, trading shelter for sex. "Some kinda do-gooder," Sam had put it, "but gay."

Littlejoe had always found it peculiar that Sam never thought of himself as gay, even though the rest of the boys, and their den mother, were. Sam was into the gay scene almost exclusively, but if he was asked, as occasionally happened, he would always claim he wasn't really gay, just "sort of trying things out." It made for a special bond between Sam and Joe, who did not think of himself as gay either.

Striding along the dark stretches of lower Seventh Avenue, Littlejoe turned in at Barrow and followed its forty-five-degree turn as it led west toward the river. There were three of these strangely kinked streets here, one next to the other, Morton below Barrow and St. Luke's below Morton.

Joe felt sure the pad wasn't on St. Luke's, which was a rather fancy segment of Leroy Street that had changed its name for just that block. The houses were one-family ones, some still with the original gas-lamps outside the front doors. One was where some ex-mayor of the city had shacked up with his girlfriend. Another was supposed to have a ghost. It wasn't the block for a gay crash pad.

He found it, finally, on Morton, between the bend in the street and the corner of Bedford, a basement apartment with windows that barely looked out at shoe-leather level to the sidewalk. There were no lights inside, but Littlejoe felt pretty sure he'd find someone to let him in. He descended the stairs and rapped on the steel door. It boomed like a drum.

After a moment it opened several inches, to show a sturdy steel-link chain holding it from opening any farther. The older man peered out at him. "It's one A.M., man," he said. "Go home."

"It's Littlejoe. I'm a pal of Sam's."

The single eye watching him shifted sideways in its

socket, then stared back at him. "Sam's asleep. Come back tomorrow, man."

"Shit he's sleeping. I gotta talk to him."

"About what?"

"You his pimp?" Littlejoe asked.

"About what?"

"Business. A chance to make himself a buck."

"Stealing what?" the man snapped back.

"You're not his pimp, you must be his mother," Joe retorted. "Let the guy answer for himself. Let me talk to him."

The older man paused for a moment. The one eye blinked twice. "You can't talk to him in here. We got people trying to sleep."

"I'll buy him a drink at some bar."

"When will you get him back?"

"What the hell *is* this?" Joe exploded. "He's over eighteen, for Christ's sake."

"That's not it. We get ripped off here regular, like a lot of basement places. I lock up for good right about now. Anybody comes back after I lock up, he can't get in till morning."

"I get it, you're not his mother, you're his warden."

"From that smart mouth on you," the man said, "you really must be Littlejoe."

"A legend in his own time. That's me."

"You're a legend, all right," the man agreed. "Sam told me you helped him out of a tight squeeze earlier tonight. So, I guess . . ." His voice died away as he left the door.

Joe stood in the downstairs areaway and waited. No traffic could be heard on Morton or even nearby Bedford or Seventh Avenue. This time of night, nobody cruised these Village streets, not even cops. This was the so-called quiet quarter of the area, officially labeled a historical landmark section. With no clubs or theaters nearby, the area had few late-night strollers.

The steel door closed, then opened wide enough for

Sam to slip out, buttoning a denim jacket over his bare chest, even though the night was still quite hot. His eyes looked wary, and his face, as always, was as grave as if carved from stone. Sometimes he reminded Littlejoe of a painted angel, but tonight he looked more like one of those thingies on the roofs of churches that the water spouts through, better-looking than most but still kind of grim.

"What gives, Littlejoe?"

"Got a business proposition."

Sam's head was already shaking from side to side as the words left Joe's mouth. Behind him, standing in the doorway, the older, den-mother type watched both men carefully, as if they were speaking a code he was trying to crack.

"Don't say no till you hear it."

"I don't have to hear it, Littlejoe."

His big black eyes looked pleadingly at Joe. The den mother moved up behind Sam. "You don't have to discuss it tonight, Sam," he said. "It'll last till tomorrow. Or even till never."

"Tonight," Joe insisted. "Now. Come on, I'll take you over to Chumley's for a beer."

He had mentioned the only bar in the neighborhood, no more than a block away, a fairly respectable restaurant and drinking place that had once been a Prohibition-era speakeasy and still did its best to preserve a slightly illegal atmosphere. But Sam knew it was basically square and straight, not a leather joint he was liable to have trouble in. The thoughts chased themselves over his stolid, deadpan face and Littlejoe could almost read them as they went back and forth. He realized he had made a good choice in Chumley's. Sam would consider it safe and nearby, a place from which he could leave without being molested, a place where he could tell Joe no and get away with it.

"Just a half-hour. One beer," Sam was saying.

Littlejoe jerked his thumb at the older man. "Clear it with the warden, Sammy. Otherwise he'll come looking for you."

"That mouth," the man said. "That great big mouth."

"It's okay," Sam told him. He took Joe's arm and almost hustled him up the steps and along Morton Street. "He don't mean nothing," Sam said once he was out of earshot of the den mother. "He's a good guy. Without him, we'd be long gone. But he, like, fusses. You know?"

"Fusses. I know."

They were heading up Bedford. Now they turned east again and found an arched entryway in a brick wall. The archway led into a kind of flagstone court-yard filled with bagged garbage and empty cor-rugated boxes in which bottled beer had been shipped. Ahead was another arched door, almost hid-den in darkness. Its wood was so thick that no sound came through it, but when Littlejoe pushed it open a blast of jukebox music hit him in the face.

The bar wasn't terribly long, but it stood at one end of a square taproom area crowded with standees nursing beers and other drinks. Beyond their chatter and the jukebox thump lay a dining room, which was nearly empty at this hour. Littlejoe planted Sam in a corner against the wall and bought two draft beers in mugs, which he tried to keep from spilling as he picked his way through the crowd back to Sam.

A woman stood talking to him, a woman perhaps twice his age, dressed in a body shirt and faded Levis, her aviator spectacles tinted the lightest shade of brown. She turned to Littlejoe as he arrived with the beers.

"Doesn't he talk?"

Joe shrugged. "It's kind of late for him to be out."

"You his brother?"

"Buddy."

"Doesn't he dig girls?"

Joe handed both mugs of beer to Sam. He turned back to the woman, who was half a head taller than he. He eyed her full breasts and narrow waist. "No," he said, "but I do." He reached for her with both hands, fingers outstretched, as if tuning two dials of a large radio. She blinked and backed out of range.

"What kind of thing is that to do?"

"Your pad around here?" Joe persisted. "Let's go there now. By the time Sam finishes both beers, you'll be halfway to heaven, baby."

She took another step back. "Who said you could come on that way?"

"Or would you like both of us?" Joe continued. "We do a great front-and-back act, baby. It's ten bucks apiece."

A look of disgust crossed her face. She turned away and lost herself in the crowd. Littlejoe retrieved one of the beers from Sam. "Now, about this proposition. You remember a closet type name of Don?"

Sam shook his head from side to side. He sipped the beer and left a faint white moustache of foam on his upper lip, like a boy drinking milk. "Chubby bastard with a nervous giggle?" Joe went on. "Works for Chase Bank. He—" He stopped and tapped Sam's narrow chest for emphasis. "He is our meal ticket to thousands and thousands in cash, Sammy."

Sam's eyes hooded slightly, as if in pain, but he said nothing. "He is the guy who will hip us to a real heist," Littlejoe continued. He felt that Sam wasn't really listening, that he had somehow tuned out the words. He poked Sam's chest again, gently, three times. You didn't want to come on rough with Sam, because that only made him pull back deeper in his shell.

The jukebox was slamming so hard that if the room hadn't been filled with warm, sweaty bodies blocking the huge speakers, the noise would have been painful. As it was, Joe could half shout in Sam's ear and know for certain that he wasn't being overheard.

"I have a deal with this Don," Littlejoe went on, choosing his words carefully so that, while he wasn't telling the truth, he wasn't saying anything that he couldn't defend later as being similar to a version of the truth.

"This Don has promised me the most important thing in the world," he said. He watched Sam's eyes move slowly to look at him. He'd finally gotten the little guy's attention. "He promised to finger a small neighborhood bank where on a particular day they make up a big cash payroll. You dig?"

Sam nodded. "I dig."

"That way, instead of the five, six grand the bank usually would have in the till, it's got, maybe, forty or fifty grand, maybe more, maybe even a hundred thousand. I mean, is that the most important detail or not?"

"The most important," Sam said in a low voice that Littlejoe had to strain to hear, "is not getting caught." His solemn face turned to face Joe fully, as if to impress him with this wisdom.

"Right. And the secret of success is speed."

"How d'you figure speed?"

"In and out. Bing, bang. No time for chit-chat. No time for somebody to do a make on your face. Just slam in there at closing time, the last customers in the place. Make the guard lock up. No more visitors, right? Now it's hand over the cash, lock everybody in the vault, out the back door and home free."

Sam's eyes, so dark and grave, had been following this action-packed adventure yarn with little up-and-down jumps, as if viewing it on a small-screen television set. Now his eyes swung up to glance into Joe's. "What makes you think it'll go that smooth?"

"Because I know banks. Christ, I did time in plenty of them. I know the routine. I know where the warning buzzers are. I know what to do about the fucking overhead cameras. I know about the marked bills they always try to hand you for loot. I know the little signals like pulling a shade or not pulling a shade. I know the whole routine, baby. You're dealing with a real pro."

"Good. Then you don't need no amateur like me lousing you up." Sam took a long swallow of beer, as if he had clinched the fact that he was out of the deal.

"I need a hotshot with a cannon," Littlejoe bounced back at him. "I need somebody behind my back I can trust, somebody to ride herd on the people while I clean up the loot. There is nobody I know on this earth I can trust the way I know I can trust you, Sam."

Neither spoke for a long moment. The tune on the jukebox changed from a strident, shouting soul number to a Latin beat. In the relative quiet, the woman who had been trying to talk to Sam let out a shriek of laughter from across the taproom as she talked to a man in flared white ducks and a horizontally striped French sailor's shirt. Whether she had told him about Littlejoe or not, both of them turned to eye Joe and Sam.

Joe wondered if this was the kind of place where he could take the schmuck in white ducks apart and still make a clear escape, the way he had in Mick's leather bar. Probably not. The place didn't have a Maf look. The customers seemed to be here only for booze and food, not for the something special only a Maf joint could buy the protection to offer.

He had a sudden inspiration. "Suppose I tell you," he said to Sam, gently touching his chest with the tip of his finger, "that this entire caper is backed up by Mick's boys?"

"Huh?"

"Suppose I guarantee total Maf cover for the whole job?"

Sam's eyes shifted this way and that, a sure sign, Joe knew, that he had begun to consider the proposition seriously. "What kind of cover?"

"Like taking care of the cops up front. Before we even make our move."

"Mick can promise that?"

"The Maf can."

"Why should they?" Sam asked.

Littlejoe answered quickly, as if speaking the prearranged truth. "For a cut of the action, what else? A cut of my share," he added immediately.

Sam's black eyes narrowed. "What's your share?"

"Well, we got three on the job, you, me, and somebody to drive the car. We got to take care of Don, too," Joe continued, fantasizing smoothly. "So that's four. Don's part isn't risky, so he gets ten percent. That leaves ninety for three guys. I take fifty. You take thirty. The driver gets ten, like Don."

Sam's lips moved slowly, adding up the numbers. "Tell it to me in dollars."

"Right. If we score big, say a hundred grand, ten grand goes to Don, ten to the driver, fifty to me, and thirty grand to you."

Sam blinked. "That much?"

Littlejoe said nothing. Instead of explaining again that it all depended on how much was in the till, he decided to let Sam mull it over on the basis of thirty thousand dollars for his own pocket. He expected that the next thing Sam's mind would balk at would be the largeness of Joe's percentage, but he was wrong.

"How much do you have to give the Maf?"

"Twenty grand."

"So that leaves you with thirty, same as me. It ain't fair, Littlejoe."

"Who's to say? With Maf cover, everything is possible."

"But you deserve more, you're dreaming up the whole gig."

Joe nodded philosophically. "That's life, baby. Without the Maf, we wouldn't move. With it, we'll all be rich." He wondered if he ought to gild the fantasy with an equally imaginary cut for Mick, then decided the ins and outs of Mafia percentages would only confuse Sam.

In truth, if he asked Mick to arrange for Maf cover, the boys would take a flat 50-percent cut, for which they might or might not deliver real protection, depending on whether they had the cops in that particular neighborhood on their pad or not. Some precincts were captained by honesty freaks, who transferred payoff cops somewhere else. In such precincts the Maf couldn't protect anybody, even itself. It simply didn't operate in such neighborhoods. Fortunately, there weren't that many honest areas in town.

He glanced at Sam, who had finished his beer. He wondered how convinced the kid was and whether he ought to come up with some other story to bolster the ones he'd already told. "Whadya say, Sam?"

The corners of Sam's beautifully chiseled mouth turned down in a gesture of resignation. "When do we move?"

"A day or two."

"You got some heat?"

"I can get a few from a relative upstate," Joe promised.

Again Littlejoe found it hard to read Sam's face. Was he in or out? "Those are details I take care of," he promised.

"Um, yeah. Listen."

"What, baby?"

"See if he can get me a forty-five Colt automatic, one of those sidearms the shore patrols carry. They're government issue. No problems with ammo, either."

Littlejoe felt a wave of relief. "You got it, baby," he said and gave Sam a slap on the back, but gently.

7

A WEEK PASSED, in which Littlejoe learned a lot about people he thought he knew everything about.

Take his upstate relative, the one who was supposed to supply guns. He ran a sporting-goods shop outside Buffalo, and a beverage-distribution company, and a small truck line, and the minute you asked him for a favor he got instant deafness. It was like a door slammed, but secretly, because in public nobody was supposed to stiff a member of the family the way Vinnie had stiffed his niece's boy, Littlejoe. Phony guinea bastard.

Anyway, Joe thought now, sitting in the quiet of the Queens bar and sipping his third Rheingold of the afternoon, he'd promised Sam that he would be in charge of such details, and he was. Cousin Mick had come up with a GI carbine with three five-round clips of .30-30 slugs, hollow-nosed for more stopping power. That was good, but awkward to have around in Gino's car.

That simpleminded father-in-law of his hadn't yet tumbled to the fact that Tina's husband had swiped the Mustang for good. A permanent heist. And, since Joe had been careful not to go anywhere near Tina or the kids or his mother, there was no way Gino could ask for the car back, unless he wanted to go to the cops, which he didn't. How would it look, fingering your own son-in-law?

So the carbine, wrapped in a green-and-blue beach

towel, had been shoved under the carpeting on the floor of the Mustang's trunk, where only Sam knew about it.

As for the .45 automatic, Littlejoe had had even more of a hassle. Mick's source wanted five cees for such a gun. It seemed to be a popular item, because a lot of guys who had been in the service were familiar with it and had qualified on it at target practice. In addition to stopping power, the tumbling .45 slugs—which chopped through a man like a hammer blow—were fairly accurate at close range.

Finally, just last night, Joe had gone for drinks with a guy he knew around the Village, a political type, young hustler eager for votes and just breaking in with Tammany. He'd taken him for drinks to his club on Thompson Street, one of those Old Country joints with a wop name which meant it was used for private target practice, down in concrete ranges beneath the basement, where the noise didn't alarm the neighborhood.

They'd had a few blasts of booze while the pol sized up Joe about his off-and-on connection with one of the bigger groups that demonstrated for the rights of gays. He was trying to figure out, Joe knew, whether there was a solid block of votes available to him if he took the risk and supported laws protecting gays against cop harassment.

He'd left Joe in the bar to make some telephone calls and Joe had wandered back into the locker room to take a leak. The amazing thing was that none of the lockers was locked, not one. The members trusted each other—typical Old Country idiocy.

In the third locker Joe opened he found two matched Colts in Marine Corps black leather holsters. He removed the magazine from one .45 and took it with the other gun, also loaded, slipping them into his belt behind his back, where his jacket would hide them. When he left the politico later on, he went immediately to his East Tenth Street pad and carefully wrapped the gun, with its two magazines—eighteen shots in all—in a dish towel of tan Irish linen. When the street grew quiet, about two A.M., he drove downtown to a deserted side street off the financial district near the entrance to the Brooklyn Battery tunnel, where he hid the wrapped gun next to the carbine in the trunk of the car.

The last person in the world he had expected to let him down was Don, who had chickened badly when faced with a real demand for information. Littlejoe had met him three times in the past week without getting a line on a likely bank. Finally he had had to threaten blackmail.

"Give me the goods," he'd told Don, "or I tell your boss at Chase about your private life."

It wasn't much of a threat, because, like most big-city banks, Chase was happy to get any kind of worker at all, let alone one with a square, steady background. If he'd told some boss that Don was secretly gay, he'd probably only have confirmed what everyone already had suspected. Maybe his boss was that way too. So as a threat it really didn't have much leverage.

Oddly enough, however, it worked. Joe had counted on panicking Don with the threat so that he didn't have the time to think about the situation but was stampeded into coughing up information. He did.

The bank stood diagonally across the boulevard from the tavern in which Joe was now sitting. His information was that on Thursday the bank always held at least fifty grand for a Friday-morning payroll from a nearby bakery, whose yeasty smell perfumed the air of the whole neighborhood.

Watching the façade of the bank now, sipping his beer and thinking about nothing much in particular, Joe saw that they were in for another heat wave, even worse than last week's. Waves of heat from the pavement and the truck traffic made the air shimmer, gave the image of the bank a ghostly look, as if it wasn't really there.

The bar was a particularly good place from which to case the bank because, unlike a lot of small neighborhood bars in Queens, it wasn't empty during the business day. Evidently the bakery worked in a series of shifts. At any daylight hour, Joe soon found out, there were a dozen people, mostly men, arguing over shots of Seagram's Seven-Crown with a Seven-Up chaser, or watching soap operas on the color TV set, or trying to make out with some of the biddies they worked with who accompanied them to the bar for a quick one.

Joe could never quite figure if they had gone off shift and were on their way home or were going on shift and had paused before work for a snort or two. It didn't really matter. He didn't want to be the lone customer in the tavern, and he wasn't.

". . . say the President is still the President and if we ain't got the President we're shit without no president," one of them was shouting.

"That's just what we are," somebody yelled back at him, "up shit creek without no president."

"Every president is a thief. Every prime minister and king is a crook."

"Shit they're crooks. Jack Kennedy wasn't no crook, Harry Truman wasn't no crook. FDR wasn't no crook. Ike Eisenhower wasn't no crook. The fucking foreigners are laughing up their fucking sleeves at us. They hate us anyway, and now they got us marked down for a bunch of feebleminded slobs."

"Who are you to go against the rest of the country, something special? We elected him President. So he's a thief president. But, shit, he's *our* thief."

"You can say that again. The whole fucking country's full of thieves cheating on their taxes, stealing from supermarkets, robbing the fucking insurance companies blind on hospitalization and auto damage, cheating on their husbands and wives, lying about expense money, cheating on overtime pay."

"Listen to who I gotta be sorry for now, the insurance companies? The biggest thieves in the whole world?"

"Next to the telephone company."

"Please, don't get me started."

Joe turned away to hide a smile. He glanced at the clock over the bar and saw the time was three o'clock. But his wristwatch, which he set every morning by the radio time check, showed that it was two fifty-eight. He watched a woman pushing a baby stroller rush up to the bank. A black guard let her in. He held the door open for a moment, glancing at his own wristwatch, then closed and locked the door.

Littlejoe continued to look. What happened next was instructive. Another customer hurried up. He rapped on the window, and the guard waved him away. Instead of leaving, the man stayed there, evidently spotting a customer inside the bank who would have to be let out. A moment later the guard allowed the mother with the stroller to leave, but he still refused to let the man inside. Time: three five.

Good to know the guard obeyed the clock no matter what. As a customer, Joe hated guards who were slaves to the clock. But he liked knowing this one could be counted on to keep out anybody who arrived after three sharp.

The routine of the branch bank wasn't that complicated. A few days of watching had uncovered it for Joe. He'd used three different places from which to do his spotting, this tavern being the most recent.

He knew the bank's morning opening procedures and he knew its closing routine, down to the fact that at three ten the guard lowered a venetian blind

on the southeast corner of the building so that, when
the prowl car drove by at some time between then
and three twenty, it kept right on going. This ele-
mentary security routine was what Joe had wanted
to know. Each bank had its own, usually involving
the raising or lowering of a blind, the placement of a
window sign, the turning off or on of a light.

Tomorrow was Thursday. Littlejoe was looking
forward to casing the job one more day, to see how
the cash was delivered, whether by bank truck or
Brink's or what, and when the delivery was made.
Then he'd have a whole week to check out the routine one more time and make sure there were no
slipups. That was the way he'd worked it out with
Don, who had been cooperative once he'd been
forced to help. As he sat there nursing his beer,
Joe couldn't help thinking that Don had been
almost too cooperative.

Was it possible he was planning to blow the whistle? There were a lot of ways of doing it, including
the good old American-as-apple-pie anonymous telephone call. But Littlejoe felt that, if he were in
Don's shoes—passed over for fifteen years, never promoted—if given the chance to play hero, he'd want
all the credit for tripping up the heist. It was a clear
shot at a promotion. In fact, looking back over the
whole thing as he sat there in the tavern, Joe began
to wonder if he hadn't been set up for this just to
make a hero out of Don.

Stranger things had happened. You didn't get to be
a hip legend in your own time by believing everything
that was laid in front of you. Or, if Don wasn't that
clever, you didn't pull off daring daylight heists on
information squeezed reluctantly out of a frightened
closet queen who might have second thoughts and
turn in your ass out of sheer fear.

It dawned on Joe as he finished his beer that he
had worked himself into a tight spot. Sooner or later

the big-shot creep whose .45 he had stolen would miss the gun and start making inquiries. Sooner or later Don's nerve would give and he'd figure a way of turning a minus into a plus for himself. Sooner or later his cousin Mick would wonder what the carbine was for and the Maf would muscle in on the whole caper. Sooner or later Tina and her father would get fed up and put the Mustang on the police stolen list. Sooner or later Lana would leave him for somebody who could pay for her operation. Sooner or later his up-state relative would start to ask questions. Sooner or later Sam would have second thoughts, remember how bad jail had been, and crap out of the whole deal. Sooner or later . . .

There were too many loose ends, too many leftovers. Too much hanging over his head. But one thing could solve all his problems.

Joe got to his feet with such a violent movement that his elbow knocked over the empty beer glass. The bartender glanced questioningly at him. Joe shook his head. He went to the door and hesitated before opening it, before going out into the thick, damp heat of another dog day afternoon.

". . . and it's thieves like you who want a thief in the White House. Otherwise his ass would've been out of there so fast it'd make your head spin."

"You better believe it, buster. Thieves like me and fifty million others. Why should we elect some honest square to front for us? We want somebody just like us, and boy, have we got him."

"What about the honest people?"

"Let 'em wake up and join the show."

Joe pulled the door open and strode out into the blast of hot air smelling of fresh bread. The traffic noise roared and shook the air as trucks rattled past. Everybody who was in on it, including dopey Phil, who was driving the car, knew they'd pull the job a week from tomorrow. That gave everything a solid week in which to fall apart, go sour, trip him up and ruin him.

Okay. In that case, they'd hit the bank not a week from tomorrow but tomorrow. One week early. Fast, hard, and so cleverly that they'd leave everybody standing around flatfooted with their mouths open. Let them learn a thing or two from Littlejoe. You don't get to be a legend for nothing.

8

T HE RENDEZVOUS was on a residential block in Elm-
hurst, another in that belt of lower middle class communities that stretches across Queens from the East
River to Nassau County. These neighborhoods bear
names left over from some earlier time when they
were independent communities or, perhaps, only a
momentary gleam in the eye of a land developer.

The block of one-family houses reminded Littlejoe of his mother's block in Corona, some miles
away. In the absolute sameness, as if sliced off a
piece of something much larger, cake or cheese or
something like that, it reminded him of the block
where Tina and the kids lived in Rego Park, and his
father-in-law's semidetached row house and garage in
Flushing, and his grandmother's apartment block in
Ridgewood. Nobody escaped.

He had let the Mustang get very dirty over the past
week. Even the windows were dusty. A slight rain
three nights before—which had been expected to
break the heat wave but never made a dent in it—
had left the fenders splashed with mud. Joe had
carefully splashed more mud on the license plates,
front and back. He bore his father-in-law no grudge,
didn't want him involved in an armed-robbery rap,
and especially didn't want any unexpected witness to
come up with a handy license number to give the
cops.

The carbine was no longer in the trunk. Now

encased in a white florist's box, it had been shoved under the front seat. The .45 lay in the glove compartment, with two tan poplin hats, the kind fishermen use. Joe had bought them in a camping-goods store on Second Avenue in the Village. He'd bought them a little too big for his head and Sam's.

He'd also bought large, cheap sunglasses, the wraparound kind with thick frames. He played around at one point with the idea of paste-on moustaches, but decided they'd be too much trouble. The glasses and the hats, jammed down, brims drooping, would be enough.

He'd driven the car from East Tenth Street, bringing Sam with him. He'd expected the kid to be wearing his usual clothes, jeans and a thin body shirt, but Sam had surprised him. From somewhere he'd borrowed a very sharp suit, six-button, nipped in at the waist, wide shoulders, the color of Breyer's vanilla ice cream, sort of a creamy white with a pattern of tiny black spots, like traces of vanilla bean. His trousers matched, and instead of sneakers he was wearing a pair of multicolored bump-toe, clog-heel boots that added four inches to his height. He'd chosen a white shirt with ruffled front and cuffs, and a wide orange tie. He looked terrific, Joe decided, so elegant he almost didn't look like Sam at all.

Littlejoe hadn't deviated that much from what he normally wore: the same shoes, a plain white business shirt like the kind he'd worn when he worked in the bank, an odd pair of chino slacks, and no jacket. Joe Anonymous. Not that he wasn't capable of dressing up to an occasion. He'd once shown on a chilly autumn evening along the Christopher Street meat rack in short shorts, sandals, and a sleeveless underwear top with big holes. They'd talked about it for weeks.

Today, however, was business. Sam was dressed so elegantly that witnesses would be certain to spend a lot of time describing a Sam who never existed, at least not in those clothes. And Littlejoe would be Mr. Anybody from Anywhere.

Now for the bad news. The driver, Phil, one of the kids Sam crashed with in the Bedford Street pad, was not going to be in on the job. Littlejoe had learned this late last night when he and Sam, leaving Mick's more reputable leather bar at about midnight, had seen a squad car stop across Christopher Street. The two young cops who jumped out of the car had proceeded to hassle Phil and another guy for a few fast minutes before packing them into the car and driving off. Exit Phil.

As if this weren't bad news enough, the replacement driver, Eddie, was worse. Thinking back over last night, Littlejoe realized he'd panicked. They'd been so close. Losing Phil had stopped him from thinking straight, and in his panic he'd begged Mick for a reliable guy. Not from the organization, just somebody Mick vouched for. He'd been given a name, Eddie. And he'd told Mick the time and place of the rendezvous.

From the moment he'd seen Eddie walking toward them, a block away, Joe had known the choice was a mistake. For one thing, Eddie was big, damned near six feet tall, which he knew would spook Sam. Secondly, Eddie was beefy, a mixture of teen-age muscle and beer-belly flab acquired in the five years or so since he'd stopped being a teen-ager. And third, as it soon developed in talking to Eddie in the car, he was a no-good son of a bitch.

"No probs, man," Eddie had said in a tone of utter confidence so fake that even to a stranger like Littlejoe it stuck out a mile. "I drive like a goddamned angel."

"I don't need no angel," Joe said in a gruff voice, trying to reestablish dominance. "I just need a fucking dummy who keeps his fucking mouth shut and don't drive through no fucking red lights. Think you can remember that?" he added insultingly.

With Eddie in the front seat, there was almost not enough room for Joe and Sam. Joe watched Eddie's lumpy profile, the fatty chin, the thick neck, the tiny pig eye, the puffy ear. He looked like some kind of club palooka, good enough to take a few clouts on the chin and then dive for the money.

"Hey," Eddie said weakly, the bully whose bluff has been called. "Listen, man, they ain't no call to rank me that sharp, okay?"

"Whatever gave Mick the idea you could drive for me?" Joe bored in relentlessly.

The air in the car was growing hotter by the second. Eddie turned his beefy hands palms up. "All he told me, this was a heavy caper and you needed a heavy driver."

"Heavy, not fat."

"Shit, man, that ain't fat," Eddie responded, almost in a whine. He pummeled his belly several times, and Joe watched the shudders traverse his flesh in jellying ripples. Another five years and this would drip with meat like Tina.

Sam groaned softly, almost under his breath. "If that ain't fat," he muttered, "then it's shit."

Eddie turned to face them with a scraped-together show of bravado. "What the fuck is this, the U.S. Marine Corps? You wan' a driver, you got a driver."

Littlejoe and Sam greeted this with glum silence. All he needed, Joe thought, was a slow-witted dumdum at the wheel. The plan was split-second and the one who needed to follow it second by second was Joe himself. Eddie had only to drive, wait, and drive again. The responsibilities were 99 percent on Littlejoe, where they belonged.

"Tell me again what you do, Eddie."

"Like, I drop you guys at the bank when you tell me, I mean, where you say, and, like, you know, keep on driving around the block and park behind the bank and keep the motor going and just cool it till you show."

"And what happens when we show in back of the bank?"

"I mean, I wait till you're in the car, right, and then I like take off for Queens Boulevard, west to Horace Harding, then you tell me my next move."

Joe glanced at his watch. Two thirty. He got out of the stifling car and stood in the hot sun for a moment. This was another scorcher, today. The sky was cloudless. New York couldn't expect a drop of rain. The temperature had been climbing all morning, from eighty overnight to ninety at the moment. Ninety-five was forecast. Littlejoe leaned forward, squeegeed his forehead with a finger, snapped the finger toward the sidewalk, and sent a spray of sweat droplets onto the cement. They vanished almost at once.

He stood by the driver's window. "Start it up. Get the air conditioning going. We don't have to die while we're waiting."

He watched with a certain distaste as Eddie fumbled with the Mustang's controls and finally got it started and adjusted the levers to produce cool air inside the car. Then Joe walked around to the opposite door and got in. They rolled up the windows as the cool air started to flow. In a few minutes, the three of them sitting on the front seat, they began to feel almost comfortable. Joe checked the time. Two thirty-five.

"Okay, Eddie. Take this street to the Boulevard. Not fast. Just a nice average slow speed. Watch the lights."

The Mustang took off with a jackrabbit start, then settled down. They reached Queens Boulevard and turned right. Two forty.

Littlejoe indicated the next turn after a mile of careful driving. Eddie could handle a car, but he was jumpy. A car cut in on him from the left-hand lane, and he jammed on his brakes so abruptly that both Joe and Sam lunged forward until their faces almost hit the dashboard. "Easy!"

Two forty-five.

They turned left off the Boulevard. In the distance Littlejoe could see the big five-story building that housed the bakery. The one-story bank building hadn't come into view yet. He watched Eddie's face as they waited through a full, long red light. Something was perking inside the tub of lard. Cool he wasn't. Sam, on the other hand, was ice. His profile was completely still. Nothing moved but his eyes, which shifted slowly now and then from the traffic to his watch.

Two fifty.

So much depended on the timing of the entry, Littlejoe reminded himself. Too early and the damned guard would keep the door open long enough for one more customer. Too late and he'd give them a hassle as they tried to enter. And the guard was the only one with a gun, wasn't he?

Joe could see the bank now and, across from it, the tavern where he'd sat at this time yesterday and had his brainstorm, the idea of moving up the whole job one week to avoid all the loose ends that were going to trip him up. Another red light. Eddie had started to drive so slowly now that a cop might stop him as a menace to traffic.

Two fifty-five.

Joe handed Sam his hat and glasses and put on his own. They looked at each other and laughed. He reached into the glove compartment and handed Sam a nine-slug magazine. He watched the kid tuck it away in his jacket pocket. Then he gave him the .45 automatic, blue steel, engraved wooden plates on the butt, a motto in Italian on a curved bunting held in an eagle's beak. "*Honore e patria.*" Shit, yes.

Two fifty-seven.

The Mustang came to a halt at the curb near the bank. The carbine, in its long, flat white cardboard box, now lay across Joe's knees. There was no string or ribbon on the box.

Now Joe opened the car door. The two of them left the dusty Mustang and moved without haste to the bank door. From the inside, the black guard was also moving toward the door. Their intentions were opposite, as were their movements.

Littlejoe pushed open the door and ushered Sam in ahead of him. The kid had tucked the flat Colt into his waistband and buttoned his jacket over it, but the bulge was obvious to Littlejoe. He carried the white florist's box under his arm, negligently. Both of them were inside by the time the guard reached the door.

Three.

Littlejoe glanced around the bank. Not a single customer. Great break! He watched the guard lock the door. He was a short, chunky Negro well past sixty, with unevenly gray hair and a face that had been punished over the years, perhaps in the boxing ring. He walked in a funny way, ducklike, as if his joints hurt.

Past the guard, Littlejoe watched the grimy Mustang pull away from the curb and disappear along the street. If he'd been the religious kind, this would have been the moment for praying that Eddie kept his cool and followed the plan to the letter. It was time now for Littlejoe and Sam to do their part.

Sam had gone up to a glass-topped table, as agreed on, and was messing around with a bank pen and some deposit slips. Joe moved quickly behind the guard. He shifted the box top to let the muzzle of the carbine peek out. It looked like the mean little eye of a pig, or the crazy eye of a caged ape. He let the guard see it.

Three five.

Terrible things were happening to the guard's face. It had gone blank at first on seeing the muzzle. Now, as Joe unsnapped the guard's holster and removed his .38 Police Positive, the man's eyes turned up in his head, showing a rim of white and pink. He seemed about to faint. Joe dropped the guard's revolver in the white box.

Sam glanced at the two of them, kept on playing with papers. None of the bank employees had bothered to look up yet. They probably wouldn't, Joe figured, until some unusual noise was made.

Three seven.

Joe went to the venetian blind in the corner and lowered it to the sill of the window. Then he reached inside the florist's box and brought out a spray can of black paint. He turned to the camera over the front door and covered the lens with a blast of black. As he moved toward the remaining television camera, a balding man seated at one of the bank desks looked up with a practiced smile. "Can I hel . . . ?"

His mouth stayed open as Littlejoe squirted the second camera lens, opaqueing it. Then he dropped the spray can onto the carpeted floor and laid the white box on the man's desk. He lifted out the carbine and worked its bolt. In the sudden silence, the click was deafening. He glanced at Sam, who brought out the .45 and aimed it at the guard.

The smile died on the balding man's face. "What?"

"Okay," Littlejoe said, "this is a stickup."

One of the tellers let out a shrill yip. Joe swiveled the carbine on her. "Do that one time more and you get it in the guts." Again he trained the gun on the man at the desk, who seemed to be the manager.

"No alarms. No funny stuff. Nobody presses the Holmes button or you get it between the balls and the bellybutton, twice, and these are dumdum slugs. Your colon will be sprayed all over this lobby."

The man started to raise his hands over his head and get to his feet at the same time. "Hands down!" Joe snapped. "No problems, shithead, no smart moves or you get it anyway." He shoved the muzzle of the carbine into the man's gut and watched his eyes bug in pain. He looked a little like Don, come to think of it. Not exactly the same, but that same banky way all these middle-aged guys got after a while. This one seemed calmer, however.

"Tell the people," Joe commanded.

"Uh, look," the manager began in a raised voice, "you can see what's happening. Nobody press any alarms, please. This man seems to know the routine. I see he's drawn the blind. He'll kill me if any of you do anything he doesn't like. So, please . . ." He ran out of words.

Littlejoe nodded encouragingly. "Nice work. Tell them the rest."

"The, uh . . . ? Oh. Look, people, clear out your cash drawers and put the money on the counters." The manager's eyes darted this way and that, as if making sure this command was being obeyed with good discipline. Joe contented himself for the moment with watching him. He had the kind of face that gave off its own warning signs.

Sam moved quickly along the counters, scooping up the money in a wastebasket, which he brought to Joe. "Keep your eye on the guard," Joe warned him. "He's gonna faint or something stupid. He's an old guy."

"He has a bad heart," the manager cut in.

"Shoulda thought of that before he got this job," Joe said. He upended the wastebasket on the manager's desk. Tens and twenties, loose and in wrapped packs, slid out. "Now, this is the important part, Mr. . . . uh . . . ?" Joe looked questioningly at the manager.

"Boyle."

"Mr. Boyle, this is where you star. I want you to go over this cash and pick out the bundle of marked money. Then I want you to show me the markings, so there's no doubt."

The manager frowned. "It's not that easy."

"That's why I picked you for the job." The muzzle of the carbine buried itself an inch in Boyle's abdominal flab.

"Right." He had a round, easy-going sort of face, Littlejoe noted: the kind of guy who might sing in the church choir or maybe captain the bowling team, typical Irish face with the long upper lip and big chin and fuzzy eyebrows.

"Here." Boyle handed over a packet of twenties. "See this here, next to the signature?" As if patiently teaching an employee a lesson, he produced a loose twenty and showed Littlejoe that the small green dot next to the Secretary of the Treasury's signature was only on the special packet of bills.

"That's the only pack that's marked?" Joe asked.

"The only one. Now, look. You have a lot of money here, maybe ten grand. It's what you came for. We cooperated. We didn't give you any trouble. We played your rules. Now you're leaving, right?"

Joe eyed him for a moment. Boyle didn't seem to be kidding. He looked as if he couldn't wait for them to leave but was determined to be polite till the bitter end. Littlejoe rummaged around in the piles of money.

"Chickenfeed, Boyle. There's maybe four grand here, if that." Nobody spoke. "Mr. Boyle," Joe said, drawling out the man's name as if it was something shamefully amusing. "I think it's time we visited the vault."

"The v—" Boyle's voice choked off in mid-word. He nodded miserably.

"Everybody out from behind the counter," Joe called. He waited till they had formed a small group near him in the lobby. Then he moved slowly past the bank employees. There were three of them, all women, two tellers under thirty and one older woman, not bad-looking, who had been working at another desk, using an adding machine.

Joe turned to Sam. "They don't look natural from

outside," he said. "Move them toward the back, behind that floor sign there. The guard too. Never mind his heart. Keep them all back there, sort of out of sight. You stand behind them so nobody sees you from the sidewalk. This won't take long."

He followed Boyle into the rear of the bank. He'd expected a smallish vault, hardly more than a walk-in, but he hadn't expected one quite this small. Evidently the only business the branch did was consumer stuff. The bakery payroll was probably its only big commercial account.

"Okay, Boyle. The payroll cash."

Boyle's wide, easy mouth opened, then closed. "Ellen," he called. "Bring your key."

A thin girl almost as young as Sam appeared after a moment. She held up one key while Boyle removed a similar one from his pocket. He nodded to Ellen, who inserted her key in one of the two locks on the vault door.

"Easy," Joe said. "Don't turn that key till his is in the other lock."

Boyle nodded. "You really do know the routine." He started to fit his key into the lock. Nothing about his face or his movement told Joe anything unusual except that Boyle was moving slowly to avoid upsetting him.

Just as the key touched the steel of the lock, Littlejoe's arm shot out. "Son of a bitch!" he yelped, grabbing the key.

He held it under Boyle's nose. "You motherfucker, this is the spur key. Did you really think you could get away wi—"

Boyle's eyes went wide with horror. "Christ! I didn't mean to do that. Honest. Look." He pulled out an identical key. "No spur. It was a mistake, I swear it was."

Littlejoe pocketed the key with the almost invisible projection, like a spur, that would have triggered an alarm if used. "Boyle," he said, "you're cute. You're gonna cute yourself to death. Now put in the right key and turn them both at the same time. No more comical stuff."

Boyle heaved a heavy sigh. "I'm not kidding, it was a mistake. You have to believe me. All I want is to give you the money and say good-bye. Nothing personal," he added, grinning weakly.

He twisted both keys simultaneously and, turning a handle, swung the polished steel gate wide open. Littlejoe could hear Ellen crying softly, but his eyes remained on Boyle. Once cute maybe twice cute. "The payroll, Boyle."

"Okay." The manager stepped into the vault. "I don't know how you knew, but you just hit the jackpot."

"Fucking ay right I did."

Boyle rummaged around inside a plain steel cabinet. "Ellen? Where did you have Wells Fargo put the—" His light blue eyes looked up from the cabinet at the girl, and when they did, his voice stopped short. "Ellen?"

She started to sob audibly. "There isn't any money."

"What?" Littlejoe shouted. He was aware that Boyle had also shouted the same question at the same time.

Now the girl began to break up. "Th-the delivery was ch-changed, Mr. Boyle. Th-they changed it l-last week. Don't you r-remember, Mr. Boyle. Oh, dear God, there's a pain—" She broke off, clutching at her left breast, her eyes wide.

"That's right," Boyle said. "Delivery's Friday morning now."

"No money?" Littlejoe yelled at him.

Ellen slumped to the floor of the vault, sobbing and choking on her sobs. "Oh, sweet Jesus, I'm sorry," she said. "I'm so sorry, Mr. Boyle."

Joe watched her for a moment. She was too

young for this sort of hysterics. He nudged her with the toe of his boot. "Calm down," he said. "It's not your fault."

"She's afraid you're going to shoot us," Boyle explained.

Littlejoe turned on him. "What the hell am I gonna do with your chickenshit four grand? Is that the best this rotten bank can come up with? Maybe she's right. Maybe I am gonna shoot somebody."

They stared at each other, Boyle's forehead damp with sweat. Abruptly, from somewhere in the distance, a telephone began to ring.

9

JOE BROUGHT THE CARBINE MUZZLE up very slowly until it pointed directly at Boyle's navel. "You're gonna do this right," he said then. "You're gonna answer the phone, find out who it is, put him on hold, and tell me all about it. Then I'll tell you what to say next."

Boyle swallowed. His beefy throat almost concealed the movement of his Adam's apple, Littlejoe noticed. He jerked the carbine left and marched Boyle out into the lobby.

The phone rang again. Again.

At once Joe saw that things had changed. Sam was no longer cool. He had his automatic at his side, but he was holding it tightly and his trigger finger was white at the knuckle.

"It's okay," Joe told him. "It's just a routine call."

Boyle walked to his desk and picked up the telephone. "Boyle speaking." His glance was riveted on Littlejoe. "Who? Lou? Hold it a second, Lou. I'll be right with you." He punched the "Hold" button on his telephone. "It's Lou."

Littlejoe grinned. "You're a real comic," he retorted. "It's like a TV sketch. Lou who? Lou what-does-he-want?"

Boyle pulled in a long breath of air. "Lou Bagradian from across the street." He started to point, then kept his hands on the desk. "The insurance office across the street."

Littlejoe turned very casually. At this distance no

one in the insurance office could see him, nor he them. But the sign did read INSURANCE, and he could even distinguish a Bagradian among the names gold-leafed on the glass door. "See what he wants."

Boyle punched another phone button. "Okay, Lou. We're sort of busy here. Sorry I kept you waiting. What?" His eyes crawled sideways to watch Joe again. "No, no trouble."

Joe felt a chill along his shoulder blades. He stepped closer until the carbine muzzle dug into Boyle's ear as he sat at the desk. "Be very good, Boyle," he murmured softly.

"Just the usual end-of-the-month routine." He paused and moistened his lips twice with his tongue. "Extra guys? You must mean the two fellas here from headquarters in Manhattan."

Joe nodded slowly up and down. He shoved the muzzle a bit harder against Boyle's ear. The steel was digging into the grayish hairs there.

"What do they want? It's bank business, Lou. Do I ask you questions about the insurance business?"

"Systems," Littlejoe hissed softly.

Boyle produced a poor imitation of a laugh. "No, Lou, they're from systems, that's all. Systems? Well, it's, uh, confidential. Right, Lou. No, no trouble. Thanks for calling. So long, Lou."

As he hung up the telephone, a bead of perspiration rolled down Boyle's snub nose and dropped on the gray linoleum top of his desk. He sighed and glanced up at Joe again. "That's okay now," he said.

"Not if I know Lou," the older woman said. She was standing with the rest of the bank employees behind a lobby sign some fifteen feet back. Behind her rather plump face, Littlejoe could see Sam's tight, anxious look. "That Lou is nosy," the woman was saying.

"Yeah?" Joe put the carbine in its white florist's box and drew out the guard's .38. He tucked it in his belt. "What's he likely to do?"

The woman eyed him. She wasn't bad, Joe noticed: nice tits and good figure for a broad about his mother's age. Not elderly, he corrected himself, but closing in on forty. They really loved it at that age, didn't they. But why was she trying to be helpful? "I asked you something, cunt."

She blinked. "I have these young girls working here. You'll have to watch your language, mister."

"Am I? Are you the one who's gonna make me?"

"I'm trying to help," she said then. "Call me Marge, not—not that other word."

"You never heard it before?"

She tried a smile. "Not recently." Then, quickly, "What I mean about Lou. Look." She indicated the street outside with a nod of her head.

"Oh, God," Boyle groaned.

Littlejoe watched a chubby man in a white short-sleeve shirt, eyes squinting against the hot sun, making his way from the insurance storefront across the street. He stopped at the midline to let some cars pass, then continued over the asphalt toward the bank door.

"I don't believe this," Boyle said. "Look at that moron."

"Okay, folks," Littlejoe snapped. "I'm the one uses shitty language. But the guy standing behind you there with the automatic, he kills. I bark. He bites. Get your asses on the double into the vault, all except you, Marge. Stick around."

"What about Leroy?" Marge asked.

"Leroy?"

"The guard."

Joe walked behind her and jammed the .38 in her back. "Leroy waves Lou away. Says the bank's closed. Right, Leroy?"

"Christ," the guard mumbled. He sat up straighter in his chair, but his face still looked panicky.

"You do that," Littlejoe told him, "or Marge gets a slug from your gun right in the left ovary."

"Lou can't be handled like that," Boyle said, getting up. "I'll take care of him."

Marge turned sideways. "Leave the ovaries alone, mister. You and I can just, uh, look at these ledgers here. Isn't that what a systems man would be doing?"

The man in the white short-sleeve shirt was standing outside the door now. He shielded his eyes to squint through the sun's glare and reflections into the bank lobby. Then he saw Leroy, flopped on a chair. He waved to the guard. When this failed to get a response, he rapped on the door.

"Get up, Leroy," Joe called softly.

Leroy pulled himself to his feet and stood there shakily. Lou watched this for a moment, then kicked the door twice, impatiently. "Hey!" he called so loudly he could be heard through the tempered Herculite glass.

Boyle went to the door. On the way he took Leroy's arm and removed the door key from his hand. "Sit down, Leroy." He continued toward the door, fitted the key into the lock, and moved the huge sheet of glass a few inches. "Lou, we're closed, you know that."

"Is everything okay?" the man asked.

"I told you over the phone it was."

"What's with Leroy?"

"He's not feeling well. Heart."

"So where's a doctor?"

"Lou, will you stop running my business for me?"

Littlejoe glanced behind him in the direction of the vault, where Sam had herded the two younger girls into a corner out of sight of the front lobby. All of them, Sam and the girls, seemed frozen in a kind of trance, their eyes on his gun, his eyes on their eyes. Littlejoe had never seen Sam like this before. He looked taller, more important. More of a man. And there was something strange about his face. What was it? Something new and sexy. He was smiling, that was it. For the first time since Littlejoe could remember, Sam was smiling.

"I didn't like your tone of voice is all," Lou was saying.

Joe turned quickly, watching past Marge's face to the two men standing at the door. It was a contest, he saw, Lou wanting in, Boyle trying to keep him out.

"You're sure it's all right inside?" Lou asked.

"Absolutely fine. Just routine."

Joe's glance shifted to Sam. Not only was he smiling, but there were beads of perspiration on his forehead. It became suddenly clear to Littlejoe that Sam was starting to lose control. A little more of this back-and-forth with Lou and there would be some dead people.

"Mr. Boyle?" Joe called. "This ledger doesn't check out."

"What?" Boyle wheeled, startled.

"Can you come here a second and explain these entries?"

Boyle's eyes, narrowed against the sun, widened now. "Right you are." He turned back to the man in the white short-sleeve shirt. "Lou, I hate to close the door in your face, but you can see we're busy."

"Just as long as everything's okay."

"Everything's okay."

"You're sure," Lou insisted doggedly.

"Positive, Lou."

"Okay, then."

"Right. So long, Lou."

Boyle waited until the chubby man had stopped holding the door open. He let the Herculite glass swing shut, turned the key in the lock, and moved stiffly back through the short lobby toward Littlejoe. It was only when he got within a yard that Joe could see how shaky Boyle was, face white with strain, dark indentations above his nostrils.

"Goddamned nosy Armenian busybody," Boyle was saying.

"Okay," Littlejoe said. "Trouble's over."

He waited for Sam to relax, but nothing in the kid's rigid stance softened. The smile seemed to have been carved on his face. "Okay," Joe told him, not wanting to use his name. "It's okay now."

One of the girls, the dark-haired one, Ellen, started to whimper again. "He's going to kill us, Mr. Boyle," she said.

"No he's not." Marge's voice cut through with some authority. "Is he?" she asked Joe.

Joe came up to Sam and touched his gun arm, very gently. "Ease off, buddy."

Slowly, Sam's glazed eyes came to life. The smile disappeared. He slumped back against the wall. "That crying broad," he said in an undertone which Ellen could hear, "if she don't stop I'll stop her the hard way."

"No need to, baby," Littlejoe said, keeping his voice light and easy. "We got our loot and we're splitting as soon as I get the travelers' checks."

Sam blinked, but said nothing. Joe turned to Marge. "Bring me the whole supply of checks and the register books for them."

"You don't miss a trick, do you?"

"And my friend wouldn't miss Ellen's eyeball if you tried anything funny."

He watched her move off toward a standing steel case with a combination lock on it. She twirled the lock and swung open the light steel doors. "Whadya mean?" Sam said then in a tight, choked voice. "Whadya mean, we got our loot?"

"Baby, we got every scrap of cash this joint's holding."

"Four fucking gees?"

"That's it," Joe agreed. "Plus maybe a grand in travelers' checks. I have to destroy the register so they can't put out an alert for the numbers, but the checks are as good as cash."

"Five fucking gees?" Sam asked, his voice rising. "What happened to the hundred grand, Littlejoe?"

Joe blinked. They had agreed not to use each other's names. He'd been so careful to keep from saying the word *Sam*, although it would have helped in keeping the kid calm. Now, in his nervousness, Sam had blown Littlejoe's identity.

"Sam," he said then with deliberate maliciousness, "the hundred gees was just talk. They won't have the payroll cash till tomorrow. You wanna spend the night here or take the five grand and split?"

The two men stared at each other, Littlejoe trying to reassert his domination over Sam. But he could see that something was seriously wrong with the kid.

"Littlejoe," he said, "maybe you don't unnastand my problem."

Joe glanced around him. He didn't need an audience for this, but he couldn't let them roam free. "We got no problem, baby," he told Sam, grinning cheerfully. "We're on top of this all the way."

Sam's head shook slowly from side to side. His normally grave expression was even glummer than usual. "You don't unnastand," he said, lowering his voice to a murmur. "You get copped for this, it's a first offense. Not me, Littlejoe. They cop me, they throw away the key. I'm a three-time offender."

"Nobody's copping us," Joe assured him. "We're home free."

"With five crummy gees." Sam's voice went even lower. "You get the point, Littlejoe? For my cut of peanuts, this job don't make no sense. When you talked big loot, I figured, okay, that makes it worth trying." His glance seemed to bore into Joe's, as if trying to implant the idea by sheer willpower. "For my cut of a big score, okay, I take my chances. But this . . . man, this don't make no sense no way."

Littlejoe paused for a moment. He understood all too well what Sam was driving at, but the job was really over. The getaway was all that remained. Didn't Sam's brain pick that up? If he were anybody else, you could lean on him a little heavy and he'd snap back into line. But not Sam. Joe knew him too well to think he could bulldoze him into obedience.

"What do you want from me, baby," Joe asked softly. "There is no big score. The fucking Wells Fargo don't deliver till tomorrow."

"Don said—"

"Shit on Don. He—"

"Anyway," Sam cut in, "why not wait for Wells Fargo?"

Joe eyed his prisoners and saw that, while all of them were listening closely, their eyes were elsewhere. Sam worried him now. He never interrupted someone talking to him. But evidently he was under such pressure that he wasn't thinking or behaving normally.

"We can't keep this whole crew quiet all night," Joe said.

"We bust a few skulls. That quiets 'em."

Out of the corner of his eye Joe could see that this suggestion went down poorly with the bank people. Actually, he thought now, Sam isn't all that crazy. He whirled on Boyle so suddenly that the manager flinched.

"How much is Wells Fargo delivering?"

Boyle's mouth twitched, his lower lip tucking under his front teeth. "Twenty thousand," he said at last.

"Bullshit." Joe moved up against Boyle's belly, but kept his hand on the butt of the .38. "Your mouth was ready to say 'fifty' and you changed your mind."

Boyle's face went red. "Okay. Now you're a mind-reader."

"Lip-reader," Littlejoe said. He felt a sudden surge of elation and puckered his mouth inches from Boyle's. "Kiss, kiss?" he said, imitating Lana's act in the back room of the leather bar. He turned to Marge. "Only fifty grand?"

She nodded. "You can't keep us here all night, mister. Some of these girls are going to crack under the strain."

"Let 'em." Joe turned back to Boyle. "When does the truck get here? No crap. Tell it straight."

"Eight fifteen."

Joe kissed Boyle's cheek. "Good for you, Boyle. Next time it's on the mouth." He turned back to Sam. "Whatya think, baby?"

"You know, Littlejoe. I'm for it."

"It's only fifty. We split, say, fifty–five."

Sam's gun hand remained steady but his other turned palm up in a what-can-you-do gesture. "We're here," he said. "Let's make it pay."

"Right!" Joe felt on top of the world. He snapped his fingers under Boyle's nose. "Back-door key."

"Back d—" Boyle stopped, began feeling in his pockets. "Here," he said, pulling a key off a leather-covered key ring and handing it to Joe.

"I don't want it. Just march it back to the rear door and use it. I'll be right behind you." Joe followed Boyle to the back door and watched him carefully switch off the alarm devices before opening the lock. He swung the door open slowly.

Joe kept his hand on the Police Positive .38 tucked in his belt. "Move out a ways. I'm looking for something."

"What?"

"You're as nosy as that insurance guy, huh?" Joe surveyed the rear of the bank. A parking area backed up all the stores on this side of the street. The grimy Mustang stood about a hundred yards away, and damned if its motor wasn't running. Eddie's big, fleshy face, as seen through the windshield, looked as gray and soft as vanilla pudding.

Littlejoe gestured to him, made a key-turning motion, and waved him to come out of the car. It took the dumb show a while to penetrate Eddie's thick head. Then he switched off the engine and hopped out of the car with such alacrity that he stumbled and almost fell. A mean little smile crossed Joe's mouth. Bigger they are . . .

Eddie trotted over to the rear door of the bank. "Here's the scam," Littlejoe told him before he had a chance to open his mouth. "We're holing in for the night. You too." He turned to Boyle. "Which car's yours?"

"That blue Merc there. But you don't th—"

"Shut up with the you-don't's. I do what I do. You do what I tell you to do. Eddie, lock up the Mustang and get back in here. Move it."

Joe and Boyle watched the heavyset young man trot through the thickening heat toward the car. He followed orders and was back in a few moments. "Listen close," Littlejoe told him then. "As far as I'm concerned, you're still the driver and nothing else but the driver. Dig? Just keep the fuck out of the way and out of sight."

Eddie's tiny eyes widened as he stepped inside the bank, but whether with awe or excitement or just relief from the hot sun, Joe didn't know. He didn't much care now, either. After starting to sour around the edges, the caper was beginning to straighten up.

At first nothing had gone right, from Don's phony-baloney tip-off to the suspicious Armenian. Never mind. It was going right now. Littlejoe hadn't earned his rep by panicking when the odds went bad. An all-night stand wasn't hard work for fifty grand, as long as Eddie kept out of the way and Sam stayed cool and nobody loused up any more than they had already. Sam's cut of fifty would keep him calm enough. As for Eddie, five grand was about his speed, or maybe less.

Keeping Boyle and Eddie ahead of him, Joe locked up the rear door and ushered everyone back into the rear of the bank. He surveyed the scene.

Had he covered everything? Cash in the cash drawers. Travelers' checks. No sense trying to get into the safe deposit boxes, because the holders' keys were needed. Littlejoe's gaze came to rest on Marge's breasts. She'd probably love a little jab or two from the old Avenger. Something to talk about later. Never had it before with witnesses, huh? Ellen's irritating snuffle broke through his thoughts.

"Dry it up," he told her.

What had he missed? Chickenfeed in their handbags, nothing in the way of jewelry. Boyle probably had fifty in his wallet, but let him keep it. He was going to donate his Merc in the morning anyway. No sense being a hog. What else? Bearer bonds? Not in a cheesebox branch office like this. The telephone started to ring again.

Boyle blinked. Sam flinched. He was the jumpiest of them all, Littlejoe noted, except maybe the crying broad. Why should he take Boyle's word that the vault was clean? Better give it a last look-see.

"Sam," he said, all business now, "move these people behind that lobby sign. Boyle, let the fucking phone ring."

"It's probably a personal call," Boyle volunteered.

"Fuck it. All of you just stand there nice and calm. First one gets out of line, Sam knocks off. He's very good with that forty-five. Boyle, tell them what a forty-five slug does to you."

"What's that?"

"No guts, huh?" Littlejoe smiled recklessly. "It goes in small, like a keyhole." His eyes were on Marge now. The phone kept ringing. "And where it comes out it carries away a chunk of meat the size of a football. Got the picture?"

He watched her sag. "Marge, you're coming with me into the vault."

"There's nothing left inside," Boyle reminded him. Ring. Ring.

"We'll see." He herded Marge ahead of him into

the tiny room. He moved up behind her and pressed himself against her buttocks. "Feel it?" he demanded.

"Y-yes." Her breathing was fast and light now.

"Want it?"

"Not here," she said after a long moment. "You know, you're something else, Littlejoe."

"You bet that sweet soft ass of yours I am."

"In a spot like this, nobody I know could even get it up."

He burst out laughing. "Tell that one to the reporters tomorrow. Baby, you're gonna be on TV. Tell them how it felt."

She pulled open some steel drawers. "Satisfied?"

Behind him the telephone kept ringing. He had gotten so excited that he'd almost blanked it out of his mind. This was a real high now. The excitement of holding someone completely in your power. This was better than Tina, who did what he told her because she liked being humiliated. But this Marge broad was a tough one. She reminded him of Flo, only his mother didn't have this kind of shape.

"Gimme your home phone, baby," he whispered in her ear. "When the heat's off, we'll get together for a few laughs."

She shook her head slowly. "You are too much, Littlejoe."

"Remember the name, huh?"

"It's just a nickname, though." Her voice sounded worried.

"Right. Open those doors."

Only ledger books lay on the shelves. Still standing behind her, he started to cup her breasts. She had a fairly heavy-duty brassiere on, and the feeling wasn't the same as when he fondled Lana's.

Ring. Ring.

Marge turned to face him, inches away. "Who tipped you about the payroll, somebody here in the shop?"

"Right. If the cops ever get me, I'll tell them it was you."

She smiled slightly off-center. He saw that she had small, white teeth with sharp edges. "With a friend like you . . ." She let the thought die away.

Ring.

"Okay, out of the vault."

They entered the rear of the lobby. Sam had that stiff look about him again, Joe saw. What was bugging him now, the phone?

"Cheer up," he told Sam.

Eddie had been standing next to him, and this, too, might have depressed Sam. "Eddie," Littlejoe ordered, "find yourself a place to sit down on the vault floor. I want you out of sight in case we get any more nosy Armenians."

"Huh?"

"Move, shithead!"

He watched Eddie's hulk waver indecisively for a moment. It had been a mistake taking this tub of turd inside the bank, but what else had there been to do with him? Under the new plan, where they stayed the night here, Joe couldn't afford to send Eddie away with the Mustang. He had to have him under control. But one thing was certain, he wouldn't give Eddie a gun. That was just too risky.

The driver disappeared in back, muttering under his breath. Littlejoe grinned at Sam. "He's not a partner, baby," he said. "We drop a fiver on him and we split the fifty grand just two ways, you and me."

Sam's dour face brightened slightly. "And you'll take care of Mick from your cut?"

Littlejoe frowned. The kid didn't have even a basic idea of security, throwing names around that way. "I said I would and I will," he told Sam in a severe voice. The phone's ringing was beginning to bug him too.

"What does that make it for me, Littlejoe?"

His frown deepened. Tell the kid anything to calm his ass. "How does twenty-five grand strike you?"

He'd expected a smile, but all Sam did was nod slowly up and down. What had made the kid smile before? Joe tried to remember. Oh, yes. He turned to face the bank people. "Here's the layout. It's ladies' night in the vault. There's enough room for the three of you and Eddie if nobody starts to let farts." He grinned boyishly.

"You, Boyle, are out here in the main room. The rules are simple. Any of your people in the vault start acting up—crying, hollering, anything—you get it. We march you back to the vault and put a slug through the roof of your mouth. Your brains spatter all over the ladies. It's simple. They get a load of your mind." He started to laugh and for a moment couldn't stop.

Now Sam was smiling. That's what it took, Joe noted.

Ring. Ring. Ring.

"Okay, Boyle, take the phone. Same deal. Put him on hold."

The manager trudged through the empty lobby to his desk. "Boyle speaking." He listened for a long while. "Hold on." He punched the "Hold" button. Then he looked across the lobby at Littlejoe. "It's for you."

A sharp jab of cold shot across Joe's shoulders and down his spine. He could feel gooseflesh crinkling the skin of his forearms. "Me?"

"Man says he wants to talk to you."

Littlejoe's legs felt strange under him as he walked stiffly across the lobby. It couldn't have been more than twenty feet, but he was aware of each time his heel came down on the vinyl floor tile.

He stared down at Boyle. "Me?"

Boyle nodded, handed him the telephone, and punched a button.

Joe cleared his throat. "Hello?"

The man's voice was thin and slightly nasal. "What are you doing in there?"

"Who is this?" Joe asked.

"This?" the voice echoed. It took on a sarcastic tone. "This is Detective Sergeant Moretti."

"Wh-what?"

"We got you completely by the balls. You don't believe me, I'm staring you right in the eye. Right now. Just look across the street at the insurance office, asshole."

THE DETECTIVES' ROOM in the precinct house had been relatively quiet at three that afternoon, also hot and smelly. The brick building was the same in which the police station had been housed since 1937. At the personal expense of some earlier detective, probably during LaGuardia's time, a heavy, noisy oscillating fan had been put in one corner of the smallish room.

Moretti looked up from his paperwork and stared at the fan. It had been making peculiar noises for at least the past ten summers in which Moretti had sweated out his shifts as a detective, but today he suddenly heard a new note in it, a second, lower, irregular hum beneath the normal one.

He frowned, his thoughts distracted for a moment by the fan, which provided just enough flow of air to keep detectives from dying of heatstroke on days like this one. When was the last time anybody had oiled the damned thing, he wondered. Of course, they made fans to last in the old days. Maybe all he had to do was get up, go over, and kick the damned thing. Or maybe he wasn't hearing a new noise. Maybe he was just cracking up from the heat.

He turned back to his typewriter, which he suspected of being even older than the fan, probably one of those office Royal 400s made during World War II. Painstakingly, with two fingers of each hand, he rapped out a brief description of the case he was just concluding, or trying to conclude, one of those misty office-theft jobs in which everybody was lying, absolutely everybody.

He pulled out a red bandanna and wiped his forehead, then got up to go to the toilet. "Jerry," he grunted at the other detective in the room, "I'm taking a personal."

The other detective looked up from his copy of the *Post*. "Squeeze it but don't stroke it."

In the toilet the urine-and-carbolic smell was stronger than in the rest of the precinct house. Sometimes, on a hot, muggy day like this one, as you stepped into the room you nearly lost your breath for a moment. Over the years Moretti had tried to work out a way of holding his breath for the length of his pee, but it never worked. Eventually he always had to take a breath. In the john.

He examined his eyes in the mirror. Normally they were average size, dark gray, bedded in a network of fine wrinkles as if they'd been carefully placed in a nest of crumpled Kleenex. Today they looked small and bloodshot. Moretti had an air conditioner in his bedroom, even though his wife never felt heat. He also had an air conditioner in the living room of his tiny two-story brick semidetached house in Hollis, farther out in Queens. The man who owned the house to his right was a fireman. The owner to the left was a transit-system cop. It was that kind of neighborhood.

Moretti also had an air conditioner in his car, a three-year-old Rambler. When he went out on assignments, interviewing people in stores, offices, homes, everywhere he went, there was air conditioning. Not in the detectives' room.

He peed and returned to the mirror to figure out what was wrong with his face today. Of course, at the age of forty, things started going wrong all over, not just the face.

The nose, small when he was a teen-ager, had thickened over the years. So had the cheeks. That was to be expected. From a sort of good-looking kid, Moretti had matured into a slightly slimmer version of his old man, with that same stocky Calabrese body, wide shoulders, short, powerful arms, big hands. *Un vero contadino,* Moretti thought, a real peasant.

Lucky for him he wasn't as short as his old man or he'd never have made it on the cops. But he was an inch or two over the minimum height and he'd scored well on his exams and he'd had a little political pull, what the boys call a rabbi, who could pull strings, after he passed the sergeant's exam, to get him this post.

That had been ten years ago, his tenth on the force. He wasn't doing that well, was he? He should have made lieutenant two years ago, but the shake-ups after the corruption exposures had turned everybody so goosy that even his political rabbi couldn't help him.

So that's why you look different, he told his reflection: You're getting old and you're getting to be a loser. You don't have to lose a lot to be a loser, he thought. You only have to lose one thing, like a lieutenant's bar.

Also, a man aged faster in this line of work. And more than that, a cop aged faster in a place like New York City than a place like, say, Dubuque.

Not that Queens was so bad—most of the loonies and junkies gravitated to Manhattan—but that still left plenty of weirdos for this borough. Not just petty thieves. Not just hustlers and con men and grifters and heist guys, not just shoplifters and check kiters and gypsy-switch artists. No, Queens had its share of hard guys, too. Armed robbery was common. Murder happened often enough in this precinct to keep Homicide busy. Rape was coming up fast as the new fad crime.

And if it wasn't bad enough, Moretti thought, what people did to people, now there was a whole new brand of loony that tortured animals and killed them.

Not that the cops got involved in crimes against animals, just that the *idea* of a mind that would do this alarmed detectives like Moretti, who understood a little about the human soul. Not much, he told his face in the mirror, but enough.

In this case, not much was too much.

He turned and left the toilet. He had been in there so long that he'd lost his sense of smell. His olfactory nerves had been paralyzed by the powerful piss-Lysol combination. As he got back to his typewriter, the telephone was ringing. Jerry jerked a thumb at it, as if to say he'd answer, but Moretti was in charge. He picked up the telephone.

"Detective Sergeant Moretti."

"Tony?" a man asked.

Moretti frowned. His Christian name was Gaetano. Only his close friends ever used Tony, and this wasn't the voice of a close friend. "Who's this?"

"Lou."

"Come on, Lou. Give me a last name."

"Lou Bagradian, for Christ's sake, Tony." The man sounded hurt. "You know. I got the Aetna agency."

"That Lou. *Wus machts du?*" Moretti spoke not only Italian and the Calabrese dialect, but knew enough Yiddish and Greek to get prompt service in any sandwich deli. He knew Bagradian wasn't Jewish, but it seemed like a thing to do, after he'd presumed to call him Tony.

"Listen, did your prowl car check the Chase branch at closing time today?"

Moretti sat forward in his chair. "Lou, stop questioning the cops. Tell me what you want to tell me."

"Don't take my head off, okay? I'm just a citizen doing my duty. I would hope to God somebody would return me the favor if I ever needed it."

"The Chase branch," Moretti reminded him.

"Yeah. First of all, two guys went in there just at closing."

"That's shocking."

"No humor, Tony, please," the caller said in an aggrieved tone. "If you want honest citizens to back up the cops, let's have a little respect."

"You got it, *mein kind.*"

"The next thing is that Leroy, the guard, doesn't pull down the venetian blind like he always does. No, one of these two guys pulls down the blind."

Moretti sat up straighter. "Yes?"

"He was carrying a florist's box, this one guy. I mean, you could hide a gun in a florist's box. Anyway, I call Boyle over there to see if everything's okay."

"And he says yes?"

"Yeah, he says yes, but it takes him about fifteen rings to get the phone and then only after the guy with the florist's box stands over him. In other words, he—"

"I get the picture. What explanation did Boyle give?"

"They're guys from Chase. Systems men, some nonsense like that. But this is the thing that bothers me, one of the guys looks like some garage attendant or something. And the other one is all dressed up like a high-class pimp. I mean, like bank guys they don't look. No way."

"Jerry," Moretti told his partner, "check Holmes. See if they had an alarm from the Chase branch." Then, into the phone: "What else, Lou?"

"I'm going across the street and get a closer look. The girls are all kind of huddled in one place way in the back where I can't see them. It's just not the way things go after closing over there."

"Lou, I think it's too bad the insurance business is so lousy you have the time to watch all these things. We'll check it out."

"Why do all you guys have to be so smart-ass? I'm only doing what every citizen is supposed to do. What if it was my place being held up? I'd want somebody to call the cops. Why should they if all they get is cheap humor?"

Moretti stifled the urge to tell his caller that the way he ran his agency there wouldn't be much cash around to tempt a heist guy. He glanced over at Jerry. "Anything?"

Jerry looked up from the phone. "No alarms."

"Okay, Lou," Moretti said into the telephone. "I'm going to check it out. Is that action or is that action? I mean, when we get an honest citizen we know how to take care of him."

"Very funny. Good-bye."

"Lou!"

"What?"

"Don't make a scene at the bank. If something's going on, you'll only stir up the animals and get yourself shot. Just, you know, take a look and move along back to your office. Promise me that?"

"Okay."

Moretti hung up. "You want to take a ride in a genuine air-conditioned Rambler?"

Jerry shook his head. "I got two reports to finish."

"Guaranteed fifty degrees cooler inside."

"Don't tempt me. What's the rumble at Chase?"

"No rumble. Just a nervous bystander with time on his hands. See you."

Once outside the precinct house, the full blast of sun and heat hammered on Moretti's head as though it were an anvil. He put on a narrow-brim cocoa-straw hat, knowing as he did so that it would make him feel even hotter, but Moretti always wore a hat, always.

He got into the baking Rambler and used the air conditioner to flush out all the heat before he closed his door and started off. The Chase branch was a mile away. He reached in his glove compartment for a small pair of binoculars, which he tucked into the side pocket of his jacket. He hoped Bagradian's office was air conditioned. This kind of August was murder, almost literally. By tonight at least a handful of old-timers would be in the hospital, maybe in the morgue.

He passed the Chase branch doing about twenty-five miles an hour and gave it the once-over without seeming to. A chubby guy in a white short-sleeved shirt was standing in the doorway talking to Boyle, whom Moretti knew by sight, as he knew all the branch bank managers in the precinct. The sun was too glaring for Moretti to make out anything happening inside the bank. He circled around behind the Aetna agency and parked in the rear. He knocked on the back door, got no response, tried the lock and found it shut.

Moretti took out his wallet, from which he extracted a sheet of stiff celluloid about the size of a charge card. He worked the celluloid between the door and the frame so that it pushed back the catch. Chances were Bagradian hadn't bolted it. Why would he? The catch slipped back and Moretti was inside the rear of the insurance office.

He moved to the front and sat down in a chair behind a loose-weave curtain that had been half pulled against the outside glare. He could see through the curtain but it hid him. He watched Bagradian make his way back across the street, dodging traffic. The terrible outside heat slowed his progress down to a near crawl. Inside the office, Moretti was pleased to note, the temperature was comfortable.

Bagradian unlocked his front door and let himself in. Moretti waited until he had walked back to the rear of the office, passing a few yards from Moretti without noticing him. "Lou," the detective called. "Don't panic. I'm inside. Don't come rushing back here. Just move around naturally."

"How the hell you get in?"

"Police secrets. What'd you find?"

"Not a damned thing. Boyle's as cool as a cucumber. The guy who had the flower box is working on some books with Marge. I can't see the rest of the people or the other guy, the hotshot pimp."

"You realize how pissed off Boyle will be if there's nothing going on over there and I start making cop noises."

Bagradian loomed up behind the counter. "Tony, I swear to God, it don't feel right. Boyle's too cool. He's too calm. And no chitchat. Usually the guy is good for a laugh or two. He's a regular guy, Boyle. But today it's all business."

"Right." Moretti took out the binoculars and tried focusing them through the loose-weave drapery. It didn't work too well. The image was interrupted by fuzz. He moved cautiously sideways until one lens of the binoculars was clear of the curtain. "Okay," he said, "this may take a while."

"What's happening?"

"You want a blow-by-blow?" Moretti asked. "None of them are in the lobby area now. Now here comes a lady with a gorgeous pair."

"Marge."

"My little Margie, I love you," Moretti said. "She's going to a cabinet. She's giving some stuff to the garage-attendant guy. He's been talking to a guy in an ice-cream suit. That's your pimp, Lou. And your pimp is excited. Yes, he's getting more excited," Moretti went on, imitating a racetrack announcer. "He's getting very excited and he's waving his hand. Yes, and in his hand is—*oi, weh ist mir*. In his hand is a gun." Moretti glanced back at the insurance agent. "You win, Louie. Congratulations."

"What? What? What?"

"Hold it." Moretti hunched forward, watching closely through the single barrel of the binoculars that cleared the edge of the curtain. "Now the garage guy and Boyle have disappeared. Sam, get me the telephone number of that branch, will you? Now the garage guy is back. He's moving everybody out of sight. He's talking to Marge. Got the number? Start dialing."

"It's ringing," Bagradian reported a moment later.

"It's ringing and nobody's paying any attention to it. The garage guy and Marge have disappeared. Bring the phone over to me, Sam. Is there another phone on a different line?"

"In the back."

"Call the precinct house, ask for Jerry Munoz in the detective room. Tell him what's happening. Move."

Moretti watched the man who wore chino pants. He was leading everyone back into sight now. He seemed to have a gun butt sticking out of the waistband of his trousers. The pimp in the ice-cream suit looked very nervous, even at this distance. Probably the insistent ringing of the telephone had all their nerves on edge. All Moretti wanted to do at this point was to ask Boyle for a clue. In the few seconds after Boyle answered the phone, he would have t—

Boyle was moving across the lobby toward the phone. He picked it up. "Boyle speaking."

"Sergeant Moretti. I'm watching from across the street. Are they going to leave or will there be trouble? If they're leaving, just hang up on me. We'll get them later. Otherwise, let me talk to the head guy. Your decision."

Boyle said nothing for a long moment. Then: "Hold on."

HELLO?" a man's voice asked. Moretti classified it as local: a Queens boy.

"What are you doing in there?" he demanded.

"Who is this?"

"This," the detective said, "is Detective Sergeant Moretti. We got you completely by the balls. You don't believe me, I'm staring you right in the eye. Right now. Just look across the street at the insurance office, asshole."

He watched the man in the chinos put down the phone and go to the window. Moretti got out of the chair and stepped from behind the drapery. He realized what a touchy spot he was in, but Boyle's decision had put him there, and all he could do was play it light, keep the guy in the chinos from panicking. Moretti lifted his cocoa-straw hat and tipped it to the man. Then he held up the binoculars. He watched the man go back to the phone.

As he picked it up, Moretti began talking fast to gain the initiative. "Listen," he said, "it's not as bad as you think. We got you, but we're not animals, understand. If nobody's hurt in there, the rest is easy. Is anybody hurt?"

He could see the man listening to him. He could even hear his breathing over the telephone line. "Let's be reasonable people," Moretti went on. "Let's not be stupid. Let's take care of each other, get me? You fold your hands over your head and come out the door. Nobody's going to shoot y—"

The line went dead as the man hung up. Son of a bitch. Moretti was cursing himself more than the man. Why had the goddamned manager put him on the line? What was going on over there that made Boyle decide to do it this way? "Lou," he called back to the insurance man. "Did you get Jerry?"

The chubby man returned from the rear of the office. "What's happening?"

"Nothing, the guy hung up on me."

"Maybe you shouldn't have called," Bagradian suggested. "You could've nabbed them when they left the bank."

"I gave Boyle that option. He turned it down. What did Jerry tell you?"

"Said he would—" The insurance man stopped. Sirens sounded in the distance. "I guess that's them."

Moretti nodded. He dialed the precinct-house number. "Abie," he told the desk sergeant, "it's Moretti. Get this message on the air to the squad cars coming to the Chase. Tell them to surround the joint and get on my walkie-talkie frequency. Do nothing else. Just take a plant, sit tight, and wait to hear from me. And get some more cars from some other precinct. Okay?"

Moretti hung up and handed some keys to Bagradian. "There's a cream-colored Rambler parked behind your office. In the glove compartment pick up two things. A box of cartridges and a walkie-talkie. Understand?"

The insurance man's face went very solemn. "Got you, Tony." He wheeled and made off. The thrill of a lifetime, Moretti thought, watching him march away. He's going to tell this story for the rest of his life. People!

"Lou," he called. "What's the bank phone number?"

The chubby man gave it to him, and Moretti dialed again. This time it was answered on the second ring. "Boyle speaking."

"Why did you put him on the line?" Moretti demanded. "I'm sorry now I phoned."

"You don't understand what's—" Moretti saw the telephone being snatched away from the manager.

"All right, prick," the man in chinos shouted over the phone. "Keep away from the bank or we start throwing dead ones out the front door. You got that?"

"Is anybody hurt in there?" Moretti asked calmly.

"No, but you're trying, aren't you?"

"I don't want anybody hurt, starting with you," Moretti assured him. He was keeping his voice level, almost hypnotic. "You're in a spot, I don't have to tell you that. But you can get out of it real easy. We're here to help you. You—" Sirens howled close by, and the line went dead again.

One squad car pulled up in front of the insurance office, blocking Moretti's view. He waved the cop driver to move the car along a few yards, and it took several minutes for him to get the message. By then the insurance man was back with the walkie-talkie.

Moretti switched it on. "This is Moretti. I see Car one oh eight. Where's the other vehicle? Over."

The instrument crackled and hissed for a while. Then: "Car four one four behind the bank. Over."

"A robbery is in progress. Two suspects, male, Caucasian, mid-twenties, armed. Have ordered reinforcements. Maintain surveillance. Car four one four report any activity at rear door. Car one oh eight maintain position till further notice. Out."

He put the walkie-talkie down on the chair, picked up the phone, and dialed the precinct house. "Moretti. Let me talk to Jerry." As he waited, he saw that some sort of argument was going on inside the bank. From the way people gestured, faced, and talked, it was clear that the man in the chinos was the leader. The pimp in the fancy suit was the enforcer. He hadn't entered the argument at all, but Boyle and Marge had.

"What's up, Tony?" Jerry's voice asked.

"Standoff, for now. Do I get my other cars?"

"You got four more coming. Plus a traffic detail to close off the street."

"I think it ought to be over quick, because they know we're here and they know they haven't got a chance. A few more cars ought to help them make up their minds."

"Any ID on them?"

"Not yet."

"Tony," Jerry started, then stopped. After a pause, "Tony, you know it's the law. This is a national bank. So I had to notify the FBI."

"Jesus H. Christ!"

"I got no choice, Tony," Jerry whined. "It's my ass if I don't."

"You couldn't delay it half an hour?" Moretti demanded. "Half an hour I could talk those two monkeys out of there."

"The last time we held up notification we got such a chewing—"

"Ah, shit," Moretti cut in. "The whole place will be swarming with Batman and his little Robins. All these Feebies know to do is chuck in tear-gas bombs and shoot whoever comes out."

"Tony, it ain't that bad. It'll probably be Baker who's the agent in charge."

"Baker? Working with Baker is like working with five pounds of chilled liver."

"But at least you've worked with him before. It's easier than some faceless John they send in out of the blue."

"Baker," Moretti repeated. "What did I do to deserve this? The next time I take a personal, you answer the phone. You take the whole case. Okay?"

"Right, Tony," Jerry said, laughing. "Give me the number there."

Moretti gave him various telephone numbers. As he

did, another squad car pulled up, blocking his view of the bank. He waved savagely at the driver and finally got him to back up.

"Jerry, have somebody pick up a high-powered telescope or something. These binoculars aren't worth shit. Get Krachmal. He's supposed to be a lip-reader, right? Send him in here with the telescope. In uniform, Jerry. I want to show lots of blue around here."

He hung up and switched his walkie-talkie to "Send." He was aware that the heavy breathing from behind him was Lou, the insurance man. Just a thrill a minute. "Car six one oh, I read you. The other car, come in for ID and placement. Over."

"Car two oh seven, behind the bank. Over."

"Okay," Moretti told them. "Walkie-talkies on 'Receive' from here on. The layout is two cars behind, two in front. I want one officer from each to leave the vehicle and move around. Show yourselves. Show your walkie-talkies. Traffic detail will be closing the thoroughfare. At that point, remove riot guns from vehicles and show weapons. Not now. When instructed. Out."

"Car one oh eight. Show the weapon now, Sarge? Over."

"Negative. Show weapon when instructed. Out."

"Car six one oh. Which weapon is that, Sarge?"

Moretti took a long, steadying breath. "The pump gun. Do not, repeat, do not show pump gun till instructed. Out."

Moretti waited for another idiot question, but got none. He opened the front door of the insurance office and stepped out on the street at about the time uniformed men in each car showed themselves. Moretti moved out onto the asphalt.

The black surface radiated a furnace heat. The soles of his shoes stuck to the tarry stuff with each step. He glanced both ways along the street and saw that roadblocks had already been set up on either side. In the distance, fresh sirens wailed. He could hear a machine-gun sound from somewhere nearby and glanced up.

Two helicopters hovered over the area, helping the traffic detail reroute cars and trucks. Moretti waved one of the choppers in. It wouldn't hurt to show the man in the chino slacks what kind of backup forces were being assembled. The police helicopter bobbed lower over Moretti and hung there, sending a fierce downdraft that rattled the brim of Moretti's hat. He waved the chopper away and it lifted suddenly, as if it were a balloon whose string had just been cut.

When he walked back inside the insurance office, the chubby man was on the telephone. "For you, Sarge," he said.

Moretti registered the fact that the gravity of the situation had somehow upgraded him from Tony to Sarge. He took the phone. "Detective Sergeant Moretti."

"I hear you got yourself a little fracas, kiddo?" The voice was rich, thick with good living, as if filtered past both an expensive cigar and a quality cognac. Moretti recognized the voice of his rabbi, a Tammany hack named Mulvey who still clung to his post as assistant commissioner, the man to whom Moretti owed everything and would like to owe more.

"Good to hear your voice, Commissioner," Moretti said. "How'd you get the news?"

"Good news travels fast."

"Good?"

"Good for you, kiddo," the man assured him. "This is exactly what you've needed for the past few years, publicity. The rest will be a lead-pipe cinch."

"If I can get them without anybody being hurt," Moretti added.

"I'm counting on you, Tony. You're my man." The voice went deeper and richer with fat overtones of patronage. "Just one thing."

"I know."

"Right. Don't let those bastards in gray steal the headlines."

"It's Baker again," Moretti said.

"You can handle him. He's not God."

"I'll try."

"You have to do better than try, Tony," the man corrected him. "This isn't just your career. The honor of the force is riding with you. I don't have to tell you that, do I?"

"Commissioner," Moretti said, "the only thing I can promise is the best goddamned try in the world."

There was silence at the other end. "Well, in a sense, I guess that's all I can ask, Tony," the man's fat voice admitted. "But as a human being who has your good at heart, who wants to be able to send you right in there for your lieutenant's bar, I can't help but hope for more than a good try."

Moretti closed his eyes for a moment against the glare through the plate glass. Why was talking to this man so difficult? Was he saying something the guy didn't understand, or was it the other way around? He wished they were face to face, but the commissioner had rarely appeared in public since the corruption scare had started.

"I understand how important this is," Moretti assured him. "I'm giving it everything I've got."

"Good. It may be your last major shot," the voice reminded him. "This sort of chance doesn't grow on trees. Make it count." He hung up without waiting for a good-bye.

Moretti replaced the phone in its cradle. God, it was nice to deal with bloodless shits like Commissioner Aloysius Mulvey. Why couldn't he have inherited a more human rabbi?

But you didn't choose your political protector. Accidents of birth, who you were and where you lived, dictated whom you had to see in the political machinery to have a good word put in for you. And the tribute exacted by a rabbi was fierce. Mulvey hadn't really leaned on him in a year or two, but there were occasions, middle-of-the-night emergency phone calls, in which Moretti was told to kill a case against a gambler, or release a heroin dealer on his own recognizance, or any one of a dozen illegal favors. And Mulvey was by no means the most corrupt pol in town.

Moretti pulled out his bandanna, removed his hat, and mopped his forehead. When he replaced his hat on his head, the leather band inside felt unpleasantly clammy with sweat. And it was cool in the insurance office. A warning call like that brought out a different kind of sweat.

So this was to be it, Moretti realized, his last chance at a lieutenant's bars. Easy. Nothing to do it. Just snake the two bandits out of there without anybody being hurt and make sure the Feebies didn't get any credit for it.

With Baker on hand, it would be touch and go. Baker was as hungry for publicity, in his own anemic way, as Mulvey. "The honor of the force." Wasn't that what that mealy-mouthed Mulvey had said? As if the man's being alive and breathing the polluted air of New York wasn't dishonor enough. But Baker probably had the same ambitions, for himself and for "the honor of the Bureau."

People! Christ!

As if on cue, a gray four-door Ford moved slowly down the street. Since it had been allowed through the barricades, and since it was gray, Moretti already knew it to be an FBI vehicle.

It pulled to a halt at an angle to the curb, as if the driver were from another part of the planet where they had never heard of parallel parking. The first one out of the gray car was Baker, gray-haired in a suit just a shade darker gray than the car.

Behind him three younger Feebies moved with tiny, economical gestures, hands at their sides. No gesticulations, no facial expressions, except that they stuck close to Baker and moved in a kind of phalanx with him. All four men wore gray hats, but one of them didn't wear a gray suit. It was a charcoal color. They stood for a moment, surveying the bank façade, and then let themselves into the insurance office.

"Oh, it's you, Moretti," Baker said.

His voice had a whisper quality to it, as if he produced it by rubbing his hind legs together. No "hello." No "how are you?" No "long time no see." Moretti nodded. "I can't have all those people in here," he started right out. "Send two of them back to the car."

Baker paused. His small-featured face was immobile. Moretti figured they were probably the same age, about forty. But Baker moved in such a tight way that he seemed like an old man, lacking the energy for sweeping movements. After a moment, he turned and nodded to two of his agents, who left the office and returned to their car.

"All right?" he asked Moretti. Then, without waiting for an answer, "Who's he?" indicating the insurance man with a nod of his gray head.

"Lou Bagradian. This is his office we're using."

"Sorry, Mr. Bagradian," Baker said. "You'll have to vacate the premises."

"B-but—"

"Lou turned in the alarm," Moretti said. He felt sorry for the chubby little guy in his short-sleeved shirt. All his fun was going to be spoiled, and he didn't deserve that. "We'd never have known about the robbery except that Lou spotted it."

"Very commendable," Baker said in his neutral, Midwest voice. "But the law is quite clear about it, Mr. Bagradian. Please vacate by the rear entrance, if there is one."

"This is my office," the insurance man protested.

"You'll be adequately recompensed for any damage incurred in the course of maintaining law and order in, on, or nearby these premises," Baker told him.

Moretti gave up the struggle. Baker was right, of course. Civilians had no place here now. But he couldn't stand the look on Bagradian's face as he picked up his jacket and left. Nor could he stand the look in Baker's eye: dead, almost unseeing, as if the removal of Bagradian were a detail only slightly less important than stepping on an ant.

"Are you going to give me any more trouble, Baker?" Moretti pounced. The only way to keep a Feebie in line was to constantly keep him on the defensive.

"More?"

"I don't want any of your snipers killing civilians," Moretti went on, maintaining pressure. "No shootouts. Here in New York we deal with people as if they were human beings. Understand?"

Baker eyed him with distaste. "You really think this will earn you that bar?"

Moretti grinned evilly at Baker. "You bet your ass, Baker. And nobody, not you and not the whole Bureau, is going to keep me from it."

★12

WATCHING THE VARIOUS SQUAD CARS wheel into place, Littlejoe began to realize he would be lucky to get out of this alive. Never mind the fifty grand tomorrow morning. Forget the five grand they already had. Forget Sam, because in a showdown he'd start shooting. Forget Eddie, the driver, because he wasn't part of the team anyway. But me, Joe told himself, my own ass. Finished.

He had been standing back from the smallish picture window of the bank as various uniformed police moved in and out of doorways across the street, brandishing walkie-talkies and guns. Big deal. But effective.

The sight of all that blue was getting to him, no question about it. What had once been a simple question of "Do we score big or small?" now became the kind of question that produces a sour churning at the pit of the stomach, "Do I live or die?"

Do I, Littlejoe thought. Is that a proper thing for Littlejoe to be thinking about? What the fuck is death to me?

He turned, to find that most of the people inside the bank were watching him. Littlejoe the leader. Power out of the muzzle of a gun. Shit, yes.

"All right," he growled, more to give them a taste of power than to have something done. "Marge, move those titties out of view. Get your ass back behind that lobby sign where Sam can keep a bead on you."

"Mr. Planner," Marge snapped back.

"Move it, baby."

"You're going to get us all killed," she countered. "Making things up as you go along. How in God's name did you ever have the gall to rob a bank?"

"Out of sight, cunt!"

"And the language," she said. "A cheap mind with a cheap mouth."

"Jesus H. Christ!" Joe burst out at the top of his lungs. "This is a gun, Marge. One more word out of you and the slug gets you right in the left tit. What the fuck is the world coming to? I hold a gun on this broad and she badmouths me to my face? What is that?"

"I'm just saying what we're all thinking," Marge spoke up.

Littlejoe moved in on her, the .38 Police Positive pressing against her navel. "You want it there?" He prodded her lower. "Or there?" He lifted the gun and worked the cold blue muzzle in and out of her mouth. "You want it like that?"

The utter silence in the bank told Littlejoe he'd made his point. He backed away from Marge. "Whatever way you want it, you get it. Just keep laying that mouth on me and you go." He snapped his fingers once. Marge blinked. "Like that."

He'd finally gotten to her. He'd gotten to all of them, probably. Good. What the hell was it if holding a gun on somebody didn't give you the power of life and death over them? Guys who heisted a plane, now, nobody dared to give them a hard time. One shot and you could depressurize the whole cabin. Hijackers had it easy.

Littlejoe moved sideways out of the window area and sat down in a chair. "You want a plan?" he asked Marge sarcastically. "I got plans I haven't even used yet, baby. Plans that'd dazzle you. Right, Sam?"

Sam's dark eyes shifted uneasily. Joe could see that

Marge's words had gotten to Sam, as had her first defiance of the gun. "Right, Littlejoe." His response sounded mechanical.

In the silence that followed, Joe leaned back and relaxed for a moment in the chair. The trick was not to get uptight. The cops were trying to psych him into panicking. Give up. No chance. Well, maybe they were right, but Littlejoe hadn't earned his rep getting so uptight he couldn't think straight any more.

"Hey," Eddie said from the rear of the bank. "The street is crawling with 'em. Jesus, Littlejoe, I didn't buy nothing like this when Mick told me t—"

"Shut up!" Joe shouted. "You got an asshole for a mouth. The second the going gets jumpy, you shit green through it. You want to leave? Go ahead. Walk out. They'll cut you in slices like pastrami."

"Let me chill him," Sam said then.

The quiet suggestion, made without the tiniest edge of feeling, made everyone turn to look at Sam. He had swung the .45 Colt toward Eddie, a few feet away from him. "Okay, Littlejoe?"

Joe got up out of the chair. "I'd love it, Sam," he said in a calm, businesslike way, as if discussing ordering some sandwiches, "but if the pig outside hears a shot, there's no telling what they'll do. Maybe storm the joint."

"You mean he lives?" Sam said. There was the faintest downturn of disappointment.

"No other way for now, baby. Sorry."

"Maybe later?"

Littlejoe watched the sweat break out across Eddie's pasty forehead. His small eyes had widened like manholes. He looked ready to faint flat on his face. The bigger they are . . .

"Maybe," Joe said, almost grudgingly. "We'll see."

If they were, indeed, riding a sinking ship, Joe thought now, dumping Eddie wouldn't hurt their position that much. He was like ballast you threw overboard from a balloon, so it could rise higher and fly free.

Like a plane. In a plane the gun was respected. Airlines coughed up millions. Governments allowed free escape. Special conditions. Prisoners released from jails. Hijacking a plane, you could ask for anything.

And get it.

Moretti was ready to turn the whole mess over to Baker and walk away in disgrace. None of this showed in his face, of course, nor in his voice. He had been a cop too long to let anything—even the major failure of his life—show to the outside world. But the defeat was clear enough to him, and soon it would be just as clear to the rest of the law-enforcement people there.

To begin with, they had stopped answering the telephone in the bank. This had happened after two more calls, during which Moretti had tried to reason with the man in the chino pants and been hung up on.

This meant that Moretti's plan of easing the bandits out by reassuring them, soft-talking them into the open, had no chance to move ahead, no chance to succeed.

Secondly, a tremendous amount of attention was now focused on this particular event. It was almost as if, on a broiling hot day in August, when everyone should have been under the shower or at an air-cooled movie, they had nothing better to do than devote all their attention to what was, so far, a rather minor bank job.

This had the effect of magnifying every wrong move Moretti made, of amplifying each weakness, each hesitation. He knew he'd made plenty of mistakes so far, but the knowledge that all of New York could see him goofing up only exaggerated his all-too-human tendency to guess wrong.

Not only had more police been summoned, but several more carloads of Feebies were on hand. In addition, Holmes Protection people were clamoring to get in on the act, because their alarm system was supposed to protect the bank. Two insurance-company investigators were flashing their meaningless badges. The whole thing had taken on the proportions of a bad dream.

Overhead, helicopters hovered like man-eating bugs, ready to pounce. The street was full of officious police with bullhorns yelling at the several hundred bystanders who had gathered behind police barricades at each end of the block. Angry store-owners, losing an afternoon and evening of business, were crying for fast action.

Moretti's own captain was threatening to take charge of the case and dump Moretti unceremoniously on his ass if he didn't show results fast. Television vans had pulled up behind the crowds at both ends of the block, and photographers with the portable creepy-peepie cameras were moving into the combat area on the strength of passes and ten-dollar bills slipped to cops supposedly guarding the barriers.

Reporters from television, the newspapers, and the wire services were swarming in and out of store-fronts along both sides of the street, trying to stake out telephones, into which they poured a steady stream of non-reportage, none of it meaning much, because nothing, actually, was happening.

Therein lay Moretti's defeat. By now something should have happened. Otherwise this was nothing more than a dry-run rehearsal for remote camera crews, crowd-control squads, and human-interest reporters, getting their adjectives oiled up and ready to pour.

The whole thing, so far, had been for everyone

else but him, Moretti noted. It hadn't even been for the luckless bastards in the bank, either the suspects or the hostages.

He winced as he thought of the word *hostages,* because that was the shape the case was taking. He knew enough about the criminal mind—which was so damned little different from the normal mind—to know that even the stupidest of bandits would eventually realize that his only salvation lay in trading the lives of the bank employees for his own freedom.

That it was taking the man in the chinos longer than necessary to realize this only indicated to Moretti that (a) he was stupid or (b) he was still hoping to score big somehow.

In an earlier conversation with Boyle, before the phones had stopped being answered, Moretti had finally learned the truth of the heist, that it had netted only five grand and the suspects were planning to wait all night for a cash delivery by Wells Fargo. They'd even brought their driver inside. It had been that prospect that had caused Boyle to bring Moretti into the open at once. Boyle distrusted the ability of the three bandits to remain cool all night and leave without killing some, if not all, of them.

So it came back to hostages, Moretti thought. He dialed the bank number again, on the off chance that the ringing would stir some action. After twenty rings he gave up.

"Let's stop playing games," Baker said then.

His flat, dull, uninflected voice startled Moretti. "What games?"

"Let's turn off their power. In this heat that bank will be a sweatbox inside of fifteen minutes."

"You got great ideas for keeping a felon cool."

"Yours isn't any better. But if you veto it, let me suggest that my men get on the roof and flush tear gas into the ventilation system. We'll have every one of them out on the street in no time."

"Except for the corpses inside."

"You're letting some two-bit punks spook you, Moretti."

"I've been watching them. My lip-reader guy has been giving me snatches of their talk. One of them I can count on, the monkey in chino slacks. He's sane. There's also a big dummy hiding in back. No problem. But the dude in the white suit is whacko bananas. Three times, my guy says, he's offered to kill anybody the other guy names. He's itching to spill blood. In such a spot, you want to gas them?"

Baker was silent for a while. "Moretti," he said then, "why is it all you ever do is find reasons for doing nothing?"

"Because at this point, the moves are up to them."

"That's defeatist thinking. I don't like no-win players on my team."

Moretti chuckled. "Since when is it your team, coach?"

"Any minute now, the way you're going."

"I got one thing I haven't tried." Moretti stood silently, eyeing the bank across the street. His man, Krachmal, was surveying the scene with a telescope partly hidden behind the drapery.

"What one thing?" Baker asked in the tone an adult uses to humor a wayward child.

"My business, Baker."

Moretti removed his hat and sponged his forehead dry. He replaced the hat and gave it a firm tug to set it in place. Then he stepped out the front entrance into the blast of August heat.

A faint cheer went up from the nearest crowd. To Moretti's ears it sounded faintly sarcastic. He saw the three television cameras at that end swivel toward him. At the other end of the street, a camera with a giant telephoto lens moved ponderously toward him like the turret gun of a warship. A man nearby lifted his camera on its shoulder brace and twisted the lens to focus.

Good, Moretti thought. Carefully, he stepped off

the curb and removed his jacket. He dropped it on the sidewalk and stood there in his striped shirt, shoulder holster and straps clearly outlined. He waited until the people in the bank had noticed him. Then moving very slowly, he unbuckled the harness and shrugged out of the holster. He laid it, with its snub-nosed Colt Cobra, on the baking sidewalk. In the same stooping movement he picked up his jacket and put it on. Then he put his hands out to his sides, a foot away from his hips, and started across the boiling asphalt. Out of the corner of his eye he could see a cop pick up his holster and gun and put them inside a squad car. The smell of fresh bread filled the moist air.

He had the undivided attention of the man in the chinos. Good, he also could sense, with his peripheral vision, that the cameras were following him closely, the red lights under their lenses bright and clear.

"Hey, looka!" someone shouted. "It's Wyatt Earp!"

Moretti forced his face to remain unmoved. Typical New York smart-ass bystander. Everything was a joke. Well, wasn't it?

"Go get 'em, Sheriff!" another civilian yelled.

"This town ain't big enough for both of yez!"

Goddamned half-wit jokers, Moretti thought. Where everything's a joke, nothing's serious. Well, wasn't it? What was so serious about a twenty-year cop with a wife and three kids risking his ass to get three dumbbell bandits off a hook their own greed had hung them on? Was that serious? Shit, it was to laugh.

He could see the man in the chinos move toward the door. The revolver in his belt looked like a .38 cop gun, probably lifted off the bank guard. But where the hell had he gotten that carbine? What the hell kind of arsenal did he have in there?

The asphalt plucked at his heels. He could feel the sweat flowing down his sides, down his forehead.

A drop gathered at the tip of his nose. How could anybody take this seriously, he thought. Except maybe this weirdo with the carbine.

Anybody had to take a carbine seriously, Moretti told himself. It was ten times as accurate as a handgun. Keep babbling, he thought. Keep the old brain idling in neutral. Don't think about too much, because it wouldn't help. *Gurnischt hilfen, bubbele*.

He reached the curb in front of the bank.

"Ain't you the new schoolmarm?" some clown yelled.

"String 'em up, Marshal!"

The man in the chinos lifted the carbine across his chest, as if doing "Port Arms" by the manual. He was old enough to be a vet, Moretti noticed. Vietnam vet meets Korea vet; object: homicide.

Moretti turned very slightly to check on the position of his men. He had snipers on several rooftops, as did the Feebies. He could now see his own reflection clearly in the glass front of the bank, and, without even trying, he could see that Baker was standing behind him in the doorway of the insurance office, holding a walkie-talkie in his hand. The son of a bitch was not above ordering his snipers to cut loose, even if they got Moretti by so doing.

The sergeant walked across the sidewalk and stood a foot in front of the glass door. His man in chinos had stopped in almost the same position inside the door. "Can you hear me?" Moretti called.

The man nodded.

"Loud and clear, sweets!" someone in the audience called out.

Moretti cleared his throat and pitched his voice as loud as he could. "There are a dozen sharpshooters zeroed in on us," he shouted. "They have orders to hold their fire." He paused. "To *hold their fire*," he repeated even more loudly, hoping the goddamned message sank in. "Nobody is going to shoot," he went on then. "I'm your protection. They can't shoot while I'm here. Now, I don't ask much. I just want you to open that door a crack so we can have a private parley. Okay?"

The man with the carbine blinked. He seemed rooted to the spot. Moretti was afraid to say any more. He'd warned off the snipers, he hoped, no matter what Baker told them. More to the point, he'd put Baker on notice not to give the order to fire. Most of what he'd shouted was directed at the law, not this poor creep standing on the other side of the door.

"Just open it two inches," Moretti said at last. "So we can talk like two human beings, instead of barking at each other."

The man with the carbine reached in his pocket and brought out a key. He inserted it in the lock. Then, with a dramatic gesture, something like Errol Flynn swinging a saber, he threw the door wide open and held it that way with his toe.

"Speak your piece," he said.

A loud cheer went up from the crowd.

Moretti listened until it had died down. "Can I come inside?" he asked in a low, confidential voice. "You saw I'm not armed."

"Stay out there." The man's eyes took in the television cameras. There were six of them now, with lenses of various lengths, all focused on the confrontation in the doorway. The man snapped an order over his shoulder. "Sam, kill the crying broad if anything happens to me. If I go down, kill everybody. Including Eddie."

"A pleasure," the dude in the ice-cream suit called back.

Moretti watched as the man put down the carbine. He pulled the .38 out of his waistcoat and laid it on the bank floor next to the long gun. Then, squinting into the sun but remembering to smile, he stepped out into camera range.

The crowd went insane. Shouting, catcalls, cheers, screams, and strange barking noises filled the street.

Moretti saw a white van pull in behind the crowd at one end and start selling cold drinks and Popsicles.

"That was a smart move," he told the man in the chinos. "Let's try and make a few more."

"You Moretti?"

"Yeah. What's your name?"

He hesitated. Then: "The bank people know it anyway. It's Littlejoe."

Moretti eyed him up and down, referring to his short size without using words. "Why don't I call you Joe," he said. "Here's where we stand, Joe. I figure you have three women, Boyle, and the guard inside. You and what's-his-name, Sam, and the big guy are going to get out of this smooth and easy. They do what you tell them. Sam's not that hard to handle, is he? So he'll do it when you tell him to drop the Colt automatic and come out here. You got that much control of him, right?"

"Bullshit," Joe snapped back. "It isn't going to happen that way."

Moretti put on a disturbed and worried face. "There's no other way you're going to make it, Joe. You just have to trust me."

"Shit to that. The only thing keeping your killers from mowing me down is that Sam will chill the broads inside. That's all. It don't look good in the papers for the cops to cause the death of broads. So you're holding fire now. The minute Sam would drop that gun, your people would chop me to shreds."

"Without hitting me?" Moretti demanded in an aggrieved tone. "Joe, I have put my ass and my immortal soul on the line. You better believe that if they open up, I go with you, mincemeat special."

Someone in the crowd with a high, cracked voice shouted: "May I have the next dance?"

"Waltz me around again, Willie," another voice chimed in.

Moretti glowered. He was distantly related to

Willie Moretti, the New Jersey Mafia don who had handled Sinatra's early career. He hated the name Willie because it stirred up people's memories, especially those of reporters smelling an exclusive. The other Moretti had gone off his nut from paresis and had been hit by his own men for the good of the cause. It was this kind of ancient history, spiced by the Sinatra connection, that might lead a reporter to dig into it.

"Never mind those clowns," Moretti told Joe. "They got nothing better to do on a hot day but fry their tonsils yelling smart-ass cracks. Just listen to what I'm telling you, Joe. At this point I am the only friend you have in this world."

"Some friend. You just want my scalp on your belt."

"Wrong. I'm here to keep everybody alive. Including you and Sam."

"What about him?" Joe pointed behind Moretti at Baker. "The undertaker there. He your boss?"

"No way. He's FBI. They shoot first and sort it out second. You want him in charge of this party? It's easy. Just fight me all the way, make a monkey out of me, and the FBI takes over. That's your death sentence, Joe. I'm your ticket to staying alive."

"What's so great about that?"

"How can you ask such a question. You Catholic?"

Joe frowned. "Hah."

"You Italian?"

"Nah."

"Don't shit a *paisan'*, Joey."

Joe turned to face the other battery of cameras. "What do you call staying alive, Moretti? Seven to fifteen for armed robbery?"

"You a first offender?"

"Yeah."

"Vietnam vet?"

"Yeah."

"It won't go bad with you, not if you surrender now," Moretti promised him.

Joe puckered his mouth. "Kiss, kiss."

"What the hell's that for?"

"I like to get kissed whenever I'm getting fucked."

"No cheap jokes. We got enough comedians watching us."

"Anyway," Joe mused, more to himself than to Moretti, "Sam won't buy the deal. He'd kill every one of them and shoot himself if he thought he was going back to jail."

"He's done time? That'd go rough for him."

"More than time. They buggered him so bad he landed in the hospital."

Moretti threw out his arms, palms up. *"Ma, che cosa?* Jail is like that. I don't run jails."

"You just fill 'em."

"What do you want, Joe? You should go free and get a medal for this?"

Joe thought for a moment, then shook his head. "No deal."

"It's your only deal."

"No, I got another." Moretti watched Joe's eyes dart this way and that, as if he were thinking furiously. The detective recognized Joe as having the worst kind of mind for a cop to outguess. Joe didn't think straight. He was a fantasist and an improviser.

"No," Joe repeated, "I got another, Moretti. Maybe to you it looks like I heisted a bank, right?"

"Yeah, you could sort of put it that way."

"Let me put it a different way. Suppose I told you I hijacked a plane that happens to look like a bank."

"What?"

"Suppose I told you that five bank people in there are dead, one by one, unless you give us a million in cash, a safe conduct to Kennedy Airport, and a plane, with a crew, ready to take off."

"For where?"

"Cuba."

"They'd throw your ass in the clink as soon as you land."

"Algeria."

"Joe," Moretti pleaded, "you're way behind the times. Nobody gives skyjackers sanctuary any more."

"Then we use chutes. I jumped once in Nam. It ain't that hard."

"That's no deal, Joe, it's suicide."

"Shift your head into a different gear, Moretti. Stop thinking bank heist. Start thinking hijack. Think kidnap. Think ransom. Think hostages. Think getaway. Then you're on my wavelength."

Moretti watched Joe's eyes dance with excitement. Joe kept turning this way and that, as if to give every camera a chance at a full-face shot and a profile. He's a lens louse, Moretti thought. He's high on publicity. And the goddamned TV people would just love to give it to him. They deserve each other.

He stepped back from Joe whose face instantly registered alarm. "Stick close, Moretti."

"I just don't want to hide you from the cameras."

"Tell them I've got a deal to offer. Let the whole town know." Joe's voice went up slightly with excitement. "Shit, the whole country's watching this, right?"

"Don't forget satellite relay to Europe." Moretti glanced around. He saw the cameraman with the creepy-peepie. "Hey, you! Is that a color camera?"

The TV man, startled, let the lens' snout dip. "Uh, yeah."

"Come over here. Where's the guy with the mike?" Moretti looked around him. "You over there, from Channel Four, is this your cameraman? So let's have the mike. It's an announcement."

The sound man, holding a Nagra recorder by a suitcase strap, brought over his microphone. "What is it, chief?"

"Detective Sergeant Moretti. We have five hostages

inside there, two men and three women. They're being held at gunpoint by a man who won't hesitate to kill them. He'll do whatever this man tells him. Does that explain why we haven't moved as fast as we wanted to in this case?" He noted that Joe was edging closer to the camera.

"This man here calls himself Littlejoe," he said. "He has a plan to save the lives of the hostages. He doesn't have my approval. He doesn't have Police Department approval. This is his own idea, and I want you to see what we're up against here, why we're somewhat paralyzed in handling this."

Moretti stepped back. The camera and microphone centered now on Joe. He brushed his hair sideways and gave a tentative smile.

"We have four non-negotiable conditions," he said. "One: a million dollars in cash, no bills larger than twenties. Two: safe passage to JFK airport. Three: a plane gassed and ready for transatlantic flight. Four: a crew no larger than three. Oh, I forgot. Five: My wife is to be brought here to the bank before we leave. She's going with me. She uses her maiden name. It's Lana Lee, and she lives down in the Village on Bleecker Street."

He stopped. The camera's red light was still on. The microphone was still extended. Moretti cleared his throat. "Anything else?"

Joe moved toward the door of the bank. The three other men moved with him. "As soon as those conditions are met, we'll release all hostages but two. They go with us on the plane. No sense taking chances."

He darted inside the glass door, shoved it closed, and locked it. It happened so fast that the cameraman lost him in his finder and had to content himself with filming Moretti's face. The detective hoped nothing showed. He stood there, breathing the yeasty smell of fresh bread and wondering whether he'd salvaged his chances for a lieutenancy or not.

★ 14

LITTLEJOE STEPPED BACK A PACE from the front door of the bank and stared out through the Herculite glass to the street beyond. The cop stood there as if he couldn't make up his mind what to do next. The cameraman and the sound man looked to take a cue from Moretti, and got none. Hot shit! Really threw a monkey wrench into their plans!

Didn't expect anything that big, Joe thought. Figured me for just another two-bit heist guy without any . . . any . . . what the hell was the word? Without *scope*. Right, scope! As if you could earn Littlejoe's rep without being something pretty fucking imaginative.

"Mister," he heard Marge say behind him, "now you really are in the soup."

He turned on her. "Listen, you people—"

Boyle shook his head. "I told you, take the money and run. You'd have been miles away and five thousand richer. No, you have to make a grab for the big stuff. Now where are you?"

"He has no plan," Marge pointed out. "He never did have. 'Let's just rob a bank.' That's a plan?"

"I had a great plan," Littlejoe burst out. "Think big? I thought huge! It would've worked except the motherfucking money wasn't here the way it was supposed to be."

Marge frowned. "I told you, I have young girls back here."

"Fuck!" Joe yapped. "Shit! Piss!" He drew a

breath and tried to hang cool. "What am I arguing with you for? You're not even people any more. You're hostages. You're our ticket to freedom. Right, Sam?"

"Right on, baby." Sam's eyes were bright. Little-joe couldn't tell if it was the prospect of splitting a million dollars or of killing a few hostages. He had thought he knew what made Sam tick, but now he suspected the kid had mysteries inside him that no one had seen.

The telephone began to ring again. Joe turned to see if Moretti was out in the hot street, broiling under the afternoon sun, but the street was empty. The dumb cop was probably trying to get at him again by phone. And now was no time to talk to cops. He'd said his say. He'd thrown down the ultimatum. There was nothing more to talk about.

Ring. Ring.

But there was a lot to think about, a lot to plan, soft spots in the thing that had to be protected. For instance, the walk from the bank to the cars that would take them to the airport. For instance, getting into the plane. Food on the plane? A real crew, not some FBI killers? Christ, a million details to try to expect, to out-think, to plan ahead for. Littlejoe vs. The Universe!

Ring!

Littlejoe snatched up the phone. "I warned you, shitface," he rasped, "keep bugging me and you start getting dead ones thrown out the door."

There was a pause at the other end. "I . . . uh, I just called," a man's voice began, "to ask Ellen what time she's getting off today."

"What?"

"Is Ellen there?"

"Who wants to know?"

"This is her husband."

Joe closed his eyes for a second. He didn't need this kind of distraction. And how did he know the guy was legit? But what the hell could he do over the phone with the crying broad anyway? So let him talk.

"Hey, Ellen," Littlejoe called. "Your hubby on the pipe. Happy-happy!"

She made her way so slowly and with such diffidence toward him that Joe realized she had been almost permanently scared out of her wits, mostly by Sam. Those eyes of his could do the job all by themselves, even without the heavy, menacing .45.

"Hey, fella," Joe told the caller, "you got your TV on?"

"No, not yet."

"Turn it on, man. You'll get a hell of a surprise." He handed the phone to Ellen. "Tell him when you're getting home, baby. And try not to get the fucking phone wet, will you?"

Joe walked back to the street windows. The mob had quieted down a bit, but that was probably because it was so damned hot out there. Another ice-cream truck had pulled up. Now both ends of the street were being serviced with soft drinks, cones with and without sprinkles, candy, and possibly popcorn. Any minute some fucking pizza wagon would show up. There was something for everybody in these things, Joe reflected. He was creating plenty of extra income for people, wasn't he?

"Sir," he heard Ellen call.

Nobody had ever called him *sir* before. He turned slowly, almost majestically. "My husband wants to know when you think you'll be through." She held up the telephone as if to prove that it, not she, was the source of this idiocy.

"Through?" Littlejoe considered the question thoroughly, despite its lunatic coloration. "I figure if the cops play ball, we should be on our way in three, four hours. But you're going to the airport, baby. And you're gonna take a plane trip. Don't tell him that. Just say a few hours."

"He says a few more hours, Dennis."

She listened silently, her eyes on Joe as the authority, the source of all knowledge. "He wants to know should he start dinner." Her eyes had gone so wide that Joe for a moment thought she had been struck blind. He realized that she was rigid with fear, and wondered how anybody could get that frightened. She stood there like a board on which two eyes had been painted.

He took the phone from her. "Listen, fella, I think you ought to start dinner."

"It's a roast," the man said. "I never made a roast. It's expensive and I might ruin it. And then, what do I feed the baby?"

Joe turned to Ellen and tried to keep his voice soft. "What should he feed the baby?"

Her lips moved several times, framing and reframing answers. Then, stiffly: "A jar of prunes and a jar of baby chicken. They're in the fridge. He has to warm them on the stove."

Joe transmitted the information and added: "Leave the roast alone, fella. Just send out for some Colonel Sanders, okay? It's gonna be a long, hard night."

"Can I say good-bye to Ellen?"

Joe handed her the phone and watched her moisten her dry lips. "Hello, Dennis. What? Yes, they have guns." She glanced hastily at Joe to see if she'd said too much. "I will, Dennis. I have to get off the phone now. What?" Her eyes were fixed now on the middle distance, unseeing. "Well . . . there are a lot of people around and . . . uh . . . kiss the baby for me." She paused. "I love you too." She hung up the phone and walked slowly, in that same rigid posture, to join the other two tellers.

Joe glanced at everyone's face. The bank people looked somber, down. The real seriousness of the situation had hit them with the last words Ellen had told her husband. Only Sam was unchanged. He winked at Joe. "A million, huh?"

Joe nodded. "If we play it smart."

"I just wanna say one thing, Littlejoe," Sam began gravely. "I just wanna say that if you think the cops don't give you credit out there for being strong . . . you know." He paused and regrouped his thoughts. "I just wanna say if you want one of these people wasted, I can do it right now and throw them out the front door. I'll be glad to do it, Littlejoe. You know that. Just say the word and . . ." His thought slowly died away.

Joe watched the effect of this on the rest of them. It was possibly the longest speech he'd ever heard from Sam's lips, and he knew it wasn't what it sounded like. It was supposed to be an offer of total cooperation from a buddy, right down the line, everything I have is yours. But Littlejoe could hear the inner message, and it frightened him. Inside the big speech was a small one that said: "I have to kill. Let me do it now. Right now."

He knew Sam to be strange, but this glimpse inside the kid was too hairy for comfort. Somebody who has to kill ends up not too choosy about a victim. Even a buddy will do.

Littlejoe decided to make the best use of Sam's offer he could. He turned to Boyle and tried to use words the manager would understand without their offending Sam. "You see," he asked Boyle. "You see the mess we're in?"

Boyle nodded slowly, heavily, his Irish face as grave with trouble as Sam's had been. "We know you guys aren't kidding," Boyle managed to say. It was noncommittal, but it told Littlejoe he had got the real message, which was along the lines of "For Christ's sake, don't stir up Sam."

"Good," Joe said, trying to sound hearty and confident. "No problems, people. Everybody cooperates and everything works out."

"You know," Boyle began slowly, "there's no way they can get a million in cash at this hour."

"Shit there ain't." Joe glanced at the wall clock, and was shocked to find that it was only four in the afternoon. Barely an hour had elapsed. "Banks close their doors at three, but the cops can tap them any time up till five or six at night." He eyed the manager. "What the hell do you care, anyway, Boyle? Your bank insurance covers you."

"I'm worried about the ransom money. If they don't get it, we're left here with you."

"All night, if it takes all night," Joe agreed cheerfully. "Don't tell me they can't locate the rest of the cash by morning."

"It's just—" Boyle stopped. He sat down on the edge of the desk. His face had gone blank for a moment. "I just want to see my wife and kids again, that's all." He glanced at Joe. "It isn't as if we haven't cooperated with you."

Something odd twisted inside Littlejoe. It wasn't the animal that slept there. He hadn't felt that shift beneath his lungs for some time now. Being on top, owning people, controlling everything they did, gave him a sense of power that pleased the beast and kept it comfortably asleep. No, this was something else, some strange little twist that Boyle's fat mick face did to him, talking about seeing his kids and cooperating.

"I know," Joe heard himself saying. "You people have been great. I got no complaint there. It's just . . ." He gestured aimlessly, as if trying to shape the air into a convincing excuse. "It's just that things happen."

"You happened," Marge told him darkly.

"Okay," Joe admitted. "But tomorrow you're crossing the street and a truck with busted brakes happens. You don't have no guarantees in this life, Marge."

She nodded glumly. "Harry," she said to Boyle, "have you got a cigarette?"

"You don't smoke."

"I want a cigarette."

"Marge," Boyle pleaded, "I've never even seen you touch a cigarette."

"Right. Now I want a cigarette."

"It's a long night, Marge. Try and hold off."

"For some of you," Joe put in, just to keep things stirred up, "it'll mean a mystery trip to maybe Algeria."

Boyle's head shook quickly from side to side. He handed Marge a cigarette and lighted it for her. Smoke came out of the burning end of the cigarette. "Puff," he told her quietly. She touched his hand, and, in return, so quickly Littlejoe almost missed seeing it, he took her hand and squeezed it once.

"Maybe you two would like to be the lucky passengers?" he pounced.

"What?"

"Second honeymoon in Algeria? Don't tell me there's nothing going on." Joe smiled slightly, coldly, trying to cut down whatever was between them to the size of a piece of dirt. "I know what happens in banks. Everybody's so moral, right? So high-minded. But it's no different than any other meat rack. You sniff it all day and if you like it, you try some at night."

The two of them, Boyle and Marge, looked at him for a long moment. When he finally replied, the manager moved off on a tangent that confused Joe at first. "You don't have to do that," Boyle was saying. "You don't need to take hostages aboard the plane, Joe." It was the first time he'd used his name. "I've been thinking. Once you're on board, the crew are your hostages. See my point?"

"That's how much you know about life, Boyle. Why couldn't the crew be FBI guys? I need a real hostage to protect us from them too."

"Then that's me," Boyle said. "I'm the manager. It's what I'm paid for."

"Nah. You're no good as a hostage."

"Why not?"

"That slob Eddie, our driver, he's as good to me as you are. Neither one of you is worth shit as a hostage."

In the silence, Littlejoe heard Eddie shifting his weight around, shuffling his feet. "Listen," he said across the bank lobby, "what's that supposed to mean, Littlejoe? I'm gonna be with you on the plane anyway, right?"

"Wrong." Joe turned away from him to face Boyle again. "Neither of you two big, strong men." He grinned evilly.

"Not Ellen," Boyle said. "She's got a kid. So has Maria. Besides, they're just working here. But for me, it's a career. So it makes sense to . . ." He stopped talking.

"Want a Mediterranean cruise, huh?"

"I don't have any illusion you'll really make it," Boyle said then. "Do you?"

Littlejoe sat down on the desk next to him. His legs dangled just off the floor. "As our ace-in-the-hole hostage, you won't do, Boyle."

"Why not? The Chase would be more interested in saving a manager."

"Stop kidding yourself."

"They've invested a lot of money and time in me," Boyle insisted. "They have to protect their investment."

"Dream on."

"It's also a matter of loyalty. I've given them fifteen years of loyalty and they owe me."

"They owe you nothing." Littlejoe shook his head in amazement. "It freaks me out the way grown-up guys with families still don't know the fucking facts of life."

"And you do."

"You bet your ass I do," Joe told him. "The ace-in-the-hole hostage ain't gonna be no middle-aged bank hack. When the crunch comes, on the landing strip or in the plane, the FBI will chop you up like so much hamburger, Boyle. You're meat to them, same as Sam and me. You're expendable. You're a calculated risk. Shit, do I have to teach you this kindergarten stuff? You read the papers. But when I have a young chick who's a mother, it's different. The publicity's bad if they chill a mother. That they only do in Nam. There they waste mothers by the carload, and babies too. Slopes don't count. This fine upstanding crying broad Ellen, for instance, she counts. Her they'd kind of hesitate to ice. They still might do it, but they'd hesitate."

"If I felt that way about law officers, I'd—"

"Shut up, Boyle," Joe interrupted, trying not to sound unpleasant. "You just don't know your ass from your elbow about life. Take the Chase. What do they owe you, man? For fifteen years you been dumb enough to give them loyalty and honesty. That's so much gravy to them.

"They're laughing up their sleeve at you, man," he went on. "They had your ass for fifteen years and they don't owe you a fart. Not a fart in the wind. To Chase you're just meat. Buy it, sell it. What did they buy you for all these years? Are you even making fourteen grand a year now? Sixteen? I don't think so. And for a chickenshit salary you put out something that money can't even buy, loyalty. What a sucker play, Boyle.

"The first time Chase profits dip below a certain point they won't hesitate to chop you off like any other bad investment. Cut losses. It isn't even something another human being decides, Boyle. They feed the problem into their computer and, clickety-click, out comes a name. Your name. Get rid of

Boyle at fourteen thousand a year. Let some young black or Puerto Rican run the joint at half Boyle's salary."

Littlejoe paused. He saw that Marge was listening to him so intently that she hadn't puffed even once on her lighted cigarette.

"Sure he'll steal you blind, because he isn't a dum-dum like Boyle. But what he steals is a business cost that's already been passed on to the poor, stupid customer anyway. So who cares? Insurance covers it, and the insurance costs are part of what the customer pays for. Fuck everybody, but start with the poor, loyal Boyles of the world."

The lobby was silent for a long time. Joe slid off the desk and walked to a point halfway between Boyle and Marge, at the desk, and the lobby sign, where Sam was still guarding the two younger women.

"I want you people to listen to some advice," Littlejoe said then. "The first thing you have to fear is Sam. He kills. The second thing you have to fear is me. I tell Sam who to kill. But the third thing you have to fear is the cops and the FBI. They kill too. At some point we're gonna march you out there in lockstep to a car or limo or bus. That's when they'll draw a bead on Sam and me and try to figure a way to scrag us without getting one of you. Well, there won't be no way. We'll be huddled up too close to each other. And that's your biggest fear of all."

"They won't shoot," Marge, said, stubbing out her unsmoked cigarette.

"Pray you're right." Joe leaned back against the counter as if surveying his own feudal holding, complete with serfs. "Pray they don't pull another Attica, where they just went in and shot everybody, including the guards and even some of themselves. When it was over forty-two people were dead with only cop bullets in them. Get it through your heads, people, your biggest danger is out there."

At FIVE O'CLOCK, Littlejoe gave everyone permission to sit down somewhere in the bank where he or Sam could watch them. The only comment he got then was from Boyle, who said: "Think they've rounded up the million yet?"

The telephone had been ringing so often that Joe had taken all the phones off their hooks. Now, at a quarter to six, he decided to let the world in again. He had worked out pretty much every angle of the escape, bringing Sam into the planning to keep him distracted from the proximity of people he could shoot. There really wasn't anything left to chance, Joe told himself. It was an airtight escape.

He replaced the telephone on Boyle's desk, and it began to ring immediately. He picked it up.

"Got the cash, Moretti?" he asked.

"This is CBS News," a voice said. "We'd like to interview you. Is this Littlejoe?"

Joe sat down behind Boyle's desk and put his feet up on it. "Speaking."

"Well, I guess you could say the world is watching you, Littlejoe. At any rate, it's listening. I'm taping this now and we'll play it over on the six-o'clock local news. It may even repeat on the Cronkite show at seven."

"Big fucking deal."

"Uh, look, is there . . . I mean, is it possible to watch the language? This is going on the air."

"Blip me, asshole. We're on tape, ain't we?"

"Oh, yeah, of course. Maybe you can tell us, Little-joe, why you're doing this?"

"Doing what?"

"Robbing a bank."

Joe shifted uncomfortably. Was this guy for real? Weren't TV reporters supposed to have a brain? "What do you want?" he asked. "Banks is where they got money. You want to steal, you go where the money is, right?"

"But why do you need to steal? Do you have some sort of compulsion?"

Joe put his hand over the phone. "Sam," he said, "this creep is not to be believed." Then, into the phone: "It's a compulsion to eat, asshole. To buy clothes and have a place to live. That's why I steal."

"Couldn't you find a job?"

"A job doing what? You want to drive a cab, you gotta join a union. Dig ditches? Run a jack-hammer? Name it and they got a fucking union. Bank teller? I been a bank teller at a hundred and five bucks a week to start. What do you make, Mr. Newsman?"

"Well, we're talking about you, Littlejoe. You're the one everybody's interested in."

"What gave you that idea? You're talking to me because you're paid to fill the air with stuff. It's hot entertainment, right?"

"You're news, Littlejoe."

"If you had to pay an entertainer to fill this slot, what would it cost? A Steve Allen? A Pamela Mason? A Jackie Susann? Christ, you're getting off cheap with me. What do they pay you?"

The man stopped talking for a moment. "You're not talking," Joe pointed out. "You're not doing your job, Mr. Newsman. How much are you paying me to fill up your air time?"

"You want to be paid for . . ."

"Fucking ay right, dumdum. Sam and me are

dying in here. We got innocent people in here, and all of us may die. They're gonna murder us the second they line us up in their sights." Joe winked at Sam and covered the telephone again. "Get it on the record," he told Sam. "Warn everybody what the cops plan to do. It gives us a little extra margin of safety, right?"

"Right on, Littlejoe."

"How is that gonna look on TV?" Joe asked the interviewer. "We got young girls, the mothers of babies. We got a guard with a bad heart. We got Marge, a zoftig number. We got a man with a family who thinks the Chase won't let him down after fifteen years of loyal slavery. When the cops start chopping us into catfood, how will that look on TV, huh?"

"You could give yourself up."

"You ever been in prison?"

"No, Littlejoe, I—"

"Then talk about something you fucking well know about."

"Littlejoe, I know we can blip your words, but it'd get your message across a lot more meaningfully if you'd, uh, moderate your language."

"You don't want to hear this shit anyway."

"We have footage and tape on your talk with Sergeant Moretti. But we'd like a little backup here in which you explain why you're doing this."

"Money," Joe said. "Lots of it."

"Another thing that's puzzled a lot of people, Littlejoe, is why you want your wife dragged into this. Are you planning to take her with you on the plane?"

"Yeah. To Stockholm." Joe was grinning.

"What?"

"Nothing. You think I'd tell you?"

"One of the things that's delayed matters, as we understand it, Littlejoe, is that the police are having some difficulty locating her."

Joe glanced up at the clock. It showed five minutes to six P.M. "Better hustle your ass if you want to make the news."

"Can you give CBS News some additional clue that we can pass along to the police to facilitate her—"

"Do kids watch the *Six O'Clock News?*"

"I'm not abs—"

"Wee-wee!" Joe called. "Poo-poo! Ca-ca! Up your giggies, kiddies!" He hung up the phone and sat there for a moment, grinning at the tips of his shoes on top of Boyle's desk. "Hey, Boyle, is there a TV in the bank?"

"In the storeroom," the manager said wearily. "Three cartons. Leftover premiums from our new-account blitz."

"Which is Maria?" Joe asked. He looked at a dark-eyed young woman who had said nothing so far. "You?"

"Yes."

Littlejoe heard a faint Puerto Rican inflection. "Get one of those TVs from the storeroom. Anybody hungry?"

Marge looked up. "Why?"

The telephone rang. "Watch this," Joe told her. He picked up. "Moretti?"

"It's about time you answered that phone, Joe."

"I been busy with CBS News," Joe bragged. "Listen, I got a hungry crew here. Send in about four jumbo pizzas, okay? Two plain, one with sausage, one with anchovies, right? And a dozen cans of beer. My treat."

He heard the detective laughing on the other end of the line. "Joe, I guess your hostages are in good shape, right?"

"Just make sure we get the pizzas."

"It's a deal. Look, I been turning myself inside out for you. It's time you did something for me," Moretti said.

"You got the million in cash?"

"Not yet."

"Then hang up and order the pizzas."

"You get the pizzas, Joe. A promise is a promise. I need something from you before I can get any final action out of my higher-ups. You can understand what I mean when I tell you they don't trust you. Your word isn't good enough for them. I believe you. I stand by your word. That don't cut any ice with my bosses or the FBI. They're reluctant to go through with ransom, safe conduct, plane, unless they get some kind of evidence of good faith on your part."

"Good what?"

"Faith," Moretti repeated. "I got faith in you. They need something more than my faith. They need evidence."

"Like what?"

"Like . . . oh, let's say . . . like releasing your hostages."

"Kiss, kiss," Littlejoe cooed. "Fuck, fuck."

"I keep telling you, Joe, I don't need evidence. They need it."

"They must think I'm an idiot. My hostages are all that keep the pig from slaughtering us."

"Don't use that word."

"Pig? You don't like pig?"

"Listen, Joe, you and I are the ones who have to understand each other," Moretti warned him. "You have to give me my respect as a man. You can't do it when you use words like that. Understand? You give me my respect and I give you yours. Otherwise, fuck the whole deal."

"Okay, okay." Joe pulled his feet off the desk. "A touchy cop, Jesus. But the answer's still no. I give up hostages, I commit suicide."

He watched Maria lugging a corrugated cardboard carton into the lobby. "Here," he said. "Open it up."

"What?" Moretti asked.

"Nothing. No deal. No hostages."

"They won't move without I show them you're sincere, Joe. I have to show them you can be trusted."

"No hostages."

"One hostage," Moretti begged.

"No."

"One. You'll still have four, right? Four is more than enough, Joe. All you need is one, really, to keep with you out to the airport."

"No."

"Just give me one hostage now. I promise I'll have the wheels spinning and the ransom here in an hour."

"Kiss, kiss. If you didn't collect the cash yet, it's too fucking late now," Littlejoe said. Boyle joined Maria in unpacking the tiny Japanese black-and-white television set. He plugged it in and pulled out the single collapsible antenna. "Channel Two," Joe said.

"Not two," Moretti begged, "just one. Give me one. Don't worry about the cash. The FBI has cash reserves just for this purpose. We'll have the million for you. But you have to show you can be trusted."

"Shee-it. Hold the phone." Joe put the instrument down on the desk. "Sam," he said, "they say they'll speed everything up if we show we're in good faith. They want one hostage. We'll still have enough to protect us."

"Which one?"

Littlejoe looked at Boyle. "I'll show you who's in good fucking faith, Boyle. You bank people choose. Pick one."

Both Boyle and Marge turned to look at each other. Then they both looked at Leroy, the guard, who had barely stirred in the past hour from the armchair in which he'd been put. Boyle glanced over at the other bank people. "How about Leroy? His heart . . ."

"Yeah, Leroy," Maria agreed.

Ellen's face remained stiff. "I . . . guess so."

"Leroy," Boyle called. "You want it to be Ellen? She has a small baby."

The guard's eyes fluttered. "Whatever," he mumbled. "Whatever."

"Ellen's out," Joe announced. "Ellen's my ace in the hole. Forget Ellen. Give 'em Leroy, then?"

Everyone nodded. Joe went over to the guard and lifted him to his feet.

"This is your lucky fucking day, Leroy. Come on."

"S-slow an' easy," the guard muttered. "My chest hurt *bad*."

"No problems, Leroy. If it was your heart you'd be dead by now. It's gas. One good fart'll clear it up." He escorted the guard to the door. "Wait there." He went back to the phone. "Okay, Moretti, you get the dinge. He says his heart's bad so the bank people voted to let him go. Isn't that democratic, Moretti? More'n they'd do for a guinea, right?"

"Send him outside."

"In front of the door, Moretti. This is proof I'm in good faith. Make sure your people keep the faith, too."

He hung up and returned to a position just behind Leroy. "Don't be nervous now, Leroy. The old ticker is strong enough for this. The cops will take you to the hospital and it'll be fine, and Chase might even give you a twenty-five-buck bonus."

"For what?"

"How should I know?" Joe unlocked the door. "Okay, Leroy, move them feet." He swung the door open and, planting his hand in between Leroy's shoulders, gave a shove.

The guard, slightly off balance, and weak-kneed to begin with, tottered forward into the hot sun. The street erupted with confusion. Joe saw dozens of guns trained on Leroy: submachine guns, shotguns, rifles, riot guns, revolvers, automatics. He saw Moretti explode out the front door of the insurance office.

"Don't fire!" Moretti yelled. "*Hold your fire!*"

Littlejoe very distinctly heard a cop nearby ask:

"Did he say fire?" From across the street another cop said: "When do we fire?"

"*Hold . . . your . . . fire!*" Moretti screamed at the top of his voice.

Tugging his straw hat more firmly down over his forehead, he started across the hot black asphalt for Leroy, who had fallen to his knees on the sidewalk in front of the bank.

Joe watched a young cop with longish hair and a moustache run squatted down, like a Western gun-fighter, to get a closer aim at Leroy. He held the gun in both hands and trained it directly on Leroy's face from twenty feet away.

"Don't shoot," Moretti shouted. "Get the hell out of the way."

The young cop swiveled and aimed the gun at Moretti, then realized what he had done and swung it back on Leroy.

Moretti had crossed the white line in the middle of the street. "Put it down, you stupid bastard," he told the cop. The young man blinked, almost winced, but held his pose.

Suddenly the street broke up into bits and pieces of action. Joe saw cops run for Leroy, throw him to the pavement. One cop got his foot on Leroy's back. Two others grabbed his arms. One shoved a shotgun against his eye.

Moretti reached him at this point. He began batting away at the uniformed cops, trying to get them to release Leroy. One of them was frisking Leroy for weapons. Another yanked his arms behind him and locked handcuffs in place.

Joe locked the door and moved back into the bank. "There," he told Boyle, "there's your law."

★ 16

THINKING ABOUT IT as he checked what each person inside the bank was doing, Littlejoe decided that if he'd been one of the hostages, or a dumdum like Eddie, he'd long ago have been bored to sleep. But, being the leader, the one who had to dream up the ideas and give the orders, he found he felt more alive, more wide-awake, more *real* than ever before in his life. This was what he'd been born for, obviously. To lead. To be obeyed.

He checked Boyle, sitting behind a desk in the far corner of the lobby, talking quietly to Marge. Joe wasn't afraid they were plotting anything. Both of them knew better than that. They were probably wondering if they could get out of this alive to continue their little middle-aged affair. Probably they both had families they went home to at night. But there was always the motel along the way from five to seven. "Late work at the office, dear."

Littlejoe wondered what Marge could see in a bald guy with a thickening middle like Harry Boyle. He had a little style, a touch of class, maybe, but handsome he wasn't. What Boyle saw in Marge, of course, anybody could see.

Littlejoe's monitoring glance shifted to Ellen, sniveling quietly into a soaked Kleenex, Sam watching her as intently as ever. Joe felt a warm rush of emotion about Sam. He was more than a good kid. He was a man. He was to be relied upon. Maybe he was a little funny about jail. You could understand that, after what'd happened to him there. Maybe some people would think he was a killer type or something. Joe did not. Sam had his odd spots, but he was solid, the right guy in the right place.

As for Eddie . . . where was he?

Joe frowned. He pulled the .38 out of his belt and moved toward the back of the lobby, where Sam and Ellen were. "What's with Eddie?"

Sam jerked the muzzle of the .45 Colt in the direction of the vault. "Back there out of sight."

Joe glanced around. "With Maria?"

"I guess."

Joe's frown deepened. He could feel the creases deepen between his eyebrows, and he made a conscious effort to smooth out the skin there. He didn't want to grow up with a permanent frown like his shitty old man. "Eddie?" he called into the rear of the bank. "What's up?"

After a long moment he heard a snicker. "Me."

Joe's glance locked with Sam's. "He's in the vault with Maria?"

Sam nodded. "Want me to look?"

"You keep these monkeys covered. I'll look."

Littlejoe moved behind the lobby sign and turned toward the vault. Even from that angle, his line of sight slanted through the bars of the vault door, he could see that Maria was on the floor on her back. As he came abreast of the vault entrance, he saw that Eddie was on his knees straddling her, his weight holding down her torso, his hands on her arms, his erect cock ramming up against her face, her nose, into her eyes.

Hearing him, Eddie turned to gloat at Joe. His face was red, skin damp. His lips looked wet. He was breathing hard, but not uncomfortably so. "This spic cunt won't give head," he complained.

"Please, mister." Maria's lips parted for an instant. "Please."

As a spectator sport, a way of spending the afternoon if your TV set wasn't working, Littlejoe thought, he could think of a hundred better things to do than watch this dumb ox brutalizing a broad half his size and weight.

"How'd you manage to get this far, Eddie," he asked, "without her yelling for help?"

"Easy," the driver bragged. "She knows if she opens it even a crack, she eats the whole thing."

"You gotta be careful with Puerto Rican women, Eddie," Joe said, keeping his voice serious. "They try to stay very pure. She's gonna bite your head off for you."

A shadow of doubt crossed Eddie's heated face, then flickered out. "No way, man."

Littlejoe backed away from the vault. The entire conversation had been carried on at a pitch he felt sure no one in the bank had heard. This Eddie, this was what came of picking up unknown helpers at the last minute. If he ever got out of this alive and loose, he was going to give his cousin Mick a piece of his mind, saddling him with this animal.

"Sam," he said as he moved out into the lobby. "You wanna see something that belongs in a zoo?"

"That one?" Sam cocked his head in Eddie's direction. "What's going on?"

"Take a look. I'll guard everybody."

Sam lowered the .45 to his side and started toward the vault. Joe raised the Police Positive and showed it to everyone. "We're still thinking of your greater comfort and convenience, folks. Just hang easy and nobody dies."

"*Bruto animale!*" Sam cursed.

Joe tried to see what was happening in the vault. After a moment he heard a single noise, once, a kind of *thock!* He stepped back to see what was happening. Sam had hold of Eddie's leg and was pulling him that way out of the vault, like a giant beached whale.

The fact that Eddie didn't seem to object to this was explained a moment later when Eddie's face came into view as Sam dumped him where everyone in the lobby could see him. Sam had obviously clouted Eddie's chin and cheek with the side of the Colt, holding it flat so that its weight knocked Eddie almost unconscious. Eddie groaned now and touched his cheek where blood was rilling up.

"Hey!" he whimpered. "Looka this?"

Sam grabbed his hair and pulled him into an upright position, his back against the far wall of the lobby. "You fucking animal," he said.

He pulled the Colt sideways in a tight arc and, pivoting like a golfer, slammed the muzzle into Eddie's left eye. Blood spurted from the skin across Eddie's temple. He started to slump to his right.

Sam brought the Colt around in a backhand swing and smashed it across the bridge of Eddie's nose, straightening him upright on the floor and producing a new wound somewhere inside the nose, which began to pump blood out of Eddie's right nostril.

Eddie leaned forward slightly, knuckles on the floor, to lever himself up onto his feet. Sam took a step back and flicked the Colt up against Eddie's chin. The front sight of the gun punched into the flesh of the throat, producing a kind of bluish-black puncture. As Eddie's head hit the back wall, the thump rattled a sign on the wall over his head that announced to everyone that their deposits were insured for up to $15,000 by the Federal Deposit Insurance Corporation (FDIC).

Littlejoe glanced past Eddie's bloody head, to see Maria, on her knees, watching wide-eyed through the open gate of the vault. He swung around to keep the rest of the bank people covered.

"We're moving right along, folks," he said. "Just a technical problem with Eddie's cock, that's all."

"Now I'm taking him out," Sam announced. He had taken another step back, and raised the Colt with great calmness until it pointed at Eddie's gory face.

"No, Sam."

"He goes."

"Sam, the shot. Remember what I said about shots."

"This *stronzo* dies."

"Not now."

"I gotta kill him, Littlejoe. You promised."

"When did I do that, baby?" Joe said in a soothing voice.

He watched Sam's cherub face darken from the blood pumping within. His eyes had gone coal black, and his pretty mouth had frozen into a line of stone. He was having trouble breathing, almost as much trouble as Eddie was through his blood-clotted nose. Joe had never seen Sam this way. But, then, he had never seen Sam under real pressure of any kind.

"You fire a shot," he told Sam, "and you could end up killing all of us." Joe moistened his paper-dry lips. "The cops could go ape if they hear a shot from inside, figure we're killing hostages and come in shooting."

"So?"

"Whadya mean so?"

"So fucking what?" Sam asked coldly.

Littlejoe took a step toward Sam. The boy pivoted until the .45 was aimed at Joe's abdomen. "Watch it, Littlejoe. If we all go, we all go."

"We don't have to."

Sam's eyes burned almost out of control for a moment, as if his inner vision of the way they would all go was too powerful, too luscious, too glorious to forsake. "Watch it, Littlejoe," he said again, his voice as dry as ashes. "Just . . . watch it."

But the fire had gone out of his words. Joe could hear it die away. After a moment, the Colt lowered slightly, until it was aimed at Eddie's groin. "You really want me to let this animal live," Sam said then, musingly, as if not quite sure of Joe's sanity.

"I don't care if he lives or dies. I just don't want any shots."

Sam nodded then. "Okay, baby, no shots." He

seemed to get shorter for a moment. Littlejoe couldn't tell what had happened, then saw that Sam was bending at the knees like a skier.

In the next second he jumped high in the air. An instant later he was coming down full force with both clog heels on Eddie's exposed penis. He landed with a thud that rocked the FDIC sign again. Eddie screamed, choked on his own blood, and fainted.

Sam stepped back daintily out of the puddle that was Eddie. He reached down, managed to find an arm, and lugged Eddie back into the vault. He returned a few moments later, leading Maria with him and looking pleased with himself.

"That's a lot better now, huh, Littlejoe?"

The beatific smile on his face seemed to light up the lobby.

". . . AND THAT IS THE SITUATION up to this hour, a complete standoff with a million dollars and the lives of four innocent people at stake. This is Ron Aronowitz, CBS News, Queens, New York."

Joe sighed unhappily and snapped off the television set. "No Oscar. No Emmy. No Tony. Huh, Sam?"

Sam shrugged. "You looked pretty good out there, though, Littlejoe."

"I was squinting too much. That fucking sun. That heat."

"Too bad you didn't have your good threads on."

"That's all right," Joe assured him. "Anybody knows me could recognize me. They must've all seen it, huh? Tina. My mother, Flo. Probably Lana seen it, too. It's a red-letter day, baby." His face grew solemn. "I'm just sorry you didn't get on camera, Sam. Next time, okay?"

"Maybe they don't give us no next time."

"You're kidding. We call the turns, baby. We tell them, not them us. You want to be on TV, Sam? Just say the word."

"I wouldn't know what to say."

"They feed you questions. It's easy."

"For you, Littlejoe, not for me."

"Whatever you want." Joe let the subject drop. Sam was a little easier to talk to now that he'd bloodied up Eddie. He seemed calmer, happier.

Of course, as someone to rely on, Sam was finished, Littlejoe told himself. From being a Rock of Gibraltar, he'd turned into a maniac of some kind. The way he'd finished off Eddie was not a sane thing to do. It went a long way beyond what a good kid would do to help a buddy. And it didn't do Eddie a whole hell of a lot of good.

Of course, in another way, Joe mused, Sam's burst of near-killing was a big help. It told the bank people they could expect no mercy. It got that lump of shit, Eddie, out of the way. And it saved them from having to cut the son of a bitch in on the caper, or worry about what to do with him later.

So Sam was insane. And I'm profiting from it, Littlejoe reminded himself. That's what life is really all about, huh?

Even the violence of the cops was working for him, Joe thought. That scene with Leroy had been worth a couple of hours of lecturing. It sort of held up a mirror for everybody to see their lives in.

Establishment idiots like Boyle—and Marge, too, for that matter—got a good look at the establishment's prize protectors. A terrific lesson, right? They knew they couldn't expect anything outside but terror and death. And inside was Sam.

Standing off to one side of the big plate-glass window in the front of the bank, Littlejoe could just see the crowd at one end of the street. The mob had grown so that he could no longer estimate how many people there were.

In addition to several ice-cream vans, a hot-dog pushcart vendor was doing a brisk business, as was a pushcart man selling Italian ices. Men in plainclothes kept passing through the police barricade with no trouble. Joe wondered what kind of people were collecting outside. The gawkers he understood. The other people, the men who looked like cops but wore slacks and sports shirts, seemed to be drifting into the combat area without being stopped.

As he watched, a knot of uniformed police ganged

up on a boy trying to push his way through the crowd carrying what was obviously a stack of flat white pizza cartons. They gave him a hard time for several minutes, until Moretti showed up and busted ass for a while. It was the detective who escorted the delivery boy to the door of the bank.

"Marge," Joe called, "pick up one of them marked twenties you were trying to give me. Pay the kid with the marked twenty." He chuckled happily as he threw her the front-door key.

She opened the door and took the boxes of pizza and two chilled six-packs of beer. The boy turned to leave.

"Hold it," Marge said, handing him a twenty. "Is this enough?"

"It's paid for," the boy said. He jerked his thumb at Moretti, standing behind him.

Two cameramen with shoulder harnesses were closing in on the scene, telephoto lenses zooming out as they moved. A TV truck with a parabolic-reflector microphone swiveled like a radar antenna to catch everything being said. Marge watched this for a moment, then carried the pizzas and beer inside.

"You can go back out for a breather," Joe called to her. "Just remember, we've got your buddies at gunpoint."

"I know."

"And we're both hardened Vietnam vets. Blood means nothing to us unless we have a spoon handy." He made a slurping noise.

"I know," Marge repeated dully.

"Hey, I got an idea. Sam, c'mere. Hold the forty-five on Marge and walk her outside. No reason you shouldn't be on the *Eleven O'Clock News*, right? Fair is fair."

"Nah, Littlejoe."

"Don't be embarrassed. Go ahead."

"Nah. You go."

"I been."

"Go again."

Littlejoe had been lounging against the counter. He straightened up and smoothed down his hair. Then he removed the .38 from his belt and came up behind Marge. "Let's meet the people," he said, nudging her left breast with the gun.

They walked slowly through the door and stood one step outside it, face to face with Moretti. The delivery boy had disappeared. "You better eat the pizza before it gets cold," Moretti said.

Joe smiled at him. The sun had gone down behind the bank by now, but the evening August sky was still glaring hot—plenty of light for the TV cameras. "You're not so bad at the publicity con either, Moretti," he said in a low undertone. Then, in a louder voice: "Thanks for the pizza."

"I hope you brought this lady out to turn her over to us," Moretti said. "Giving us the guard was a smart move. You're earning points, Joe. Every little bit helps. My bosses figure you to be a responsible person who'll live up to an agreement. Am I right?"

"Are you ever," Joe said, still grinning, but maliciously now. He painstakingly adjusted the long muzzle of the .38 so that it poked into Marge's left ear. When he spoke again, his voice was loud and clear. "I'm glad you don't think of Sam and me as a pair of high-strung Vietnam combat vets who learned mass killing from Uncle Sam. That would be the easy way to think of us, Detective Sergeant Moretti. That would be the cheap cop-out way. I'm glad you see us as responsible Americans, anxious to do the right thing."

"You don't have to talk like that," Moretti muttered. "Stop conning the people."

"Me con the people? You got it backwards, Detective Sergeant Moretti. It's vets like Sam and me who were conned. We're the ones who were trained to kill slopes till we killed so many, a few more deaths don't make any difference to us."

Moretti removed his hat and mopped his forehead. "Knock it off, Joe," he said in an undertone. "You're turning this into a joke. Are you giving us this lady? Yes or no?"

"Why don't you ask her what she wants?"

A TV reporter carrying a microphone had started to move in on the trio of people. Joe spotted him before Moretti did. "Here's the guy to ask Marge questions. Are you Ron Aronowitz?"

"I'm Rick Ericson of Channel Five."

Littlejoe executed a sweeping Errol Flynn movement with his free arm, as if presenting Marge at court. "Okay with you, Detective Sergeant Moretti?"

"This isn't getting us anywhere," Moretti grumbled.

"What is?" Joe countered. "I'm not doing any of this for myself. Everybody else is copping big from it but Sam and me. They're selling hundreds of dollars of ice cream and beer over there. You're getting a promotion. You couldn't escape it if you tried. And this creep is earning his bread from Channel Five. He'll get a bonus, won't you, Rick Ericson?"

"Let me interview all three of you," the newsman suggested.

"Just Marge. And kind of remember the gun in her ear. You remember it too, Marge. And Moretti, you remember the three people inside with Sam."

"I don't forget Sam," Moretti told him. "You're not the only one worrying about him."

Joe started to say something, but the on-target aim of Moretti's remark stopped him for a moment. "Go ahead, Mr. Newsmaker."

"Uh, well, I understand you're Marge."

"Mrs. Marjorie Haines," she volunteered.

"How are things inside the bank, Mrs. Haines?"

"Well, everyone's all right."

"No one hurt?"

"No. We got one girl crying, but so far everyone's fine, as long as nobody starts shooting. For a minute there I thought they were going to kill Leroy. They were like animals, all over him."

"Yes, well, what about the suspect inside the bank? He's something of a mystery to us, Mrs. Haines. Can you tell us something about him?"

"He's quiet."

"Is that all?"

"Yes. I'd like to go back in now." She glanced aimlessly around her.

"You mean he doesn't talk at all?"

"No, he talks."

"What does he say, Mrs. Haines?"

"Oh." She glanced at Joe, who nodded. "He asks Joe here, 'Joe, do you want me to shoot this one or that one?' That's about it."

"Do you think he's serious, Mrs. Haines?"

"I would say so, yes."

"Does he seem like the killer type?"

She looked around her again, blindly. "What is that?"

"A killer type?"

"Does a cop look like a killer type?" Marge asked. "Leroy might have been dead if it hadn't been for this man here." She indicated Moretti. "I'd like to go back in now."

"Joe," Moretti piped up, "let her stay out here."

"Why? That only leaves us Boyle and the two girls."

"That's more than enough."

"You're playing me for an idiot again, huh? Tricking one hostage after another from me. I gave you Leroy and that's that. Talk about good faith. Where's yours?"

"Joe, she's out. Let her stay out."

"Cut the shit!" Littlejoe exploded. He knew his voice was shrill with anger. He knew the microphones and cameras were recording the outburst. He didn't care. "You cops are all the same," he shouted. "Whatever you do is right. Lie, cheat, go back on your word, trick, hide, steal. If I do it, I'm an ape, a killer type.

If you do it, you're upholding the law. I'm sick of your law, Moretti. It's a goddamned lie."

He tried to cool himself down by taking long, slow breaths of the yeasty air. After a moment it worked. He took another breath and held it awhile. "Ask her," he said then. "Ask her what she wants to do."

"And you'll abide by her decision."

"I didn't say that. I said ask her."

Moretti faced Marge. "You're out of there, Mrs. Haines. I think we can convince Joe to let you stay outside if you want to."

"I can't do that," Marge said.

"What?"

"Those two young kids inside. They're my girls. I'm responsible for them. They're frightened to death, both of them. I'm going back in." She turned and brushed past Joe on her way into the bank.

"That was Mrs. Marjorie Haines," Rick Ericson was intoning into his microphone, "in a rare demonstration of courage that we have seldom—"

"See, copper?" Joe cut in triumphantly. "She'd rather take her chances inside."

"She explained why. She's afraid for the two girls."

"Maybe. Maybe she figures it's as bad out here as it is inside. Holier-than-thou cops. Tell me something, Detective Sergeant Moretti, when the city issues you a license to kill, does that make you feel terrific?"

Moretti stood there for a moment. "When the President of the United States issued you your license to kill, how did *you* feel, Joe?"

For a moment Joe didn't know what to say. Then a slow grin crossed his face. "Hey," he said softly. "Not bad, Moretti. Not bad."

One of the cameramen atop a TV van yelled: "Wave to us, Joe."

Joe held out both arms at shoulder height and gave a V sign with both hands. "I want to make one thing perfectly clear," he yelled. "After this is over I'm retiring to San Clemente and live off my pension of seventy-five grand a year. And you're gonna keep paying it till the day I die."

The crowd went wild with hooting and catcalls. Moretti's frown deepened. "Nobody loves a smart-ass, Joe."

"And another thing, Moretti. I'm through talking to city dicks. Heisting a national bank is a federal offense. I want to talk to a higher-up."

"Oh, do you." Moretti pushed the microphone away. "If you're not careful, you're going to get just that." His voice sank to a whisper. "You asshole, I'm your only chance. They would've picked you off long ago."

"What about the million in cash? What about the safe conduct? What about bringing my wife here? What about the plane?"

"We've got your wife," Moretti said. "She's on her way here now. The million we'll get. Everything takes time."

"You're stalling, that's all. While you fill the area with plainclothesmen. I see them filtering in. I'm not blind."

"Those are off-duty cops. They heard the news on TV and they're coming in from all boroughs of the city, some of them even from Long Island."

"The smell of blood attracts them, huh?"

"It's up to you, the smell. Drop your gun. Get Sam to drop his and the problem ends. It's solved. Just that fast."

"Kiss, kiss."

Moretti turned away. "It's no use, is it?"

"Not without the ransom, my wife, the getaway car, and the plane. You're making me sound like a fucking broken record, Moretti."

But the detective had already started back across the street, the lenses of the creepy-peepies on him. Joe went back inside the bank. Sam was standing just next to the door, his glance shifting from side to side. He looked uptight again.

"What were you talking to him about so long?" Sam demanded.

"Deals."

"You told them the deal. There's nothing more to talk about."

"Nothing has changed, Sam. You gotta trust me, is all. We only have each other in this. They talk about good faith. But it's you and me have to keep faith. I won't do anything you don't want to do."

Sam's big eyes scanned his face. "Okay," he said at last. "You I trust."

"That's how it has to be."

"But we're getting out of this," Sam went on. "Either that or they kill me. I don't go back to jail, Littlejoe, not ever. And I kill as many of them as I can before they get me."

"Sam," Joe said soothingly. "Sam, we're getting out of it. We're—"

The telephone's ring cut off his words. He'd run out of them by now anyway, and it was with a certain sense of relief that he picked up the telephone. "Grand Central Station," he said.

"This the Littlejoe guy?" a man asked.

"Right."

"Good. I looked up the number in the phone book. Do me something."

"What?"

"Kill them."

"What?"

"Kill them all. Now."

"Fucking creep!" Joe burst out, slamming down the phone. He turned to Sam. "Christ, Sam you wouldn't believe the kind of people walking the streets of this town."

★ 18

At SEVEN THIRTY, Moretti finally concluded that —short of a miracle—it was all over.

He hadn't said anything to any of the cops assigned to him. He hadn't, of course, mentioned it to Baker, the FBI agent in charge. Nor had he even hinted anything of the kind to Assistant Commissioner Mulvey, who had called only three times in the past hour. Finally, when the mayor of New York had gotten on the phone for a direct talk to Moretti, he had fed him the same optimistic lies he'd given everyone else.

But the fact remained that the situation was damned near lost unless he got an unexpected break. Moretti had had Sam's record pulled out of police files. He'd also pulled two arrest citations for Joe Nowicki, alias Littlejoe.

He now knew something more about the suspects across the street, not much, but enough to realize that both had serious problems. It was amazing how much undiluted garbage lay in the files of the computer system that coughed up dossiers on both men. There was even a note on Joe that indicated he had supported Goldwater and Nixon in previous presidential elections, but had been overheard to make damaging remarks about Nixon subsequent to 1972. Moretti wondered how any system, even one as expensive as this, could sweep up such uncorroborated bullshit and, what was worse, retain it on permanent call.

Joe's dossier was sketchy because he'd never been

brought to trial for any of his offenses. They ranged from hubcap stealing as a kid in Corona to uttering menaces, a complaint of one of his neighbors in Rego Park. Charges had never been made. His file indicated he had a hair-trigger temper, nothing more.

But Sam's record was disheartening. He'd obviously had such a bad time in prison that he might not want to be taken alive if they closed in on the bank.

It was always a touchy business with hostages. Moretti was never one for meeting it head-on, the way Baker might, charging in like a bull and trampling whatever got in the way. Moretti liked a bit of the old soft shoe. He liked to tiptoe into the thing, size up all the factors and try to guess what would happen if he did this, or that.

Often enough, when the showdown came, Moretti had had felons surrender peacefully rather than spill a hostage's blood and their own. It could well be that way with Joe, if no one got that blow-top temper of his riled. But the chances of Sam giving up quietly were nil.

That meant they'd get their million bucks, and all the rest, too.

He'd already said as much to Mulvey, and been chewed out unmercifully. "Where the hell does the Department get that kind of loot? Out of your budget, Moretti? They'll remember you as the guy who cost them a million bucks. And they won't be in any hurry to promote you for a thing like that."

"Commissioner," Moretti had responded, holding on to his temper as well as he could, "does that go for the plane charter, too? Am I going to get this kind of magnificent cooperation all down the line?"

"Easy, Tony. Watch the mouth."

"Am I?"

"You'll get," Mulvey said, "what you'll get. My crystal ball is no better than yours."

Reviewing the problem now, as he watched the

light begin to fade out of the sky and grow rosy-orange in the west, Moretti reminded himself that Baker would not be having such money problems. The FBI simply never had money problems. But if Moretti held his breath waiting for Baker to offer a helping hand on the budget, he would strangle to death.

He was dying, as it was, unless saved by a miracle. The crowds were now huge. The TV and radio, the newspapers, the wire services, some of the news magazines, even publications like *New York* and *Playboy*, already had in-depth reporters nosing around, asking for permission to do such lovely things as go inside the bank and tape a confidential interview.

As if this thing had been staged for them. That was one thing Littlejoe had right. Once these things started rolling, they were for everybody else, never for the hardcore of it like Moretti and Joe and, God help him, Boyle across the street.

". . . telling you Al, you should send another two trucks at least," a voice behind Moretti was saying.

The detective turned to watch one of his own uniformed patrolmen on the telephone to his brother-in-law, the *gonif* who owned the ice-cream and pizza wagons that had flocked to the scene in record time.

Moretti had heard him make two previous calls, both of them for more wagons. Of course the cop shouldn't be using the phone. Of course there was a conflict of interest. Of course his brother-in-law slipped the cop a few bills for spotting and reporting such concentrations of gawkers. But Moretti had better things to worry about now than the usual penny-ante cop grafting.

". . . yeah, but not hot pretzels. Cool stuff, Al. Another wagon of them Eye-talian ices would go good."

"See if he has any Fudgsicles," Moretti growled.

The cop's eyes shifted sideways. "Uh, Al, you got any Fudgsicles?"

Moretti shook his head sadly and walked out on the street. Baker had been standing there for the past fifteen minutes, steely blue eyes fixed on the bank, where, inside, both hostages and culprits had just finished the last of their pizzas.

"Give you a warm feeling, Moretti?" Baker asked. "The world is getting to be quite a place when you can stick up a bank, take hostages, and for your reward you get three kinds of pizza, a million dollars, and a trip to the moon."

"Don't forget having your wife hand-delivered to the scene," Moretti added. "Has anybody heard what's keeping them with her?"

"She's on the way," Baker said. "Maybe she can talk some sense into him."

"Not Nowicki. He doesn't listen to anybody. He's what they call inner-directed."

Baker's eyebrows went up. "Fancy talk for a pint-sized Polack punk."

Moretti waved a finger from side to side. "Careful, Baker, his mother's Italian."

The two men eyed each other. Baker assayed a tight smile that barely disturbed the steely set of his lips. Man of iron, Moretti noted. Able Baker, Stainless Man of Steel.

"Let's . . . have . . ." a voice from the crowd howled, the words spaced out as if shouting them were agonizing, ". . . some . . . action . . . coppers!"

Baker inclined the top of his close-cropped gray head in the direction of the yelp. "The animals are restless."

Moretti nodded. "I wish the boys across the street were getting itchy. Maybe I could talk a deal with them."

"With animals like that?" Baker's cold eyes lidded halfway. "You can't talk to garbage. You can't make deals with filth."

Moretti nodded again. "Let me ask you something, Baker," he said then. "If that's the way you feel about the crowd *and* the crooks, what are you in this business for? Why stay in it?"

Baker snorted. "It's a career, Moretti, same as yours. You do the best you can, you get more authority. I don't have to tell you how the game is played."

"Yeah, but why a career keeping crooks from creaming the crowd, if one is garbage and the other a bunch of animals?"

Baker started to answer, then thought better of it. "I'm no sociologist."

"It's just that I can't figure out why a bright person spends his life trying to protect the public from the criminals it spawns. If you believe they're not worth it."

"I didn't say that."

"Okay, I picked up too fast." Moretti removed his hat and mopped the top of his head. "I misunderstood. Let it go at that."

"Fine." Baker thought for a moment. "There are some fine people in the world," he said then. "But you don't find them gawking around a police stakeout, do you?"

"Depends what you mean by fine. I said let it go. *Zeit gezundt.*"

"No, I want to straighten you out," Baker insisted. "I don't hate these people. Get that straight. I may feel sorry for them. I may think they need straightening out. But I don't hate them. How could you? Most people are children, anyway."

"Um." Moretti turned and went back inside the insurance office. He picked up the telephone and got his precinct house. "Dave, what's holding up the car with the wife?"

"Any second now, Sarge. They tracked her down in Manhattan. She's not in good health, apparently. I don't know the whole story. But they're in Queens now. It's a matter of minutes."

Moretti hung up. He watched Baker through the window. Even inside the air-conditioned office Moretti was still damp and uncomfortable. Outside, in the heat of the evening, Baker didn't even look rumpled. But, what the hell, the FBI didn't hire anybody with sweat glands. Moretti made a face.

He had to stop blaming everything on Baker. Baker wasn't the enemy. He was just another guy pretending to be a machine. The country was full of them, dehumanized people programmed to "do a job," to "handle the situation," real "take-charge guys" who would "walk over their grandmother" if ordered to because they were "hard-nosed, can-do guys" who "played to win," even if it meant "acceptable losses." The first loss was themselves.

The detective grinned lopsidedly. Imagine Gaetano Moretti walking over his grandmother. She'd hit him with a broom, old and tiny as she was.

Maybe dealing with crime did that to people like Baker. Moretti had seen his own morality sink over the past twenty years, not just the deals Mulvey demanded from him, but smaller things, slippages of morality that were justified by the need to "get along" so as not to "rock the boat" or "let down the team," compromises in the name of "the way it is" in a "cold, cruel world" where "nice guys finish last" and if you didn't do it "they'd find someone else."

Slowly, you sank to the level of the people with whom you spent most of your life, criminals. Slowly you began to share not only a common jargon but a common view of life and a common morality, based on "taking care of Number One."

All those crummy, second-hand slogans borrowed from high-school athletic teams.

Moretti supposed now that it was this that accounted for the high divorce rate among non-Catholic cops. It wasn't the late hours or the irregular duty. It wasn't the new wife trembling at home for the safety of her bridegroom among the uncaged street animals. It was the fact that after two, three years, the boy she had married was gone. A stranger had taken his place, who acted and spoke and thought like a hood.

He watched Baker coming in. "I think the wife's here," he said. "Listen, before you go out there, give a thought to what I suggested before."

"What, the tear gas?"

"No, just pull the switch on their power across the street. In the excitement, while you deliver the wife, we just cut the power. There's a terrific psychological edge when they're sitting in the dark like rats in a hole, sweating in the heat with searchlights blinding them. It works, Moretti. You know it does."

Moretti stuck his head out the door. In the distance a phalanx of four burly cops was making a route through the crowd for a tall, sleek woman, made even taller by her platform shoes with six-inch heels. Even at this distance, her platinum hair looked unreal.

"Here she comes," Moretti hummed, "Miss America." He turned back to Baker. "I don't like the idea of shutting off power, but I haven't got anything better to suggest."

"I'll handle it," Baker assured him.

Moretti advanced into the combat zone, walking to the center stripe of the roadway. The cops had cleared a way for Joe's wife and were escorting her toward Moretti. From the crowd behind them came a few whistles.

"Joe!" Moretti called. "We have your wife."

He watched Joe drop an unfinished wedge of pizza and come to the door. As the woman advanced toward Moretti, her walk became looser. Her hips swayed with the effort of walking on the platform shoes. The crowd began to yip and hoot.

"Oh, Joe!" someone called.

"Oh, Joey, oh, Joey!"

"Hey, doll, I'd rob a bank for you any day."

The comments were drowned in rhythmic clapping in time to the woman's saunter. Finally, when she got within a few yards of Moretti, he saw the runny mascara as thick as cake frosting, and the wide-rouged mouth. He saw the immense false lashes. He also spotted the stubbly cheeks and chin.

"What is this?" he asked one of the escorting officers.

The man produced a wide grin. "You tell us, Sarge."

"This is the one he asked for, Lana Lee?"

"Little wifie-poo in the flesh," another cop said.

"Christ," Moretti said as Joe walked out into the street. "Faggots!"

"Hey," Joe said weakly, "Moretti, what about all that mutual respect you were asking for?"

Moretti's head was shaking. "Faggots," he repeated softly, as if to himself.

Whether they had just heard it or had just realized what Lana was, people in the crowd quickly got the idea.

"Faggot!" one man cried out.

"Faggot drag queen!" somebody else shouted.

The air was suddenly choked with hooting and booing and the sound of wet kissing and sucking noises.

"Suck this, Joe!"

"Douse 'em with gasoline!"

"Burn the faggots!"

Abruptly, Lana moaned, a harsh sound, like some exotic bird of prey. Moretti turned to her. He saw her dropping. She went down in a sexy tangle of long bare legs, fainting dead away on the hot pavement. Her tight miniskirt slid up over her legs almost to her crotch.

Moretti's glance went up her legs, a conditioned reflex of discovery, the constant search for a quick, snickering peek at what lay at the juncture of a woman's legs. Then the detective grinned shame-facedly at himself. What a reflex it was, how power-ful. Knowing this was a transvestite, knowing he had the same thing between his legs as Moretti, and yet still programmed by a lifetime to snatch a peek. Moretti shook his head at his own stupidity.

Nevertheless, he thought, drag queen or not, this red-hot cutie could be the miracle I need.

19

THE SILENCE INSIDE THE BANK was profound. No one spoke as Joe came back through the heavy glass door. No one said anything as he stood just behind the small picture window and watched the scene outside on the street. Not even Sam had a comment to make when Lana went down in a dead faint.

Littlejoe watched Moretti trying to bring Lana back to consciousness. Joe knew her "faints." She was as strong as an ox, but she was tripping on so many uppers and downers that she hardly knew whether to shit or wind her watch.

He'd seen her pull faints before, once even on him, who knew her better. She always asked herself, "What would a lady do in a situation like this?" and if the answer was to faint, she flopped.

Sighing bitterly, Joe turned away from the window. He saw that everyone, even Sam, was watching the long-legged figure sprawled on the asphalt outside, a small knot of cops around her.

"She's getting better at it all the time," he called to Sam.

The boy's dark eyes blinked. "Lana Lovely. What a phony."

Slowly, almost unwillingly, the glances of the bank employees broke away from the scene on the street as the significance of what was happening began to sink in. Marge was the first to pull her head together, Joe noticed.

"Hey," she said then. "Listen, Joe."

"Yeah, doll?"

"Joe, is that . . ." Her voice died away. Then she started up again after reframing her thought: "I can hear what the crowd is shouting out there."

"Yeah?"

Marge's eyes shot sideways to Boyle, as if looking for support. His glance was fixed on the top of his desk, as if unwilling to look up at any more crude reality. "I mean, that girl is your wife?" Marge persisted.

"Yeah."

"But she's not—uh . . . she's really . . ." Marge stopped. "I mean, she's a fella, is that it?"

"Yeah."

"But . . ." Marge's mouth worked for a second, framing words and letting them die unsaid. "But that's why the crowd is shouting 'faggot' then."

"Yeah."

"At her. Him."

"Yeah."

"And at you?" She'd finally spit it out, Littlejoe saw. It was like a big hunk of phlegm stuck in her throat and she couldn't swallow it or cough it up, but, by God, she was going to try. And succeed.

Having hawked it out on the floor for everybody to look at, Marge now fell silent. Joe watched her for a moment, then turned to Boyle, suddenly, savagely. "Let's hear from you, Mr. Family Man. Any shouts of 'faggot' from you?"

Boyle's chubby face looked drawn. His eyes refused to rise, but shifted sideways to examine something completely fascinating at the edge of his desk that he had never before noticed in his entire life.

"I'm talking to you, Boyle," Joe bored in. "Now you know who heisted your precious little corner of Chase's precious little world. Two asshole bandits. Two fatherfuckers. And it's killing your Irish soul, isn't it."

"Hey," Boyle said in a weak voice.

"The language," Marge chimed in. "I got young gir—"

"Fuck the young girls," Littlejoe cut in. "And I've fucked my share. You too, huh, Boyle, and some of the older ones too, right? Zoftig titties and all, Mr. Guardian of Catholic Morality?"

Boyle's eyes finally lifted to look at Joe directly. "Hey, listen," he said then. "Listen."

"I want to hear. I'm listening. Speak."

"Joe," Boyle said at last, his voice so quiet that it hardly reached across the lobby. "I'm out of words, Joe. This has been quite a shock."

"You'd have plenty of them if I wasn't holding a gun."

"Don't say that."

"You'd be quick with the judgments, Mr. Holy Name Society."

"Take it easy, Joe."

"But I don't only hold the gun, I hold the cards, the whole fucking deck, Boyle. I'm like Superman. I can see through steel. I can see your little scummy office love affair, and that gives me more power than this thirty eight. I can tell Sam to wipe you out in the next five seconds and that would be it. But that's only life-and-death power. I also have the power to bad-name you till the end of time. I can hang a sign on your tombstone that will keep your wife and kids and mother and sisters and priest in tears forever. Adulterer. Christ, it's almost too good. What if that crowd out there wasn't yelling 'faggot' at the top of their lungs? What if they were yelling 'adulterer' at a good Catholic husband and father like you?"

Boyle's baldish head had started to shake from side to side. Marge touched his arm. "Take it easy on him, Joe," she said. "You made your point."

"No, I didn't," Littlejoe said in a lower voice. "Because you know what? Nobody'd yell anything like that at him. 'Adulterer' isn't a curse word. Only 'faggot' is."

"But you're not really . . . ?" Marge's voice died away again.

"What?"

"I mean, back there in the vault before?"

"I copped a feel?" Joe found himself grinning suddenly. "And that somehow is too wild for your brain, huh?"

Marge watched him for a long moment. Then her lips twisted slightly in an answering grin. "I'll be damned," she said then. "You're really something, Joe. You . . . you want to get the best of both worlds, is that it?"

Neither of them spoke for a moment, because Boyle had started to come out of his trance. He moved around his desk and walked toward Joe. "Let me get this straight," he began, his voice higher than normal. "What went on there in the vault?"

"You mean," Joe said, "the vault where Eddie is lying in a pool of blood now?"

"I asked you something, mister."

"You mean where you're going to be lying on top of Eddie in a double pool pretty soon?"

Boyle stood still. He had stopped about a yard from the tip of the .38 revolver Littlejoe was holding. Now his puffy face started to wrinkle. His eyes squeezed shut. He covered his face with his hands and turned away, sobbing. "Jesus," he mumbled. "Jesus, what's happening?"

"Go back and sit down," Joe ordered. He watched the manager turn and stumble back to his desk. Boyle buried his face in his arms, as if to shut out everything, sight, and sound as well. Marge bent over him warily, then began stroking the hair at the back of his head. Boyle shook his head impatiently, and she stopped.

"Love is funny, or it's sad," Littlejoe crooned softly. "It's a good thing, or it's bad." He started to laugh softly and looked up at Sam. "Some day when this is all over, Sam, and we're lying on some beach far away from here and remembering the good old days, remind me to send Boyle a wire and ask him to write me all those thousands of bad words he would have laid on me. Right now he's got them all corked up inside him, huh?"

"Bad to keep that stuff inside," Sam agreed.

Littlejoe's eyes, watching Sam, began to unfocus slightly. The scene grew fuzzy for a moment. The two of them on a beach? Some day? Did he really want to spend the rest of his life with a guy who liked to kill? Had to kill?

20

B Y THE TIME MORETTI had gotten things quieted down in the block-long corridor of hell he was supposed to be controlling, the time was past eight and the sky was really beginning to darken.

Through his shoulders, feeling it like a jungle cat, Moretti could tell that the crowd was doing two contradictory things at the same time: settling in for a long wait and losing patience. He could stand on the center stripe, as he was doing now, his gaze on the glass façade of the bank, and feel the mob's mood through his arm muscles, or his guts. He'd been a New York cop too long to ignore such feelings. They meant he had a whole new problem. In addition to settling the standoff with Littlejoe, he now had to keep the mob in line as well.

A doctor had done several things to Lana as she sprawled rather artistically on the pavement. He had propped up her head on a rolled coat. He had snapped an ampule of amyl nitrite under her nose, and he had laid a handkerchief, wrung out in cold water, over her forehead. He had also injected 5 c.c.s of glucose-saline solution, on the not altogether sound hunch that the faint was from heatstroke.

Littlejoe had retreated into the bank in the face of howls of "fag-got, fag-got, fag-got" from the crowd, which now, finally, had a universal slogan to chant.

Until this moment, Moretti knew, the mob had been of two minds, for and against Joe. Now they could no longer afford to support any of his actions, for fear of being considered as gay as he.

Moretti knelt on one knee beside the lengthy sprawl of limb that Lana was displaying. Her lashes had been working up and down now for some time, and she had, with a certain finicky distaste, removed the cool, wet cloth from her brow.

Behind Moretti, the glass façade of the bank was in darkness. It was impossible to know if anyone was inside or not. Baker had pulled the power, shut it off completely about fifteen minutes before, as the doctor was ministering to Lana. It had been a good choice of timing, because Littlejoe had failed to react, in his anguish over Lana. So had Sam. Or at least, Moretti surmised, Joe had been able to control Sam in this one instance.

Heavy-duty searchlights were even now being wheeled into place, both the normal kind and a pair of immense klieg lights of the sort used at supermarket openings.

Once the full candlepower of all these lights was concentrated on the front of the bank, Moretti hoped, it would establish a certain psychological supremacy, as Baker had promised. God knows, they could use every little bit of leverage they had, real or imaginary.

This one, now, this number sprawled on the hot pavement. She wasn't exactly the miracle he'd thought she'd be. But, on the other hand, miracles often needed a little help. She felt better. Now was the time to start shaping her up into as much of a miracle as possible.

"Mrs. Littlejoe," Moretti began in an undertone.

From the crowd the huge, tearing sound of someone sucking, mouth pressed against his curled-up fingers to amplify the noise, echoed like a trombone blast.

Lana glanced at the detective. "I am not into that whole entire insane scene, Lieutenant," she murmured. "I am not Mrs. Littlejoe or Mrs. Anybody."

"You are Lana Lee?"

She sighed heavily and made her over-rouged mouth into a petulant pout. "Is this going on my record?" she asked.

"No. You're not under arrest." Moretti tried to keep his voice low and reassuring without sounding as if he were trying to make her. It wasn't that easy.

"But, I mean, you're going to have to find out," Lana went on. "It's a little confused. I mean, we did go through a form of, like, unreal marriage. But there was a priest and all. So, I guess you could say I was Mrs. Nowicki." She giggled helplessly for a moment, and her breasts heaved.

"Bite 'em, Sarge!" someone in the crowd shouted.

"Fag-got, fag-got, fag-got!"

"I don't have to know your legal name," Moretti said.

"It's Albert R—"

"I don't have to know," Moretti insisted. "You're not being booked for anything. Just tell me you'll cooperate with us. You'll talk to that husband of yours. You'll talk some sense into him."

"Is that why you fellows brought me here?" Lana simpered.

Moretti shook his head. "Littlejoe asked for you."

"Me? Like, insane."

"You are part of the deal he's demanding," Moretti told her. "If he gets you, and a million in cash, and a safe conduct to JFK airport and a jet across the Atlantic, he'll vacate the premises and give us our hostages unharmed."

"Oh, my God."

They eyed each other for a long moment. Then Moretti took her hand and helped her to her feet. "Let's talk about this inside, where it's cooler. The doctor thinks you may have a mild heatstroke."

As he escorted her back to the insurance office,

the crowd began to hoot again. "Be gentle, Sarge!" one voice called.

"Faaa-guht!"

He ushered her inside and put her in a chair out of range of the crowd but where Littlejoe could see her. Baker, watching, said nothing at first, but it was clear to Moretti that the FBI man was starting to bubble over like an unwatched percolator.

"I told you," Baker said then, in a dead undertone. He seemed to have the knack of ventriloquism. It was as if one of the walls had spoken, not he. "Lowest form of animal life," a chair told Moretti as Baker walked away.

Lana made a kissing face at Baker's retreating back. Then, to Moretti: "You don't have to worry about Littlejoe. He won't kill anybody. He takes out his entire insane hostility on me, baby. Nobody but yours fucking truly."

"He's got Sam in there with him."

Lana's heavily mascaraed eyes widened, the fake eyelashes flipping far up for a moment. "Ugh. Unreal. No way."

"Huh?"

"I hate, abhor, and detest that little Sam vonce," she told him. "He's so screwed-up it isn't funny. Him . . . *him* I would worry about. He could kill anybody if he thought he was facing prison again."

Moretti nodded calmly, but her statement had plunged him into despair. Mustn't let it show. He didn't care if this freak saw how badly he took the news about Sam. But Baker couldn't know. If it was true, and Moretti knew it was, then they had no way out except total capitulation to Littlejoe's demands. Or one other way.

That was why having Lana in custody was so important. She might make the difference, might convince Littlejoe he had to betray Sam.

That was what it had come down to. Sam was the

186 DOG DAY AFTERNOON

stumbling block. Only Littlejoe could betray him. And only by betraying Sam could they get the hostages out alive.

Moretti walked to the window and put his back to it so that if Littlejoe was watching—he had to be!— what went on now would be hidden from him. "How close are the two of you," Moretti began.

"Sam and me. Like rat poison, honey. I mean—"

"You and Joe."

"Oh. Unreal. Nowhere."

"Come on. He calls you his wife. He obviously wants you with him when he takes off with the million in cash."

"No way. Insane."

"Come on, Lana, level with me."

She splayed her long fingers way out, flashing her dark red nails. "Not that I'm turning down a million," she went on conversationally, "but all I asked him for was three grand. That's all it costs."

Moretti nodded sympathetically. "What costs?"

"The operation. It's a month in Baltimore or Stockholm, but if you go to Casablanca, it's only two weeks."

Moretti closed his eyes. Something he'd read was coming back to him. "The sex-change operation," he said then, still in his underplayed, sympathetic voice.

"Of course," Lana said, as if nothing else could have been meant.

Moretti's eyes opened. "You're saying he robbed a bank to pay for your sex-change operation?" He could almost read the *Daily News* headlines now.

"He loathes and detests the idea. He wants me as I am." Her glance lowered seductively. "But I can't be the person *he* wants. He doesn't own me. I want to be the person *I* want. A woman."

Moretti nodded again, as if this made the greatest sense in the world. "Of course you do," he said reassuringly. "But once you're a woman, what's wrong with the million he's going to have."

"Half a million," she reminded him. "That vicious little Sam gets his cut."

"Not necessarily."

Moretti walked over to the door, opened it, and looked out. He had no reason to, but simply wanted Lana to think over the sudden possibility that it wasn't Sam and Littlejoe against the world, but Lana and Littlejoe against Sam.

"What is that supposed to mean?" Lana demanded after a moment.

"You look like an intelligent wo—person," Moretti began, correcting himself in mid-word. "I don't have to tell you that if Sam starts shooting, the whole thing goes up in smoke. There's a man back there from the FBI who thinks all of them are garbage. He thinks you don't deal with garbage, you just burn it. If Sam starts shooting, that's what'll happen. We have the firepower concentrated on that bank now to burn Sam and Joe into cinders. Unfortunately, four innocent people will die with them. And, more than that, there's no ransom, no safe conduct, no jet to Casablanca."

Lana's wondrous eyelashes flickered up and down like hummingbird wings. "A jet to Casablanca?"

"There is one thing you have to do," Moretti said. "It's not hard and it's not dangerous. Nothing bad can happen to you whether it works or doesn't work. Even if it fails completely, you'll still look good in the newspapers and on TV. But if it works, you'll be a hero." He started to correct it to "heroine," but decided it was too late to be that accurate.

Lana's glance grew calculating. She did this by wrinkling the skin between her eyebrows. "You mean it's no skin off my ass either way?"

"Right. But if it works, you score big."

The furrow between her brows deepened. "What do I have to do?"

21

I'M SUFFOCATING," Marge complained.

"When they turned off the lights," Joe explained, "they turned off the air conditioning."

"Just the news I needed," Marge retorted.

"What a mouth." Littlejoe peered through the darkened lobby at the lighted window of the insurance office across the street, where Moretti was now handing a paper cup to Lana. She drank greedily from it.

She looked better now. By rights, Littlejoe thought, I should be with her. But he couldn't bring himself to face the shouting on the street yet. That word. That ugly label. Those ugly people with their sick need to label everything.

"Littlejoe," Sam said then, his voice seemingly far away as it came out of the darkness at the rear of the lobby. "You know, in this dark, it ain't as easy to keep track of these people."

"They'll behave," Littlejoe assured him.

"They better."

"Stop terrorizing the girls," Boyle said. He was seated behind his desk, his chin propped on the palms of his hands. "Just stop it. There's a limit to how much of this abuse we can take."

"Yeah?" Joe asked. "If I really started abusing you, Boyle, baby, you'd feel it for a week."

"What is that supposed to mean?" Boyle retorted.

"You know," Marge murmured. "He's talking dirty."

"Tell him, Marge," Joe teased. "Tell him if he isn't careful, he'll have to turn tail and play nice little girlie."

"Stop that," Boyle snapped.

"I need a cigarette," Marge moaned.

"Here." Boyle handed her his pack.

She shook one loose and put it in her mouth. "Got a light?"

"Hey," Sam interrupted. "I thought you never smoked before."

"I never did."

"Don't start," he begged her. "You're clean. Stay that way."

"What?"

"I mean it, Marge," Sam pleaded with her. "Once you start, you're hooked. But you've stayed pure all these years. Just hold on. Just hang in there and stay pure."

"All what years?" Marge snapped back. "I'm not that old. And as for pure . . ."

"It'd be a real crime if you started smoking now," Sam insisted.

"I don't believe what I'm hearing," Marge announced to the darkened room. "It's okay to rob a bank but it's not okay to smoke?"

"I'm serious," Sam said.

She stared into the darkness in the direction of his voice. Then, to Joe: "Got a light?"

Boyle snapped his lighter for her. "Here, Marge. One time can't kill you."

"What do I do?" she asked. "Just pull in smoke?"

"Till it's lit."

"Marge." Sam's voice sounded terribly down.

"You're not my father," Marge called to him.

The telephone began to ring. Joe picked it up. "What?"

"Kill them all," the same peculiar voice whispered.

He slammed down the telephone. "Every creep in

New York is on the phone," he muttered. "This is their night. This is all for them, what we're going through, so they can get their jollies. Sam, you realize what we'll be in a few hours?"

"Free?"

"Men without a country. We'll never be able to go back to the U.S. after this."

" 'S all right with me, Littlejoe."

"You're taking it awful easy. It's a lot to give up," Littlejoe mused. "I fought for this country. I might've died for it." He tried to see what was happening with Lana across the street. "I was born here," he maundered on. "There's a lot wrong with it, but there's no better place, is there?"

"Tell 'em, Littlejoe," Marge mused. "You're quite a patriot."

At that moment, as if a box of flashbulbs had exploded all at once, the street outside flared brilliant white, and intense glare struck into the depths of the lobby.

"Searchlights!" Sam yelped, as if in pain.

"Cool it," Littlejoe said. "It's a trick."

"To do what?" Boyle asked.

"To psych us out."

As if the searchlights weren't sharply enough focused, the cops began to move the beams of light this way and that. Abruptly the door of the insurance office opened. Moretti came out, holding Lana by her arm to help her teeter across the pavement on her high platform shoes.

Several of the searchlight beams zeroed in on the two of them as they started across the street, moving slowly, as if down an aisle to an altar. With her spun-floss hair and sleek figure, Lana looked dressed for some festivity, but perhaps not this one.

Littlejoe watched them come toward him with mixed feelings. He wanted to talk to Lana, but not in front of the whole world.

"Sucky-suck-suck!" someone yelled at the top of his lungs.

"Faaa-guht!"

Joe went to the door of the bank, which had remained unlocked for some time now. He swung it wide and propped open the heavy Herculite glass with a massive floor-type cigarette receptacle. The outside air was cooler than inside. But there was no breeze to waft it into the bank. Moretti and Lana were halfway across the combat zone now, passing over the center line.

Joe glanced back into the lobby and saw that Sam had singled out Ellen as a kind of superhostage. He had her sitting straight up in a chair while he stood behind her. With his left hand he cradled her face. His other hand held the .45 automatic against her right eye. She had stopped crying or saying anything some time ago.

Joe took a stride out into the street.

"Fag-got, fag-got, fag-got!"

"Joe sucks!"

"Burn, faggot, burn!"

He stood there blinking in the hot lights, one hand shading his eyes, the other holding the .38. His appearance now, for some reason, stirred the dozens of police around him to renewed attention. They seemed to remember him suddenly, and raised their various weapons to draw a bead. He could see muzzles of every caliber pointed at him like so many hungry snouts sniffing the wind for blood. Maybe the searchlights hadn't had any luck psyching him out, Joe thought, but they seemed to rouse the hunter in the cops again.

"Look at this street," he called to Moretti. "Wall-to-wall pig."

"That word."

"I haven't heard you toning down the crowd's language."

Moretti paused and removed his hand from Lana's arm. "Here," he said then, "this is the first part of your demands. Paid and delivered."

Lana gave Moretti a haughty look and then turned the same look on Joe. He felt his heart constrict slightly. The strange animal that lived under his heart seemed to stir in its sleep. She could do that to him. Worse yet, she knew it.

"Well," Lana said then.

"Hi, baby."

"What an unreal, insane mess that Sam has dragged you into."

"Huh?"

"I thought you were smarter than to let a little shit like that use you," Lana went on.

"Christ," Joe agonized, "keep your voice down. If he hears you—"

"Let him. Nasty little animal."

"That's what he calls you," Joe said then. He had started to get very jumpy, with Lana coming on as salty as she was. She had never bad-named Sam before, and now was exactly the wrong time to start. "Just cool it, bitch. Sam isn't using me. I'm u—" He stopped himself. Wrong approach.

Lana closed the gap between them so that her breasts touched him. The crowd hooted so deafeningly that individual shouts were drowned out. "He's using you to settle a grudge against the world, baby."

Joe's hand clamped down on her slender arm, halfway between wrist and elbow. He knew from past experience that if he squeezed hard enough he'd leave her with a bruise. She knew it too, so she stopped talking.

"What kind of shit did Moretti pump into you?" Joe demanded, his glance swerving for a moment to the detective. "He's standing there right now like a fucking peeping tom, getting off his rocks watching you do his dirty work for him."

"That's so much shit," Lana said. "The sooner you cut loose from Sam, the b—"

He stopped her simply by clamping harder on her arm. "You stir up Sam," he said grimly, "and the first slug is for you, bitch. You got a nerve. The only reason I'm in this mess is because of that crazy operation you have to have."

"The operation you don't want me to have," Lana retorted. Her last word was spoken in a gasp as Joe tightened his grip. "You're deliberately doing that," she moaned. "It'll be all purple tomorrow morning."

"In the morgue," Joe asked, "who cares?"

"You're not shooting anybody," she said in a low voice. "It's Sam who wants to kill people. But you'll end up dead because of him."

The obvious truth of this stopped Joe from saying anything further. He glanced past Lana at Moretti, trying to pull his head together. "She does a great job for you, copper. You really programmed her, huh?"

"She's got your best interests at heart, Littlejoe."

"And that's bullshit too," Joe responded.

He felt better trading insults with Moretti. It was easier than trying to find answers for Lana. She was right: If he ended up dead, it would be because of Sam.

But he couldn't betray the kid. He'd talked him into the job to begin with. He'd *conned* him into it with his horseshit about Mafia coverage and all that crap. Now he couldn't abandon him, not the way Sam felt about going back into stir. Worse than that, he couldn't even let Sam suspect he was thinking of such things, because the kid would start shooting.

"Just think it over is all we're asking," Moretti said, using a version of the same low-pitched voice he had used with Lana.

Joe's eyes narrowed. He could see through Moretti's bluff. He knew Moretti's game. Let everyone else get frustrated and start making bad choices. Let Moretti play cool man in town. It didn't have to be true so long as it looked and sounded true.

"Oh, God, Moretti," Joe heard himself complain, "the world is so full of bullshit."

The detective nodded in agreement, but said nothing. "I don't think I ever heard anybody level with me in ten fucking years," Joe went on, more to himself than either Moretti or Lana. "It's all bullshit, meant to score one-up on you. Or make themselves bigger. Nobody levels. Flo, Tina, nobody. Not even you, Lana. You know the times I've caught you cheating."

"I like that," she said petulantly. "The way you stud it up for anything that'll hold still for it."

"That's different," Joe explained. "A man takes whatever comes along. That's what makes him a man. And I'll tell you something, both of you. I know Sam gives head. I know he works the trucks. But that kid is a man, you understand? He gave me his word and I gave him mine. And that's it." He could feel the anger rising in him, even though neither of them had said anything.

"That's fucking it!" he growled. He knew why he was angry. He knew they were right, that he had to sell out Sam if he wanted to live.

"Fuck-anything stud shit!" Lana spat at him. "Who do you think you are?" Her eyes looked wild, circled with black and wildly flickering lashes. "You think I would really associate with such unreal cheap stuff as you? Do you think that's all I've got to do is dirty myself with rough trade like you, baby? I tolerate you. To-le-rate," she drawled nastily. "You're like an insane roach I let live today. I might step on it tomorrow. That's you, baby. A murderous little Polack roach. You've tried killing me before. I'm lucky to be alive. Well, you don't get another chance at killing me, cheapie. Dragging my name and my body into your cheap little tricks with Sam. Keep me out of it!"

Her voice suddenly zoomed into an upper register. She wrenched her arm out of his grip. "You scum! You unreal scum!" She turned and ran across the street, hobbling unsteadily on her platforms.

"Faaa-guht!"

"Fag-got, fag-got, fag-got!"

★ 22

WHEN HE WALKED BACK into the bank, Joe saw that Marge had turned on the TV set and was trying to make it light up, forgetting there was no electricity. The lobby was thick with heat now, heat and the moisture of people inhaling and exhaling.

Joe stood for a moment with his back to the door, surveying them. They were lighted like actors on a stage caught in the glare of spotlights, or circus clowns pinpointed under the big top by a few hot beams.

Unreal, Lana had said. Everything was turning unreal. And she, who had always been some kind of acted-out wet dream, was as unreal as the rest of it. To think that it was all resting on his shoulders, Littlejoe mused. To think that soon enough they'd all be dead, or rich and free.

He shook his head, realizing that the chances of ending up dead were a lot better than of ending up rich. The telephone started to ring. He let it. He had no more heart for the kind of calls he'd been getting in the past few hours.

The man who wanted him to kill the hostages was bad enough, but there were others, people in bars who wanted to chat, a Jesus freak who had a lot of meaningless crap to unload, Ellen's husband, who wanted her to say good night to the baby, now and then a call from Moretti, TV reporters, everybody

wanting something. It was as if by robbing a bank
he had somehow set up a booth with a sign that said:

WANT SOMETHING? NOW'S THE TIME TO GET IT.

Whatever you wanted was yours, even if it was
just to act out a fantasy of torturing and killing helpless people, or, in the case of Ellen's husband, to get
one-up on her, make her feel like shit because she'd
been careless enough to get caught in a robbery.

"He's always hated me working," Ellen had said
forlornly as she hung up the telephone after telling
her baby to sleep tight.

"He's always after me not to work, how does it
look to the neighbors, how can the baby grow up
without a mother, all that. As if the neighbors' wives
don't work. You know? He lives in some kind of
dream world, my husband, where it's okay to live on
the money I earn while he'll be looking for work, but
any time he can stick it in and twist it a little, he
does."

Sam had finally led her away to stop her from talking, her big eyes wide not with anger or hatred but
with vision. Right, Littlejoe told himself. Even for
her this is a surprise treat. She's in danger of having
her brains ventilated, but the danger gives her the
power to see her life. Christ, the whole city ought to
take up a collection for me. I'm giving them the
chance of a lifetime.

The telephone kept ringing. Boyle reached for it.
"Okay, Joe?" he asked.

Joe watched him for a moment. The guy was still
playing the game, still pretending that if he was a
good little hostage nobody'd get hurt. "Play manager.
Answer it."

"Boyle speaking." Eyes up. Eyes right. "Yes, Sergeant." He handed the telephone to Littlejoe.

"Got the million?" Joe said by way of greeting.

"I called to say good-bye," Moretti responded.

"We're leaving? Good."

"I'm leaving," the detective explained. "You wanted to deal on the federal level, Joe, you got your wish. From now on, it's between you and Mr. Baker of the FBI."

"Hey, hold it," Joe snapped. "I wan—"

"Joe Nowicki?" Baker's voice.

"Put Moretti back on the line."

"You want to talk," Baker said, "you talk to me."

Littlejoe felt his face constrict in a movement of disgust. He'd disliked Moretti, but they'd been able to talk on the same level. Even now, at the beginning, he could feel that Baker was dealing down to him from on high. "I got nothing to talk about."

"Can anyone hear what I'm saying?" Baker asked. "Is anyone on an extension line?"

"No. Is anybody eavesdropping on your end, Feebie?"

"This is just between the two of us, then."

"The two of us," Joe agreed, "and your tape recorder."

"It's something Sam must not hear," Baker explained. "This is for your ears only. I'm offering you your life, Nowicki. I'm offering to handle your sidekick for you. Just do what I say and there'll be no problems."

"You gotta be out of your shit-eating mind."

"Don't say anything the other man will find suspicious," Baker warned him. "We've got your million in cash. It arrived in the past ten minutes. We've got your jet. It's fueled and crewed and waiting on a separate runway all its own at JFK. When I come across the street to tell you this—" He broke off. "Are you getting this?"

"I been lied to by experts. Keep talking."

"When I come across the street to tell you this, officially," Baker repeated almost by rote, "you will be hearing it for the first time. You'll confer with Sam. You'll convince him this is it. You'll agree to the deal and we'll bring in an airport limo Caddy. We'll park it at the curb in front of the bank. Got that?"

"I'm listening."

"The order of leaving the bank is as follows. Boyle comes out first with one woman behind him. You're all in lockstep. Then you. Then two women. Then Sam. Understand? Sam is the last one out. The rest of it doesn't matter, Nowicki. Just that Sam is the last one in the line. Then you move into the car on the side next to the bank. There are six of you. It'll be a little crowded in back, because only five can sit there. You take your time getting into the car. We do the rest."

"What rest?"

"That's our business. The less you know, the less you have to worry about."

"It don't take no genius to figure out the plan."

"I warned you," Baker said. "Don't say something to arouse his suspicions."

Littlejoe stood there in silence for a long moment. They'd pick off Sam. Some sniper would get him without too much trouble. And if the first shot didn't take and Sam could still work his .45 Colt automatic, there would be a few more bodies. That was the Feebie way. You relied on experts. No problems. But even experts don't bat .1000, so there are mistakes. Sorry about that. Doing the best we can. Beautiful.

But there was a way Baker's plan could be turned against him. He wasn't God. Even *his* plans had loopholes.

"You still there?" Baker demanded.

"I'm thinking."

"You're taking too long. It's a simple decision, Nowicki. You trade Sam for everybody else, including yourself."

"Tell me some more about the jet out at JFK. Or is that just bullshit."

"Damn it!" Baker shouted. "I told you not to get him riled up."

"Let me handle this. I asked you a question."

"There's a plane," Baker admitted grudgingly. "It exists. It's fueled and staffed and cleared for takeoff to Casablanca."

"Casa what?"

"Isn't that where you wanted to go?"

Joe paused again. Let them think whatever they want. But how could he believe Baker about the plane? "Put Moretti on the line."

"I told you, I'm—"

"Put him on," Joe insisted. "You can listen in."

There were confused sounds over the wire. Then: "What is it, Joe?"

"Moretti, he says the plane's ready to take off. Why don't I believe him?"

A silence at the other end. Littlejoe wiped beads of sweat off his face. He turned to Sam. "I think we're home free, baby," he whispered.

Sam's face, wet with perspiration, brightened. His grave eyes looked almost happy for a moment. "No shit, Littlejoe?"

"Maybe. Hey, Moretti, what's taking so long?"

"Just getting the details. Yeah, it's real, the plane. They're charging the Department eighteen grand each way, rental and fuel. That's real enough. The crew volunteered their time."

"That on the level?"

"On the level. If you think this is going to earn me that lieutenant's bar," Moretti went on slowly, "you got another think coming."

"And the cash?"

Another moment of confused noise. Suddenly, Lana's voice, squeaking with excitement. "It's here, baby. I mean, like, unreal, in tens and twenties."

Baker's voice followed at once. "No more playing around, Nowicki. We can skip the official parley on the street. Just confer with your buddy and give me the word now."

"I'll call you back." Joe hung up the telephone.

The people in the lobby looked soggy, tired beyond normal fatigue. Sam's crisp ice-cream suit had started to soften into mashed potatoes. He had begun by looking elegant and sad. Now he looked messed-up and happy.

All of them look like shit, Joe thought, and so do I, probably. This kind of caper took a lot out of you, starting with the starch.

He began to crave solitude. Too many people had been pressed up against him much too close for too long now. He wanted to be absolutely alone.

It wasn't just today, it was forever. First his mother, Flo, with her demands, entering his life like some huge tapeworm, curled up inside him sucking goodies from what he ate, wanting to know every little corner of his life, meet all his friends. Flo had a shit life of her own, so it was easy to see why she wanted to live Joe's for him. Okay, granted. But then there was Tina, slopping her meat all over him, drowning him, demanding, taking, swallowing even the air he was trying to breathe.

And now Lana, a cunt like the rest. No matter what kind of shit she dumped over your head, she was always ready to snuggle in under your armpit and gnaw away at the ribmeat. She was as phony as the rest of them, maybe worse, because she hadn't been born that way. She'd sort of molded herself into being that way, and, boy, she could show the real women a trick or two, huh? A trick or two in the "gimme" department? Shit, yes.

And now there was Sam, pressing in on him. Using this whole caper for what he wanted out of it, like a vampire sucking it dry. Money, yeah. But the chance to kill even more so.

Christ, these were all sickies. He didn't want any of them on his back. Lana was finished. No more Lana. She had just fallen off the earth, and good luck to her. Sam?

Baker could take Sam off his back, Joe mused. But

Sam betrayed was going to be even harder to handle than the way he was now, trusting and obedient.

"Well," Littlejoe began. "Here it is. They wheel up a Caddy and we lockstep into it. We're zipped out to the airport and the plane is waiting to go. Sam, you and I take the loot and Ellen. We board the plane. We take off. She's our good-conduct pass for the whole trip. Sorry about that," he added to the girl. "But you already told your kid good night. So you'll be back tomorrow sometime. With a bonus from the bank. And a bunch of red roses. And two weeks off to rest up. And maybe a deal from the newspapers and TV to pay for your experiences. So, like everybody else in this deal, you're coming out smelling like a rose. Whadya say, Sam?"

"I say let's go."

"One thing."

"Huh?"

"We're leaving Lana behind," Littlejoe said.

Sam's cupid mouth opened and closed. Then: "Man, you don't know how happy that makes me."

"I figured."

Joe picked up the telephone. But before he could dial, Sam's voice cut across his thoughts. "Christ, Littlejoe. It's your old lady!"

Joe turned to stare into the hot searchlights. There was some sort of commotion across the street. Two cops were trying to hold Flo, who was struggling to get free. "Aw, shit!" Joe yelled. "Put Ellen up front in the window, Sam. Hold the fucking gun against her. Keep your eye on me."

He dashed out the front door. A dozen muzzles zeroed in on his face, his heart, his abdomen. He stopped in his tracks at the curb. "Get her outa here!" he called across the street.

"Fag-got, fag-got, fag-got!"

Joe could feel the animal under his heart stir dangerously. He whirled on the crowd. "Shut up, you motherfuckers!"

"Faaa-guht!"

"Once more!" Joe screamed, "and the girl dies!"

Moretti was running toward him, holding a bull-horn. He reached the center stripe. "Quiet, you peo-ple!" His voice thundered down the street. "A woman will die if you don't shut up!"

The bullhorn's amplified voice echoed from the sides of the buildings.

"Fag-got, fag-got, fag-got!"

"Quiet!" Moretti shouted. "Quiet down! No more shouting!"

He waved the cops forward. "Shut 'em up!"

The police paused for an instant. Then they formed a loose wedge. They shoved forward into the crowd of people. Barricades toppled with shouting bystand-ers beneath them. A mounted cop charged, club swinging.

Three burly civilians picked up pieces of a shat-tered wooden barricade. They began swinging them at the cops. One found a sharp splinter of wood. He drove it like a lance at the mounted policeman's horse. A shower of empty beer cans rattled down. There were cries and screams from the crowd.

Joe stood there, mouth open. It was hard to believe what he was seeing. He glanced back at Sam, standing in the bank window. The kid was holding his gun to Ellen's head. Joe saw that the girl had fainted. Sam was actually holding her erect.

A television crew of cameraman, sound man, and reporter was cut off. A small flying squad of onlook-ers had looped past them. They were trying to escape the flailing clubs of the police. The civilians began to beat up the TV crew. A phalanx of cops drove through the swirling mob and rescued them.

Two men were slugged unconscious. They were handcuffed and dragged away. Joe saw Baker and two of his FBI underlings. They stood in the doorway of the insurance office. They conferred briefly, but remained where they stood. A rock hit Moretti on the cheek. Blood started to run down his face in a thin trickle.

He touched his cheek. He inspected his fingers and held the bloody hand in the air. With his other hand he brought the bullhorn to his face. "All right!" His voice boomed out over the melee. "Everybody cool it." The shouting began to die away. "We have an important announcement," Moretti said then.

Joe heard the noise almost shut itself off, as if a door had been closed. Even cops in the act of swinging clubs held back, posing, clubs above their heads.

Moretti dabbed at his cheek with a handkerchief. The bleeding had stopped. He nodded to the crowd and put away the bullhorn.

"Thank you for your courteous cooperation," he said then, in such a tone that the crowd began to laugh. Moretti walked back to Joe. "Make sure Sam doesn't do anything sudden."

"He's okay. It's them that went crazy, not Sam."

"Them?" Moretti jerked his thumb over his shoulder at the quiet crowd. "Who are you to call them crazy, Joe? Listen, we got your mother over there. I guess you saw her before. You don't have to talk to her if you don't want."

"I don't want."

"Okay. It was Baker's idea you might want to."

"Guys like Baker," John said, "think like the shit they print in the *Reader's Digest*."

Moretti laughed. "I'll tell him what you said."

"Listen."

"Yeah?"

"I guess I better say hello to her."

Moretti's eyes went wide. "Now you're talking like Baker. Hold on a minute." He returned to the insurance office and went inside. But it was Baker who escorted Flo out onto the street and brought her to the center line. Her face was streaked with crying, mouth set in a half smile. Her hair hadn't been combed in a while. It looked damp with heat. The crowd began to murmur sympathetically.

"Oh, Christ," Joe said, "who needs this shit?"

They stood there a yard apart and looked at each other. "What are you doing down here, Flo? You should've watched it on TV like everybody else." She continued to stand there, and, abruptly, more tears welled up. In the glare of the searchlights they could be seen coursing down her long cheeks. "I don't need you down here," Joe said.

"You didn't tell me," his mother said at last, "that you needed money."

"I need three grand for an operation for Lana. What're you saying, you got three grand?"

"I got two hundred and fifty in savings. I—"

"That only pays for the castration."

"What's the matter with her the way she is, then?" Flo asked. "Didn't you marry her the way she was? That lovely ceremony down in the Village? Why does she have to get operated on?"

"Please. I'm going away on the plane. I don't want to think of you and Lana arguing. You're supposed to take care of each other."

"I told them you were a wonderful boy. Never any trouble."

"Told who?"

"The FBI. They're very nice men, Joe. They understand. I told them about Goldwater. I said you were never a faggot, never."

"And they said?"

"That you had problems and they understood, and if you came out you'd get the best possible treatment because you protected the hostages."

"Beautiful. Next they'll send in Tina against me. The heavy team."

"She comes down here, so help me, I'm gonna mash her brains in," his mother told him. "Everything in your life was sunlight and roses until you met her. Since then, forget it."

"Please get off Tina."

"Me? God forbid I say anything against that fat cunt."

"Flo!"

"I knew you wouldn't need a . . . a thing like Lana if Tina was treating you right."

"Ma, this is old stuff."

"Come out of that bank."

"I can't. Sam will kill them all."

"Then run."

"Run? Christ! What dreams you live on!" He tried to cool it. "Did Pop come down?"

"No, he's really pissed off. He says he don't have no son."

"He's right. No more punching bag. He used to whale the living shit out of me. Five years old, he clobbered me with a broom handle. Why did you let him do that, Flo?"

Her tearful eyes went wide. "He's your father, Joe. He was doing it for your own good. To make you tough."

"Five years old, I'm walking across the room, he lets me have it behind the head. Wham! 'That's for nothing,' he tells me."

"To show you it's a tough life."

"It is with sons of bitches like you and him walking around."

Her lips trembled. She said nothing for a moment, and then, with an apologetic smile, she said: "I remember how beautiful you were as a little boy. I had such hopes."

Joe pulled back as if she had spit at him. "Fuck you. Fuck your hopes." He turned, and was about to run back into the bank.

"Wait," Flo called. "Lana wants to go with you."

Littlejoe stopped, his back still to her. "She what?"

"Isn't this all for her?" his mother asked.

As he turned back to her, Joe saw that Baker was leading Lana out into the street. The hooting of the crowd went into falsetto. The whole scene was weird, Joe thought. Not to be believed. Everybody was getting off his rocks like some kind of amateur night, stepping out into the spotlights to play their musical saw or sing "Stardust" or whatever turned them on and made them walk tall. Jesus, he thought, people!

"Littlejoe, honey," Lana was saying, "I humbly apologize for all that shit I dumped on your poor head before. I know you got a lot on your mind right now, but—"

"But you wanna fly to Casablanca free, right?" Joe cut in.

His glance went to Baker for a moment, and if ever he'd seen a man pretending not to be there, the FBI guy was it. His eyes were averted, although he had a hell of a grip on Lana's skinny arm.

"Did I say that, lovie?" Lana simpered. She had fixed up her face a little, and looked halfway presentable now. "I just want to go where you go."

For the first time, Littlejoe began to feel that maybe there really was a million dollars, really was a plane waiting. He'd believed Moretti only because he wanted to, but in the back of his mind he'd been worried. Now he believed. If Lana was ready to suck up to him in this outrageous way, even using his stupid mother to help, there really must be ransom and an escape ready to go.

"Kiss, kiss!" someone in the crowd shouted.

It came with such force that Joe flinched. He supposed the guy had heard him say that to Moretti. Now it seemed to be the slogan for today.

"Forget it," he told Lana. "You come along, it makes you part of the job, accessory. Right now you're clean. They might get you for wearing too-high heels, but you're clean on the bank job. Right, Baker?"

The man who was trying not to be there nodded once, then decided he had to say something. "That is correct."

"So no loot, no Casablanca, baby," Joe told Lana.

"I'll mail you a check from somewhere sometime." He started to laugh at the look on her face.

"Kiss, kiss!" a bystander yelled.

Joe reached for Lana. Baker, startled, started to pull her back. "It's okay," Littlejoe assured him. "Just following orders." He planted a big kiss on Lana's wide-rouged mouth.

The crowd went insane. There were no cries of "faggot!" but simply the kind of wild cheering that accompanies a home run at Shea Stadium. Joe stepped back from Lana and lifted his second finger upward at the crowd. For some reason this drove them to even noisier heights of cheering. Grinning now, and flushed, Joe turned and headed back into the bank.

★ 23

"LADIES AND GENTLEMEN," Joe said, addressing the damp, tired group inside the bank.

Sam in his wilted white suit, still looked the nattiest, but Boyle, without a tie, looked like a bum, and Marge, with her blouse half open, looked like a tramp, Joe noticed. Ellen's eyes kept rolling up into her head from time to time, and Maria, the Puerto Rican woman, continued to say almost nothing. Joe had never figured out—nor had the inclination to check—whether she understood everything that was going on or not. In either event, smart girl, she kept a low profile.

"Gang," Littlejoe went on, clowning slightly, "here's the game plan. We are now dealing directly with the Feds. That man out there in the gray suit who don't sweat, he's now handling everything and all of a sudden we got no problems."

"What's that supposed to mean?" Sam asked. His voice sounded huffy, as if Joe had insulted him.

"I mean we're home free. The limo from the airport'll be here any minute and—"

"And you're taking Lana with us," Sam finished for him, his voice dead with pain.

"Sam. Come on. I kissed her off. No Lana. Goodbye Lana. Finished." Littlejoe waited until Sam's face showed a little less pain. "Would you believe it? We're ten, fifteen minutes away from freedom. I could call anybody in the whole world, an astronaut, the Pope, any of them. Who do I call?" he asked, dialing a number. He waited. Then:

"Tina?"

"Hey, Joey!" Tina's glutinous voice was hopping with excitement. "I'm watching it all on the TV, Joey!"

"I want to talk to the kids."

"They're at Stella's. I sent them over there. Too much excitement." Tina ran out of breath for a moment, gasped, then rattled on: "Jesus, Joey, I can't believe what I see. It's not you. You never hurt anybody in your life."

"Tina, I'm in trouble here," Joe said slowly. "It's very touchy from here on in," he added, thinking of the way they wanted to pick off Sam but wouldn't really worry too much if they shot him too.

"I blame myself," Tina surged on, hardly listening. "You been tense. I knew that. Like leaving me at your folks' house last week. Boy, what a wasted evening. And swiping my father's car. I could tell—"

"Shut up!" Joe shouted into the phone. "Will you for once shut your fucking mouth and listen?"

"See?" she countered. "You're screaming already with the language. A person can't communicate with you. You're a stranger in your own house."

Joe held the telephone away from his ear. He glanced at Boyle. "I needed this?"

Boyle shrugged. "You dialed the number."

Littlejoe put the telephone back to his ear. ". . . because you hurt me," Tina was saying. "God, how you hurt me. Can you imagine, kissing that . . . thing? In front of the TV an' all. Did I ever once turn you down, or anything?"

"Tina."

"Did I ever say no, you should get so horny you have to turn to a, to a—"

"Tina."

"What?"

"Come down here, will you?" Joe asked.

"Me?" She shrieked so loudly he had to take the phone away for a moment. "Me get-shot? You should see it on the TV, Joey. It's gruesome, I mean it. It's scary, all them cops and machine guns and cannons and God knows what. You never did have any feeling for what another person is feeling, Joe. You never had a drop of compassion. All my life, I—"

He slammed the telephone down on her voice.

Outside the crowd had begun to chant something rhythmic. Littlejoe couldn't get the gist of it. He went to the door and poked his head out into the street. The air was cooler. Now he could see that behind the mob at one end of the street was a new group of bystanders, holding placards, one of which read:

GAY IS BEAUTIFUL!

As the new people caught sight of Littlejoe, one young man shouted: "Joe! Joe! You are gorgeous, Joe!"

Littlejoe stepped back into the shelter of the doorway as a TV crew rushed over to film a confrontation between the young man who had shouted and some older onlookers who were telling him to get lost.

"I don't care!" the young man was screaming at the top of his voice. "That man has put an end to all that pansy limp-wrist shit. You know what I hope? I hope he shoots it out with the cops. I hope he takes some with him."

Behind him a group of six young men and two young women were busily hoisting a longer banner into place, suspended from three poles. When they finally got it arranged it read:

WE LOVE YOU, LITTLEJOE!

Joe grinned and waved at them until the cameramen noticed him and their lenses swung around to record his reaction shot. An instant later the banner wavered and dropped as some of the original by-standers charged it and knocked it down.

Joe stepped back inside the bank. "Folks, this is my day!" he exulted. "Did you see that banner?"

"Who could miss it?" Marge asked. "What I want to see is the airport limo."

The grin faded from Joe's face. In all the excitement he had forgotten that the arrival of the limo would be the moment of greatest danger. He was determined to doublecross Baker and, by putting Sam in the middle of the line of people getting into the car, to protect him from sharpshooters.

At the same time he knew that, with orders to shoot, the snipers might try to pick Sam off anyway. Chances were not, but you never knew with real killer types. That meant someone else would get it, probably the one in front or behind Sam. It wasn't an easy decision to make.

"What's up?" Boyle asked, watching his face.

"Nothing."

"Something."

"Nothing. Say, tell me, you got a notary?"

Marge held up her hand. "I'm the notary. You want to, uh . . ." Her voice died away. The inside of the bank was unusually quiet, although outside the two sections of the crowd were busily screaming at each other. It had an odd effect on Joe, as if what was happening in here, amid deadly silence, was a matter of life and death. Which it was, of course.

"Lemme dictate it," he told Marge. "You write it. I sign it. You notarize it, okay?"

"Shoot, I mean, uh, go ahead."

"Start it off with all that being-of-sound-mind-and-body shit, okay?"

Marge drew a piece of paper and pen to her and began to write. "Go ahead."

"To my darling wife, Lana, I leave three thousand

from my life-insurance policy for a sex-change operation. Got that?"

"Operation. Right."

"To my sweet wife, Tina, I leave the rest of the insurance, seven gran—seven thousand, to take care of my children and make sure they remember me."

". . . member me. Right."

"To my mother . . ." Joe stopped and sighed. "You never understood me, even though you tried. I'm me. I'm different. I leave you my stamp collection. It's worth something."

The bank lobby was terribly quiet, except for faint shouting from outside. Sam had come over to listen to the dictating of the will. He nodded now and then, as if in approval.

"I want a military funeral," Joe said, "to which I am entitled free of charge. God bless everyone till we are joined in the hereafter, sweet Lana, my Tina, dearest Lori and Larry and my mother." He fell silent for a moment. "Okay. Lemme sign it."

"Littlejoe," Sam said then in a small voice, "it's a will, ain't it?"

"Right."

"You ain't gonna die."

"No way of knowing that, Sam, baby. It's a long flight over water." He turned to the rest of them. "And just when I let my Blue Cross lapse."

"Nobody's getting killed," Boyle said. "We're going to do just what we're told to do and nobody's going to shoot, either, not you boys and not the men outside."

"From your lips to Baker's ear," Littlejoe intoned. He was feeling great now. Dictating the will had cheered him up a lot. He turned to Sam and clapped him on the shoulder. "You wanna make your will, man? I know a cute notary does it cheap."

"A will? Me?"

"Your folks're still around."

For the first time in several hours, Sam's mouth

turned up slightly at one corner, in what was for him a bit of a smile. "Fuck 'em."

"Got that?" Joe asked Marge.

"Smart-ass," she responded primly, shaking her head. She handed him his will, and when he had signed it she stamped the bottom of the page, filled in the stamped legend, signed it, and embossed a seal over the whole inscription. "I'd like to see somebody break *that* will," she said then.

She folded it twice and started to hand it to Joe. He refused to take it. She looked around her, confused. Then, finally, she tucked it into a Number Ten envelope and sealed it. On the outside she wrote "To Whom It May Concern," and propped it on her telephone. "There."

Joe found himself wondering how to line up everyone when the limo came. He decided not to try, but just to make sure Sam was protected. He had no illusions that, once they shot Sam, he himself would have the guts to keep going. He had started Sam in motion originally, but Sam was now keeping the whole job moving. Boyle had read something of his worries from his face.

Sam now moved closer to him, as if what he had to say was not for other ears. "It's like the crunch, huh, man?"

Littlejoe brightened for a moment at the business-like sound of the word. "Yeah, crunch," he said. "But between us, baby, we're too tough to crumble, right?"

Sam shrugged, a neat, minimal gesture. "Either that or a lot of other people crumble with us."

Joe nodded vigorously. "Right, baby. Right." He could hear how false his own voice sounded. Joe wondered why he was bothering to protect Sam now, when, obviously, he'd already decided to sell him out in some other way. But delay the moment. Put off the betrayal. Not now. Not in front of people like Boyle and Marge, who thought he was pretty hot stuff.

Christ, if only Moretti were back in charge. The detective stood for something you could deal with, the thing that kept this crummy city turning over, without which it would have frozen into a pile of ice: compromise. That was what New York was all about. You never brought things to a total face-off. You always left room to maneuver. Baker didn't understand that, never would. Dealing with Baker got things done fast, all right. But sometimes you didn't want speed.

"Sweet Jesus, here it is," Ellen moaned. Her huge eyes protruded slightly as she stared out the window of the bank.

Littlejoe turned to see a long black Cadillac limousine, six doors, luggage rack on the roof, moving slowly through the crowd and into the center of the combat zone. It had been hurriedly requisitioned from somewhere, and the side of the vehicle still bore a garishly lettered sign reading:

TOTAL RELAXATION BATHS—
OUR HOSTESSES MAKE LIFE WORTH
LIVING—24 HOURS NO WAITING

Joe went to the window to stare at the vehicle of his release.

Baker, Moretti, and several other men were converging on the limousine as the driver got out. He stood, confused for a moment, holding a clipboard. He was a tall black in broad Afro hairdo and a sleeveless sheepskin jacket, dark glasses and pants with a flare as wide as an evening skirt. Joe noticed that his boots had rhinestone buckles. He went outside and moved toward the driver.

"Keep back," he yelled at the FBI and police.

The driver held out his clipboard. "You the relief driver, man?" Joe asked.

Joe moved past him and began lifting seats, searching under them for bombs or guns. He checked the glove compartment, then moved into the capacious rear of the limo.

"Hey, man, like, somebody gotta sign me out, you know?"

"Stick with me," Joe muttered. "Help me with these seats."

Together they searched a while longer. "What's all the pig doing out after dark?" the driver asked then.

"Some guys are holding up this bank."

"No shit? They still in there?"

"Guns," Joe assured him solemnly. "Hostages. Smile, you're on TV."

"I be goddamned." Joe gave him a long, slow smile, and the driver's eyes lit up. "Hey! You the bandit, right?"

"Yeah."

"Shee-it." He glanced around for the cameras.

"Fun, huh?" Joe asked. "Here, lemme sign your sheet." He did so and handed it back to the driver. "That was on TV, too."

"Oh, man, I gonna remember you."

"I hope somebody does."

Baker had moved in closer with a younger man beside him, who was wearing the same shade of gray suit. "This is Murphy," Baker said. "He drives you to JFK." He jerked his thumb at the driver. "Take off, buddy."

Two cops hustled the black driver away. Joe eyed his replacement. Murphy, like his boss, had the knack of seeming not to be there. He didn't actually look at Joe, but at a point to one side of him. Although his hair was not gray, like Baker's, it probably would be some day. He had already mastered the trick of not sweating. It probably came from knowing that he had a license to do anything he wanted in this world and call it justified.

Joe pictured him killing. He looked even better at it than Sam. "No way. Not this one. I want him." Joe indicated the original driver.

"I can't allow that," Baker said.

"*You* can't allow! I'm running this show. Get this bastard out of here and get the dude's black ass back over here. Now!"

The cops were hustling the black driver back. "Hey," he was protesting. "No way, man. Not me."

"You," Joe said, sealing his fate.

He turned to the gay demonstrators, who had raised the big banner again, waved, and blew them a kiss. A roar went up from the homosexual contingent. One of the TV crews, standing on top of a van, had missed the whole thing.

"Hey, Joe," the cameraman shouted. "One more time."

Joe nodded, smiled, waited until the telephoto lens was trained on him, then gave him the old Sicilian up-yours sign, ramming his right arm forward and chopping his left against it. Both sections of the crowd, gay and straight, burst into helpless laughter. He turned back in time to find Baker and Murphy with identical looks of disapproval on their bland faces.

"Just drive us to JFK," Joe told the black driver.

"Do I got a choice?"

"No."

The driver eyed Baker, who, reluctantly, nodded. Littlejoe then patted down the driver in a rather professional way, checking his pockets and lingering long enough on the inside of his groin to start another chorus of sucking noises from the original bystander group. In a pocket, Joe came across a small decorated bottle with silver miniature spoon attached by a chain, a coke-sniffer's kit. He glanced at it and then at the driver, whose eyes had widened apprehensively.

"Not on duty, man, right?" Joe asked.

"Right."

Joe shoved the bottle out of sight and slapped the

driver's rump. "You're gonna do fine, baby." He turned to Baker. "I'm ready."

"Remember," Baker said grimly, "they come out lockstep and Sam is last. Don't forget that."

The driver rolled his eyes. "You mens shoot, you aim for white meat, dig?"

Joe smiled at him. There was still a remnant of the smile as he turned to Baker and Murphy. "Tell him how to get there."

"Just follow me. That gray Ford." Baker frowned at Joe. "What about the third perpetrator? There was a third man inside there with you."

"Eddie? He's sleeping it off in the vault. He's out of it, Baker."

Littlejoe walked back into the bank. Everyone looked up. "This is it," Joe said. He watched Sam straighten the knot in his tie. "That's right, baby. Show them you cared enough to wear the very best. Marge, tuck in those luscious titties." He watched her quickly button up the front of her blouse, which had been open because of the heat.

"Boyle, you're a mess."

The manager got to his feet and tucked his shirt more firmly into his belt. "Can't let down the old Chase image."

Joe shook his head pityingly. "Still Chasing rainbows, huh?"

"What else is there?"

"I don't know, Boyle. My life could end in the next five minutes. Nobody gives a shit if I live or die. I bust my gut and nothing do I get back in this life. Even tonight, I mean, who knows what'll happen?"

Boyle rubbed his chin. As he talked, he raked his fingers nervously through his sparse hair, in lieu of a comb. "What makes you so special, Joe? We're all pissed off at life. Kids get sick and die. The roof leaks. I cheat on my wife. The dog gets run over. Joe, it's one long tale of disaster, not only here, all over. Bombings, famine, earthquakes, napalm. The name

of the whole thing is life, Joe. So stop your bitching."

In the silence that followed, Marge cleared her
throat. "Another cigarette, please, somebody."

"No more," Sam said.

"Okay," Joe shouted, "let's snap into it. We form
a line and we close it up very tight. Everybody takes
a left step at the same time. Then a right. We move
into the back of the car. There's plenty of room."

"In what order?" Boyle asked.

Outside the crowd was yelling for action. The gay
demonstrators were chanting, "Say it clear. Say it
loud. I'm gay and I'm proud."

"Well?" Boyle persisted.

Littlejoe knew he was biting his lower lip. He
tried to stop it. Didn't look right at this point for him
to seem that nervous. "Boyle, you're so eager, you
lead off the line."

Boyle nodded and went to the open door of the
bank. The limo stood about three yards from the
door, nine or ten feet in which a sniper could chew
Sam to chunks.

"Okay, a few more people and Sam. Then a few
more and me. I come at the tail end."

Sam was shaking his head. His big, dark eyes looked
very solemn; his cupid's-bow mouth was tight with
tension. "Boyle first, then Ellen, then me," he said.
"That makes sense. But then, like, Maria and then
you, Joe, and Marge at the end."

"No, that's okay."

"Marge at the end," Sam insisted, "or we don't go."

"Why Marge?"

"Okay, anybody but you or me. Make it Boyle."

"I'll bring up the rear," Marge volunteered.

"You don't know what you're saying," Littlejoe
began. "It's a—"

"I'm bringing up the rear," she announced firmly.
"That puts the two senior bank people at the front
and back of the line."

"Hey, man," the driver called through the open door. "I am sweating a whole lot out here."

"We're coming," Joe promised him. "Sam?"

"Let's go." He moved behind Ellen and shoved her up against Boyle. Then, very ostentatiously, Sam brought the .45 automatic up to her ear. "Let's go, man," he repeated shakily. A rim of white showed all the way around his irises. "Let's for shit's sake go."

THE HEAVY PLATE-GLASS DOOR of the bank was
propped open. Littlejoe saw snipers on rooftops
begin to nestle in for a steady shot, the muzzles of
their high-powered rifles cradled on bits of coping.
With the caliber and charge of the slugs they were
using in the interests of accuracy, a bullet could easily
tear through two people front to back.

The sandwich took one step forward, unsteadily.
Joe realized he'd have to count cadence if he was
ever to get all of them in step. His life and Sam's—all
their lives, in fact—depended on being squeezed
tightly together. He saw that Sam had rammed himself
up against Ellen's tight little behind as closely as if
she were a boy.

"Halt!" he called. "When I say 'left,' everybody
moves their left foot one step forward." He remembered a wisecrack from Nam. "You all know which
one is your left foot?"

"Come on, Littlejoe." Sam's voice sounded agonized. Maybe he knew what the problem was, Joe
thought, maybe he didn't. Either way, he was tense,
and it wasn't good when Sam got tense.

"Okay, left. Right. Left. Right. Halt."

They paused for a moment just outside the bank.
Boyle was within a yard of the open limo door.
Marge, in the rear, was a yard from the bank door.
Joe had draped Sam's jacket over the middle of the
line, from his head forward over Maria's, Sam's, and
Ellen's. He hoped it would confuse matters, but he

doubted it. He took a deep breath. The smell of fresh bread had begun to nauseate him.

"Joe, for shit's sake, Joe," Sam muttered in a tight undertone. "Let's move it, Joe. Move it."

The sound of panic turned Sam's voice into a staccato burst, like a machine gun being fired in short bursts. "Left," Joe called, "right, left, halt." Boyle inside. "Okay. Left. Sam, this is it."

"Quick, man, f-f-Chrissake, quick."

"Ellen and Sam. In! Move! Go!"

There was a moment of silence. The sandwich that remained consisted of Maria, Joe, and Marge. "Nowicki!" Baker's voice thundered over a bullhorn. As he had from the very beginning, the FBI man pronounced Joe's name correctly. Not like a Polack, Joe told himself now, but close enough.

Littlejoe had retained Sam's vanilla-colored jacket. It was draped over Maria and himself now. He held the carbine cradled in his left arm, his left hand raised to hold the jacket in place.

"Nowicki!"

He knew what was bugging Baker. The Feebie hated to be doublecrossed. He thought he'd made a deal for Joe to sell out Sam. Slowly, letting go of the hem of Sam's jacket for a moment, Littlejoe extended his arm in the air and proffered his second finger to Baker in a last salute. The crowd loved it.

"Okay," he muttered in Maria's ear, "this is our turn, *querida*. Ready, Marge?"

"Any readier and I'd pee in my pants."

"Snuggle up. Here goes. Left, right, left, right, in!" The three of them tumbled into the rear of the limo and slammed the door shut.

Joe dropped the carbine on the floor and produced Leroy's .38, which he held to Marge's head. "Roll down the window."

When she had he turned to Sam. The muzzle of the Colt .45 automatic had never left Ellen's temple. In his near panic Sam had pressed the blued metal so tightly to her skin that an angry red showed just beyond the outer corner of her eye. "Home free, Sam," Littlejoe told him.

"Let's move this thing, man. We ain't home free yet."

The wideness of Sam's eyes bothered Littlejoe. Cautiously he leaned forward to the open window. "Move it out, Baker!" he shouted. "Otherwise they die right here in the limo!"

"Aw, naw!" the driver said. "No shooting, man. Give me a break."

"Tell Baker," Joe suggested.

"Can we start moving?" the driver called out from his window.

"Otherwise, he's got a hell of a laundry bill," Joe added in a carrying voice. The crowd broke up with laughter. But the gray Ford refused to budge.

"Please?" the driver called. "I ain't too proud to beg."

The Ford's right-hand door opened and Moretti got out into the glare of the searchlights. As he had when Joe first saw him, hours ago, he gave his cocoa-straw hat a tidy little tug. He moved slowly toward the black Cadillac limo and came to a halt by the open window.

"Joe," he said then. "You got Baker so pissed off, he's going to welsh on the deal."

"What deal?" Sam snapped.

"You see?" Joe told the detective. "Why did you let that fucking Feebie in on the act?"

"I had no choice, Joe." Moretti's eyes searched for his for some sign that they were talking the same language. The brilliant lights picked out hot stars amid the beads of sweat on his forehead. "This is a national bank. Heisting it's a federal rap. They let the local cops try their hand, but once they decide to take charge, that's it. I warned you. I said if you didn't cooperate with me, you'd be up against the Feds. How does it feel?"

Littlejoe moistened his lips. It was even hotter inside the limo than it had been on the street. "Driver," he called, "are we air-conditioned? Turn it on, man."

"I thought you'd never ask." The motor turned over, and a moment later cool air began to filter back into the rear of the limo.

"Listen, Moretti," Joe said then. "There is no way Baker would ever get a real man to do what he wanted. There is no human being that low. You know it. I know it. Only Baker don't know it."

The detective paused a moment before speaking. "That's all water over the dam. We're past that now. We're into a new phase."

"Which means?"

Moretti produced a deep Calabrese shrug, lifted up from his very toes. "Only Baker can tell you that."

"Cut the shit, man," Sam said. His teeth had started to chatter faintly. "Cut the talk. Let's move. Otherwise this kid dies."

"They all die," Joe told Moretti. "Tell that one to Baker."

The detective's glance went past Joe to Sam's face. He stared for a long moment. Then he turned and went back to the gray Ford. He got in and slammed the door. Joe rolled up the Caddy window.

"This is the coolest I've been for hours," Marge commented. "Harry," she said, "are we going to last the night?"

The manager sat huddled in a corner of the first rear seat. Sam sat in the middle and Ellen sat on the far end, slumped back against the seat as if she'd been thrown there. "Ask Joe," Boyle suggested.

"Ask Baker," Joe corrected him.

"Let's move, Littlejoe," Sam chattered. "Let's moo-ove."

"Amen, brother," the driver added.

The four people from the bank, Joe, Sam, and the driver now turned forward to watch the gray Ford.

Joe could only guess what was going on inside between Moretti and Baker. Minutes passed.

"Hey, getcha cold beer here!" a vendor chanted.

"We love you, Littlejoe!" a woman's voice yelled.

"Kiss, kiss!"

"Kiss, kiss!"

"Kiss, kiss!"

At last, slowly, as if reluctant to move, the gray Ford began to inch forward toward the far end of the street. Uniformed police cleared a path through the crowd.

"Hot shit," the driver said. "Here we go."

He let the heavy car inch forward. At the other end of the street the police relaxed their guard, and bystanders began to swarm into what had once been the combat zone. The Caddy moved slowly through a thickening crowd of people, like a whale through sprats. Joe glanced left and right, alert to a possible trick. But what could they do now? The moment to have picked them off was past.

Standing between two uniformed cops, Lana leaned forward and made a kissing face, her over-rouged lips opening and closing. Joe failed to respond. The limo was moving slowly, a few feet at a time. Flo's face loomed on the opposite side of the car. She too pantomimed "kiss, kiss." Joe faced forward. "How about some speed, man?" he called to the driver.

"Any second now."

A young gay demonstrator began running beside the limo as it picked up speed. He was carrying a hand-lettered sign:

WE LOVE, LOVE, LOVE YOU, JOE!

Littlejoe stared straight ahead at the tail lights of the gray Ford. A moment later they had turned out of the block and onto a side street that led to Queens Boulevard. A revolving red beacon on top of the gray

Ford began to turn slowly, twiddling long beams of red light. There was a low growl of nearby sirens. Two cops on motorcycles began to keep pace with the limo, one on each side.

Now they were moving along Queens Boulevard as if in a dream, no traffic, not even bystanders. Apparently the entire route had been cleared by traffic cops. Joe saw some of them standing on overpasses, glowering at the small cavalcade of cars and motorcycles.

They were in Rego Park now, his home. Up ahead a TV van was parked on the parallel service road. A camera with a long lens followed the Ford and the Cadillac as they swept past. Tina would be watching, of course, Joe thought, but she didn't even have to haul her droopy ass to the window. She could see it all on the tube.

They were speeding through Forest Hills, past delicatessens, Chinese restaurants, bagel bakeries, a movie theater. Now they were in Kew Gardens. Never in his life had Littlejoe moved so quickly through the borough of his birth. It was as if, in saying good-bye, the whole place was flashing before his eyes.

"Man, this is slick," the driver was saying. "I'm doing sixty-five."

Sam produced a peculiar noise from somewhere in his throat. Joe realized it was Sam's chuckle. "I feel better." Sam said then. "Don't you feel better, Littlejoe?"

"We all feel better," Boyle cut in.

"Baker don't feel better," Joe amended.

The gray Ford swerved right onto the approaches to the Van Wyck Expressway. The cavalcade edged over, road by road, and sped toward the airport. Green-and-white signs heralded its approach. They were only a few miles away, speeding through the hot night from Kew Gardens into Jamaica.

Up ahead, the sign for the airport loomed big. The gray Ford turned into a cloverleaf that led to the

Belt Parkway, but before it could feed into the arter-
ial the car swerved into a service road that ran along-
side a high cyclone fence. A moment later it slowed
at an open gate, manned by four armed airport
guards. It turned in, and the limo followed closely
behind. The motorcycles fell back. The sirens were
silent.

Littlejoe peered into the darkness ahead. They
seemed to be on some sort of deserted runway. He
could see a plane standing there in the distance, but
he couldn't tell what kind it was. Suddenly the gray
Ford stopped.

"What now?" Joe asked nobody in particular.

"I'm stopping, man," the driver told him.

After the long burst of turnpike speed, the sudden
stop felt strange to Joe. He had been lulled by the
speed. Now all the old anxieties swarmed over him
again. "What're they doing?"

"They're out of the car," Boyle said. "They're, uh,
talking on those little radios."

"Can I leave you gentlemen and ladies now?" the
driver asked.

"Shit you can, man."

"I got a nice life," the driver went on, more to himself than to anyone in the car. "I got a nice young
chick for an old lady. Everybody meets me likes me.
I feel real good with my life, you know? I just want
it to go on, man."

"Nobody's interested," Joe told him.

"Look!" Sam yelped.

The landing lights of the plane had been turned
on. Now the immense craft was taxiing toward them.
It looked huge, with its four engines, a 707 or DC-8,
Joe decided, more than enough range for an ocean
hop.

"It's there, Sam!"

Joe watched Baker striding toward the limo.
When he got to the Caddy, Joe had rolled the window partway down. "There's your jet, Nowicki. I

want your hostages now."

"Kiss, kiss!"

"I want your hostages or you don't get the jet."

"Then you get dead hostages."

"I cannot let a multi-million-dollar aircraft out of my authority without some sign from you that you're willing to respect our arrangement."

"Oh." Joe thought about it for a minute. "Okay, Baker, take Boyle and Marge." He nudged Marge. "Out of the car, baby. It was great fun, but it was just one of those things. Boyle, move."

The two older bank people moved stiffly. Now Joe's gun was pressed to Maria's head, and Sam's continued to bore into Ellen's temple. "Baker," Littlejoe called, "these two young ladies are mothers of small children. You—"

"You only need one of them, Nowicki."

"Two is better than one."

Marge and Boyle stood outside now, watching the interchange. Baker snapped something at a subordinate, who stepped forward to lead the two bank people away. "No," Marge said. "These are my girls. I'm not leaving till I see how this works out."

"Marge," Littlejoe said, "you know I gotta do it this way."

"You don't need both of them," she argued. "Give me Ellen. My God, hasn't she been through enough? She's out on her feet."

"That makes it easier to handle her." Littlejoe watched Sam for a moment in the strange half light coming from the aircraft's landing lamps. He knew what would happen if he took Ellen away from Sam. They were welded. They were one. Ellen represented Sam's only chance of keeping alive and out of jail.

"Baker," he called, "where's the money? Pass over the ransom and you get Maria."

The FBI man conferred briefly with his assistant, who left for the gray Ford. "Where's Moretti?" Joe asked idly.

"He's not in charge," Baker reminded him. "I am."

"Think he'll make lieutenant?"

"I wouldn't know anything about that."

"You wouldn't? I think once you turn in your report, he'll be lucky if they let him keep his sergeant's stripes."

The other FBI man returned with a valise, which he handed to Baker. "It's all here," Baker said, handing it through the car window.

Littlejoe snapped open the valise. He spent a moment contemplating the banded packets of tens and twenties. So far so good. He wondered about letting Maria go, but realized abruptly that he had to let her go sometime. So long as Sam's .45 was pressed to Ellen's head, there was no real worry, was there?

"Okay," he told Maria. "*Vamos ahora.*"

As she left the car, Littlejoe could see that, all along, she had been holding her rosary beads. She stood next to Baker and looked back into the car. "I am praying for you," she said then.

"Thanks, Maria."

"I am praying you have a safe flight."

"You're a good kid," Joe told her. He watched a faceless FBI man in a gray suit escort her off the runway into the hot, empty night.

"It's you and me, Sam," Joe mused aloud. When Sam said nothing, he glanced at him. "Okay, baby? We're in."

"It's getting out of the car that bugs me," Sam said. His teeth had started to chatter again.

"No problems," Joe said. "You move her out when I start to move out. Just keep a grip on her and a grip on the Colt and we're home free."

Nobody spoke for a while. The driver cleared his throat. "Listen," he said then, "maybe I can split this car before you mens do. Okay?"

"No way," Littlejoe decreed. "Ready, Sam?"

"Ready."

Joe started to move out of his door of the car. At

the same time, Sam pushed Ellen out their door on the same side of the limo.

Baker reached for Joe, as if to steady him. Another FBI man reached for Ellen. The driver turned halfway around in his seat to face the rear.

There was a gun in the driver's hand.

"Sam!"

Baker was yanking Joe off balance. The other man pulled Ellen toward him. Sam's gun lost contact with her temple for an instant.

The driver fired point-blank.

Sam's head flipped back. A great splash of blood spouted into the air. Littlejoe hit the asphalt runway face first.

The driver fired again. The top of Sam's head flew off. Hair and brains spattered the inside of the Cadillac.

The .45 Colt automatic arced through the air and fell to the cushioned floor of the limo. Joe, twisting as he hit the runway, looked straight up into Sam's eyes. They were already dead.

He glanced at the driver and saw the muzzle of his .38 magnum S & W aimed at his face. "Shoot!" Joe screamed.

The driver's eye was lined up along the gun's sights, staring along the barrel directly into Joe's eyes.

"Shoot me, for Christ's sake!" Littlejoe shouted.

Baker reached down and locked Joe's hands behind his back. The driver lifted the gun, broke the cylinder, removed the unfired cartridges, closed the gate, and handed the gun butt first to Baker. "Tag it and file it," he said then.

Joe was lying face down on the soft surface of the asphalt, still hot from the long day. The tarry smell filled his nostrils. In the distance Moretti approached slowly, as if against his will. The driver got out of the car and stood next to Baker.

When Moretti came up, the three law-enforcement

officers stood there watching Joe. From his prone position, head craning up off the asphalt, they looked huge, like giants. Joe eyed the black driver. "You I won't forget."

"Yeah, well." The driver glanced at Baker. "We all gotta be somewhere." He walked away.

"And I won't forget you neither, prick," Littlejoe told Baker.

The FBI man's face didn't change at all. "You," he said then, as he started to walk off, "I've already forgotten."

Joe glared up at Moretti. "Walk," he ordered. "Walk away."

Moretti stared glumly down at him. "It's been a long day, Joe." He hunkered down on the asphalt, as if talking to a small child, his head just a foot or two above Joe's. He took off his hat and mopped his forehead with a bandanna. Then he put the hat back on and gave it a tug. He patted Joe's shoulder.

"My God, Moretti," Littlejoe burst out, "people!"

★ EPILOGUE

THE TELEVISION STUDIO was smaller than Flo had expected. She'd been brought here by special limo from the scene of the bank robbery, once the cars with Littlejoe and the FBI had left for the airport. Now the news was in. Sam was dead. Joe was unharmed. And in forty-five minutes the eleven-o'clock news would start to roll. Accordingly, they ushered Flo down a long hall to a small studio with two cameras, a desk, and two chairs.

The woman who was going to interview Flo was young and black. Her hair was done in a neat short-length Afro. She herself looked Italian to Flo, with a narrow, aquiline nose and big eyes. She looked like an Italian with a deep tan, but Flo refrained from telling her that.

"I'm Ann Anderson," she said, shaking Flo's hand. "And you are Mrs. Florence Nowicki? That's, uh, Polish, okay?"

Flo got the idea that to the colored all whites looked alike. "The name is Polish," she admitted. "My husband, Augie, he's Polish. Me, I'm Italian."

"Right," Ann Anderson said. "But, like, I mean, can you pronounce it correctly for me one time, okay?"

"No-wick-ee," Flo said.

"No-wick-ee?"

"No-wick-ee," Flo echoed weakly. "Are they taking our picture now?"

"Oh, no. It's, like, we're just talking a little up

front. Like I chat a little with you and then we do it again for TV, okay?"

Ann Anderson patted the underside of her Afro hairdo near her right ear. She shuffled some typed papers. "This Joe Nowickee is your son or your husband's?"

"The both," Flo responded. She was suddenly very self-conscious of her pronunciation, and she knew she was speaking sloppily. She knew she had actually said "Da boat," and it was because she was tired and upset and it was late in the night of a very bad day. She sat up straighter in her chair. "The both of us's kid," she said with great care.

"Right," Ann Anderson said. "And the first inkling you had of Joe's like, bizarre lifestyle was, like, this afternoon at the robbery, okay?"

Flo shook her head. "No."

Ann Anderson had been shuffling through papers. She now looked up, and Flo could tell that she was actually seeing this white woman for the first time. "You mean, like, you knew what kind of life he was leading?"

"If there is any human being on this here earth," Flo said with as much decisiveness as she could muster, "that I know what's inside of their head, it's my own dear son, who never once harmed nobody, and now he's going to jail. Sure." She stopped and sniffed. "Sure I knew what kind of life he was leading. I mean, my son never hid nothing from his mother. He was a good son. I was there both times, at both weddings."

Ann Anderson placed all the papers she was holding in a neat pile on the desk in front of her. She caught the eye of one of the cameramen and gave a small "not now" headshake. Then she placed her hands palms down on the desk, and with her eyes on the wall clock she said: "Mrs. Nowickee, maybe you better, like, start at the beginning, okay?"

"The beginning was when he married that cun—" Flo's mouth shut down tightly. She glanced around. No one seemed to have heard anything, least of all the black woman, whose eyes were fixed on the clock. The time, Flo saw, was a quarter to eleven.

"I was at both weddings, to Tina and to Lana," she said then.

"And you knew Lana was, like, a transvestite?"

"I don't know from that. I knew Lana was a fella," Flo admitted. "But there was a priest at the wedding. All right, maybe a faggot priest, and maybe it wasn't in no church, but I knew my son was gonna be happier with Lana than Tina had ever made him."

Ann Anderson opened her mouth and then closed it. After a moment, she opened it again. "I have a quote from your son's, uh, female wife." She started to rummage through the papers on her desk.

By now the small studio was crowded with technicians, about twice as many as necessary. In addition to two cameramen, helpers, and a boom man, people began to file in out of camera range and lean against the walls.

"Here," Ann Anderson said. "This is Tina Nowickee speaking. Quote: 'I know in my heart that my husband did not commit this crime. I mean, his body functions may have done it, but my real husband, deep in his heart, he is innocent of this crime.' Unquote. Can you comment on that?"

Flo blinked. "Comment on what? It's Tina's usual horseshit."

Some of the onlookers snickered. Ann Anderson looked up. "We start taping any minute now. Give me room to work, fellas, okay?" She turned her large eyes on Flo. "But, I mean, what does Tina mean by what she said?"

Flo's shoulders rose and fell in a mammoth shrug. "Who knows what goes on in that lardhead's brain? Are we talking about her or my son?"

"Right. We're trying to get a line on your son."

"I mean," Flo continued, "just look at the two wives. Look at Tina and look at Lana. One look and you know one of them is a no-good pusbag who never had a thought for anything but her own mouth and the other has class, real class, star class, like a movie star."

Ann Anderson's mouth opened and closed again as she tried to choose the next words. "But yet," she said then, "it was for Lana that he robbed the bank."

Flo nodded. "It's that operation." Her voice dropped. "You know the one I mean?" she murmured. "We're not on the air yet?"

"Not yet."

"Lana wanted it. My son is a real man. He wanted to give her the money for it."

This time Ann Anderson's mouth stayed halfway open. No words came forth. She glanced down at her papers, shuffled them helplessly, and then looked up. "Mrs. Nowickee," she said then, "like, I don't think we're getting anywhere this way, okay?"

"Getting?"

"We're trying to find out, like, what makes Joe tick. You tell me you of all people know. I can see he didn't hide anything from you. But we're not getting anywhere and pretty soon we have to tape this, okay?"

"Just ask me questions, then," Flo said somewhat grumpily. "Don't expect me to do all the work."

Ann Anderson's mouth was a tight line for a moment. Then: "As a little boy, did Joe show any special, uh, trend toward anything, uh, out of the ordinary?"

"He was a beautiful child, just gorgeous."

"And did he show any signs of—"

"And he grew up just fine," Flo went on, not hearing. "He grew into one real man. Strong. Smart. Good to his mother and his kids."

Ann Anderson looked up from her papers and caught the eye of the floor director, a man wearing earphones attached to a long cord that plugged into one of the cameras. "Jimmy," she said, "can Paul hear this?"

"Yeah. He says start whenever you want. If it plays, it plays."

Ann Anderson nodded and glanced through her papers again, and then turned sideways to face Flo almost head on. "During the time you talked to your son on the street in front of the bank this evening."

"Yes?"

"There was some talk about his father's brutality to him?"

"No such thing."

"About being beaten as a child."

"Never."

"We seem to have taped something to that effect."

"It's a goddamned lie!" Flo burst out.

The black woman glanced at the floor director. "This isn't going to work," she said then.

"Why not?" Flo demanded. "I'm his mother. If anybody knows the truth, I do. You talk to me. Anything else you get, it's lies."

"But we understood his father used to bea—"

"*He ain't got no father!*" Flo burst out.

"I beg your pardon?"

"I don't mean that," Flo muttered. "What the hell, yes, I do mean it." She glanced around her, feeling trapped. "Forget what I said, huh?"

Ann Anderson looked at her for a long time. Then she turned to look at the clock. Ten fifty-two. The black woman cleared her throat carefully. "Right." She glanced up at the floor manager. "We'll start taping now, Mrs. Nowickee. You know what sort of questions I'll ask. You get your answers in order, okay?"

The room had grown very quiet. "Okay," Flo said. She could hear her voice tremble a little. "Okay."

"We're going to move right along without stopping, even if we make any mistakes, okay?"

Flo nodded. "Okay." She took a breath to steady her breathing. "I just wanna say, if there is anything I can do now or some other time for a son as brave and good as my Joey, you can bet, don't worry, miss, I'm ready to do it."

The black woman stared blankly at her. "Right. Jimmy?"

"Tape rolling," the floor director intoned. "Sound rolling. Five . . . four . . ."

His voice dimmed in Flo's head. Her throat was dry. The red light below the camera lens went on. The floor director pointed at the black woman.

Flo sat in silent misery, ready to tell any lie. She couldn't really hear what the woman was saying. All she could think about was what she could ever say about Littlejoe that would make sense, now or ever after.